PENGUIN BOOKS

TRUTH AND CONSEQ

Alison Lurie is the author of many novels, includ... *The Truth About Lorin Jones* (winner of the Prix Femina Etranger), *Foreign Af-fairs* (winner of the Pulitzer Prize), and *The Last Resort*. Her most recent book was *Boys and Girls Forever: Children's Classics from Cinderella to Harry Potter*. She teaches writing, folklore, and literature at Cornell University and divides her time between Ithaca, New York, and Key West, Florida.

Praise for *Truth and Consequences*

"A delightful writer whose novels are a pleasure to read, Lurie [is] . . . a writer well worth cherishing for giving us novels that are as gracefully ed-ifying as they are incontrovertibly entertaining." —*Los Angeles Times*

"There is not one wasted word in *Truth and Consequences*. . . . Lurie's lan-guage is as sharp as the claws of pain that rule Alan's life and the pangs of guilt that threaten Jane's. The book is delightfully readable. You are into it and out of it before you know it, but not without a fresh look at the ma-neuvers inside marriage." —*Chicago Tribune*

"This is a comedy of adultery with a comedy of academia thrown in . . . as in the best comedies, everyone gets justice, and no one escapes it." —*The New Yorker*

"Amiable, quietly witty and readable." —*The Washington Post*

"Lurie . . . is back doing what she does best." —*The Miami Herald*

"Another razor-sharp satire of upper-class social norms and male-female relationships . . . a fascinating peak at the complexities of love and mar-riage . . . a brilliant romp . . . Lurie has created a novel that both pokes fun and commiserates with her characters, a tough feat and a wonderful read." —*Rocky Mountain News*

"Alison Lurie is a master at writing about how relationships—even the best of them—can come unraveled faster than you can say 'affair.' *Truth and Consequences* strikes a chord because its protagonists must answer a dif-ficult question we can all relate to: What happens when, as Jane repeatedly says, life is 'all wrong'? Lurie's characters are believable because they force us to ponder this. . . . Her ability to probe the complexity of human rela-tionships becomes apparent, and the story offers plenty of tough insights about what it means to love someone and about the often illogical nature of human relationships." —*Star-Telegram* (Fort Worth)

"Lurie's direct writing makes her novel a compelling read, and her plot drives her characters successfully. The reader is allowed the near-voyeuristic pleasure of watching old ties die while new ones begin. Even readers who aren't fans of romance will be enticed by Lurie's ability to fill her story with engaging characters." —*Richmond Times-Dispatch*

"A biting, funny glimpse behind the scenes of a prestigious college. . . . Lurie . . . has a light touch with college comedy, here, and her characters are true to life—spend any time around a campus and you'll know them all . . . fun reading." —*Buffalo News*

"The characters are what make this book flow. Lurie is whip-smart and very funny." —The Associated Press

"*Truth and Consequences* is wise and funny, with a sublimated sexiness that keeps the pot bubbling in a way that transcends the narrowness of academic novels. Lurie is at her best when she's sly, and she's plenty sly here. In *Truth and Consequences*, she's in top form, carefully portraying a range of deluded people but never subverting them." —*Palm Beach Post*

"Lurie is a poison-pen satirist who particularly enjoys skewering academics and writers. In this tightly wound, fairy-tale parody about the ruthless self-regard of creative people and the revenge of the good and steadfast, Lurie toys with the conventions of romance. Lurie is wickedly entertaining as she mocks everything from the ego of the artist to the bossiness of the meek, and everyone lives happily ever after." —*Booklist*

ALISON LURIE

TRUTH AND CONSEQUENCES

A Novel

PENGUIN BOOKS

PENGUIN BOOKS
Published by the Penguin Group
Penguin Group (USA) Inc., 375 Hudson Street, New York, New York 10014, U.S.A.
Penguin Group (Canada), 90 Eglinton Avenue East, Suite 700, Toronto,
Ontario, Canada M4P 2Y3 (a division of Pearson Penguin Canada Inc.)
Penguin Books Ltd, 80 Strand, London WC2R 0RL, England
Penguin Ireland, 25 St Stephen's Green, Dublin 2, Ireland
(a division of Penguin Books Ltd)
Penguin Group (Australia), 250 Camberwell Road, Camberwell,
Victoria 3124, Australia (a division of Pearson Australia Group Pty Ltd)
Penguin Books India Pvt Ltd, 11 Community Centre, Panchsheel Park, New Delhi – 110 017, India
Penguin Group (NZ), cnr Airborne and Rosedale Roads, Albany,
Auckland 1310, New Zealand (a division of Pearson New Zealand Ltd)
Penguin Books (South Africa) (Pty) Ltd, 24 Sturdee Avenue,
Rosebank, Johannesburg 2196, South Africa

Penguin Books Ltd, Registered Offices: 80 Strand, London WC2R 0RL, England

First published in the United States of America by Viking Penguin,
a member of Penguin Group (USA) Inc. 2005
Published in Penguin Books 2006

10 9 8 7 6 5 4 3 2 1

Photograph courtesy of Brand X Pictures/Getty Images

PUBLISHER'S NOTE
This is a work of fiction. Names, characters, places, and incidents either are the product
of the author's imagination or are used fictitiously, and any resemblance to actual persons,
living or dead, business establishments, events, or locales is entirely coincidental.

THE LIBRARY OF CONGRESS HAS CATALOGED THE HARDCOVER EDITION AS FOLLOWS:
Lurie, Alison.
Truth and consequences : a novel / Alison Lurie.
p.   cm.
ISBN 0-670-03439-8 (hc.)
ISBN 0 14 30.3803 6 (pbk.)
1. College teachers—Fiction.   2. Back—Wounds and injuries—Patients—Fiction.
3. Chronic pain—Patients—Fiction.   4. Married people—Fiction.
5. Older people—Fiction.   6. New England—Fiction.   I. Title.
PS3562.U7T74 2005
813'.54—dc22   2005042253

Printed in the United States of America
Designed by Nancy Resnick

FOR ALISON VAN DYKE

TRUTH AND
CONSEQUENCES

ONE

O
n a hot midsummer morning, after over sixteen years of marriage, Jane Mackenzie saw her husband fifty feet away and did not recognize him.

She was in the garden picking lettuce when the sound of a car stopping on the road by the house made her look up. Someone was getting out of a taxi, paying the driver, and then starting slowly down the long driveway: an aging man with slumped shoulders, a sunken chest, and a protruding belly, leaning on a cane. The hazy sun was in her eyes and she couldn't see his face clearly, but there was something about him that made her feel uneasy and a little frightened. He reminded her of other unwelcome figures: a property tax inspector who had appeared at the door soon after they moved into the house; an FBI official who was investigating one of Alan's former students; and the scruffy-looking guy who one summer two years ago used to stand just down the road where the ramp to the highway began, waving at passing cars and asking for a lift downtown. If you agreed, before he got out he would lean over the seat and in a half-whiny, half-threatening way ask for the "loan" of a couple of dollars.

Then Jane's vision cleared, and she saw that it was her husband Alan Mackenzie, who shouldn't be there. Less than an hour ago she had driven him to the University, where he had a lunch meeting at the College of Architecture, and where she had expected him to stay until she picked him up that afternoon. Since he'd hurt his back fifteen months ago, he hadn't been able to drive. Jane snatched up her basket of lettuce and began to walk uphill, then almost to run.

"What's happened, what's the matter?" she called out when she was within range.

"Nothing," Alan muttered, not quite looking at her. His cane grated on the gravel as he came to a slow halt. "I didn't feel well, so I came home."

"Is it very bad?" Jane put her hand on the creased sleeve of his white shirt. Crazy as it was, she still couldn't quite believe that the person inside the shirt was her husband. Alan wasn't anything like this, he was healthy and strong and confident, barely over fifty. This man had Alan's broad forehead and narrow straight nose and thick pale-brown hair, but he looked at least ten years older and twenty pounds heavier, and his expression was one of pain and despair. "You said at breakfast you were all right—anyhow, no worse than usual. . . ." Her voice trailed off.

"If you want to know, I had a fucking awful night, and now I'm having a fucking awful day." He moved sideways so that Jane's hand fell from his arm, and made a slow detour around her.

"Oh, I'm so sorry. Is there anything I can do?" She was following him now, speaking to his long stooped back. How could I not have known him? she thought. It wasn't my fault, it was because the sun was in my eyes and he was in the wrong place at the wrong time. I was surprised, that's all, the way you are when you run into neighbors when you're abroad, so at first you can't quite identify them. *But Alan is your husband,* her conscience said. *You should know him anywhere.*

"No." He paused by the kitchen door. "Well, maybe. You could help me off with my shoes. It just about kills me to bend over. And if you're going upstairs, you could bring down my pillows."

"Yes, of course." It occurred to Jane for the first time that there was a pattern here. Lately, Alan usually refused any offer of assistance at first, but soon corrected himself, asking for various objects and services. On other occasions he would wait longer, until she was somewhere else in the house and in the middle of some other activity, and then he would call for help.

"I can't go on like this. It's worse every day," he muttered, leaning over the kitchen sink, gulping water and pills. He wiped his mouth on the cuff of his shirt, which should have been thrown in the laundry basket two days ago.

"I'm so sorry." Jane put her arms around the soiled shirt and began a hug—but Alan winced, and she let go. "Sorry," she repeated.

Not acknowledging either her sympathy or her apology, he shuffled into the sitting room and slowly, with a muffled groan, began to ease himself onto the big flowered sofa, which was now placed diagonally across the middle of the room. It had been moved around last fall so that Alan could watch television while lying down, and an end table and coffee table had been positioned awkwardly beside it. The sitting room of their hundred-and-fifty-year-old farmhouse was low-ceilinged and small, and now resembled a crowded antique furniture store. It was difficult to have more than two people over, because with Alan stretched out on the sofa there was nowhere for them to sit. They hadn't had a dinner party for months, and they couldn't have had one anyhow because Alan couldn't sit in a straight chair for more than five minutes without excruciating pain. He had to eat standing up, or balance a plate on his chest as he lay on the various squashed pillows and cushions that now covered the sofa.

Only five—or was it already six?—years ago, Jane suddenly remembered, Alan had lain on this sofa in almost this same disarray of cushions, and she had lain there with him. The sofa was new then: it had just been delivered. After the man from the furniture warehouse left, Alan and Jane stood there admiring it. Then they sat on the sofa, bouncing a bit on the thick down cushions, laughing lightly. They congratulated themselves on their purchase; they kissed, and kissed again.

"We should launch it," Alan said presently, pressing closer.

"What? Oh yes."

"Let's."

It was a mild, sunny autumn day, and their clothes came off easily, falling to the carpet like the bright leaves outside. And then something strange and wonderful happened: the sofa, though of course it did not actually move, seemed to slide into a warm sea, to be borne through gently turbulent waves, which lifted and dropped them, raised and rocked them. When she was a small child, Jane had used to pretend sometimes that the big sagging green couch in the sitting room was a ship, sailing over the carpet. Now her story had come true.

"Look, we match the slipcover," Alan had said afterward, raising himself on one elbow. Jane sat up, and saw that it was so: the creamy beige and soft brown and subdued crimson of the eighteenth-century flower pattern were echoed in their nakedness.

"Yes," she said.

"You're so beautiful, and so lovable," Alan said.

"You too."

That sea voyage, that afternoon, had been one of their best moments. And now, again, Alan lay there on the same sofa in a confusion of cushions, but he was no longer beautiful, and the expression on his face was one of pain and despair.

It wasn't fair that he should suffer like this, Jane had told her mother only last week, it wasn't right. But Jane's mother, who went to the Congregational church almost every Sunday, did not agree. "We can't understand these things, dear," she had said, as she had said before in other circumstances. "We just have to accept them, and ask God to give us the strength to bear them."

In a moment of despair, Jane had passed on this advice to Alan, who thought her mother a well-meaning ninny. He also did not believe in God and, as far as she knew, had never asked him for anything. "Yeah?" he had said. "And what if he doesn't give us the strength? Even among true believers, the record for answered prayers isn't that good."

Now, with a cheese-grater groan, Alan turned over on the sofa. He stuck out his feet, and Jane sat on the narrow edge of the sofa beside him. Awkwardly, she untied and removed the oxfords she had put on and tied earlier that morning. It was like taking care of a giant toddler, she thought—but this child's bare feet were not soft and smooth and lovable, but hard and knobby, with horny toenails. "Is it really bad?" she asked.

"I already said it was bad." He spoke impatiently, angrily.

"Where does it hurt?"

"The back. Always the back. And I've got that shooting pain in my left leg again."

"I'm so sorry," Jane repeated weakly.

"It just won't quit. Fifteen months." Alan eased himself over onto his side, facing away from her, and in the process rucking up his shirt and revealing the back brace he now habitually wore, a kind of stiff heavy white plastic corset, all straps and Velcro, that made him look even more overweight than he was.

"Could you get me the pillows now? And maybe a couple of icepacks out of the freezer."

"Yes, of course."

Jane stood up. Who is this man lying on our sofa? she thought as she looked down at him. He's still called Alan Mackenzie, but he's not the same person. And I'm not the same person either, she thought as she climbed the stairs. I'm tired and worried and no fun for anybody, including myself. In a way we're not really husband and wife anymore. We're housekeeper and employer. Or maybe, in the language of a blandly instructive pamphlet she had read while waiting for Alan in some doctor's office, caregiver and caregetter.

At first they had both thought his back trouble couldn't be anything major, anything permanent, because it had begun in such a small way. Last year the departmental Memorial Day picnic had been held at one of the local parks, and Alan had joined his graduate students in a vigorous game of volleyball. It was a hot day, alternating sun and brief showers, and most of the other faculty members weren't playing—he was the oldest person on the court by at least ten years. But watching him you would never have known that: he was so tan and strong and he moved so lightly and quickly.

The ball came over the net, and Alan reached for it—a long elegant reach, too long. He skidded on the bright wet grass and fell in an awkward heap, with one leg out sideways. Everyone stopped playing; people gathered around and asked if he was all right. Alan stood up at once, a little awkwardly but smiling and replying, "Fine, just winded." But he didn't go on with the game—instead he came to sit on the bench by Jane, saying something about getting his breath back. After a while, he suggested that they leave. He thought maybe he'd pulled a muscle, he told her, and wanted to get into a hot shower.

The shower had seemed to help, and Alan was cheerful the rest of the evening, but the next morning his back was worse. It would get better in a few days, they kept assuring each other, but it did not get better.

For a while life went on more or less as before. Alan was uncomfortable and impatient to be well, but good-natured and affectionate, just as he had been after other, earlier minor accidents or during brief illnesses. But instead of moderating, his pain grew worse. He began to move more slowly, to favor the injury. One day, Jane caught him dragging a garbage can across the floor of the garage rather than lifting it as usual; she heard the coarse scraping sound of plastic on cement that she was to hear again so often—louder after a few months, when she took over the job.

It was not the only job she took over. As time passed Alan began to do less and less around the house. He began to put on weight from lack of exercise, and to show signs of what he called "grumpiness." But of course this was temporary, Jane told herself. In a few weeks more, a month or two at the most, he would be himself again—healthy, handsome, slim, athletic; good-natured, affectionate, and often passionate. He would love her again and make love to her again, instead of apologizing and explaining that he really wanted to, but it just hurt too goddamn much. Now, when they tried to meet, as they called it, it never really worked. Jane could never let herself go: she was always afraid of hurting Alan by a sudden movement, and sometimes she did hurt him, or he hurt himself. Then he would groan, or even cry out in pain. So she held back, and watched herself constantly, and soon their meetings had become tentative and awkwardly self-conscious, as if they were two adolescents on a date. Often Alan would break off halfway. "I'm sorry," he would say. "I want to go on, but it hurts too goddamn much."

"Yes, of course, I understand, that's all right," Jane always said. But it wasn't all right, it was all wrong.

Alan hadn't complained of pain much at first, but as time went on he mentioned or showed it more and more often: he groaned when he got out of bed or lay down, and cursed violently when he dropped anything. Of course, everyone complained when they were ill or injured, Jane told herself at first, and then they got better and stopped. Or, if they didn't get better, they got medical help. And indeed, when his back didn't improve after a few weeks, Alan, with the upbeat decisiveness that had for so long been part of his character and had made him such a successful department chairman, sought this help.

According to the experts, his problem was something called a slipped disk, which as Jane understood it meant that a kind of spongy pad between two of his vertebrae had slid out of alignment and was pressing on the spinal nerves, causing continual pain. Sometimes these disks slid back into place after a while, the doctor told them, and sometimes they did not. There were, he was told, many different treatments that might help.

For the next ten months, therefore, Alan consulted a series of health professionals. Each one approached his problem with new suggestions, and each time Alan and Jane hoped for a while that they had found the solution. But every treatment ended in disappointment, and some of them in rage and despair and increased pain. By Christmas Alan had seen what one of his colleagues had described as four physical therapists, three orthopedic surgeons, two neurologists, and an acupuncturist in a pear tree: a peculiar pale woman who worked in a cloud of smoky fruit-flavored incense and had inserted needles into Alan's back and shoulders and then left him to lie in pain for half an hour listening to oriental music while she spoke on the phone in an unknown language. He had submitted to agonizing injections of cortisone and other substances, and practiced many different sets of exercises. He had sat and bounced on various inflatable devices, including one that looked like a dull black rubber donut and another that resembled a giant shiny electric-blue beach ball.

In April, when nearly a year had passed without any change, Alan and Jane went to stay in a pretentious and unpleasant luxury hotel in a large city four hours' drive away, so that he could undergo what was called a diskectomy. According to the surgeon, this operation was usually relatively painless and had a ninety-five percent chance of success. In Alan's case, this turned out not to be so. After the operation, in spite of large doses of narcotic drugs, he was in continual agony, and his pain did not improve; rather it spread and worsened. As one of Jane's less sympathetic friends said at the time, "Well, somebody has to be in the other five percent." Before the operation the doctor had announced that usually there was immediate relief. At the follow-up interview afterward, however, he claimed that sometimes it took several months. But by this time, Alan did not believe a word the doctor said.

Since then, he had treated his pain himself. He used heating pads and icepacks, and wore an electronic device called a Tenz Unit that was supposed to block nerve impulses and sometimes did so. He also took a great many prescription and nonprescription drugs. Unfortunately, the drugs all had side effects and led to new complications and ailments. Alan now suffered intermittently from constipation, severe headaches, insomnia, chills, leg pain, groin pain, weakness, and fatigue. The Tenz Unit had caused an ugly raw red rash to appear on both sides of his lower back. He was also eating too much, and not only at meals. Jane would come upon him in the pantry gobbling peanuts out of a can, or cookies from a cellophane package. Late at night she would sometimes hear a noise in the kitchen that could be mice or burglars and would tiptoe down the stairs to find Alan standing in the half dark in front of the fridge, spooning vanilla ice cream from the cardboard carton into his mouth.

"Jane?" called a grating voice from below. "What the hell is going on up there?"

"Just coming." She snatched three pillows of varying size and consistency off his side of their bed and ran downstairs.

"Sorry I yelled at you."

"That's all right," Jane assured him, thinking at the same time that Alan now yelled at her, or at something else that had irritated him, more and more often. Afterward he always apologized, and seemed to assume that canceled out the yell.

"And the ice," Alan reminded her. "If you could get me the ice now."

"Sure, right away." She headed for the kitchen and opened the freezer, which over the last year had become crowded with refreezable plastic icepacks.

"Here you are." Jane held out a large white sagging object.

"Not that one, it's too heavy." He shoved her hand away with a grimace of irritation. "Jesus Christ. I need the little blue packs. Both of them."

"Sorry."

"That's better," he said a minute later. "And could you maybe bring me a towel to wrap them in? It keeps them cold longer."

"Yes, of course." Jane climbed the stairs again, found a clean hand towel, brought it down, wrapped the icepacks in it, and helped Alan settle them between his back and the back of the sofa. "Is there anything else?"

"Not just now, thanks." He groaned and closed his eyes.

Though Alan had not said so directly, Jane knew he now suspected that his back would never get better, and in fact would probably get worse. He was in almost constant severe pain, except when he was so full of drugs that he was woozy and unsteady on his feet as he had been this morning. In the late afternoon and evening the pain sometimes became so bad that he would have a shot of vodka, or two, or three, though labels on the pills he took clearly stated that it was dangerous to mix them with alcohol.

Pain, according to the nineteenth-century novels that Jane's Aunt Nancy had loved as a child and presented to her at Christmas and birthdays, could be ennobling and inspiring. In *What Katy Did* and *Jack and Jill*, thoughtless young girls, injured in accidents at play (like Alan) had to lie in bed for months, during which time they matured wonderfully and their characters changed for the better.

But Alan hadn't needed to change for the better, Jane thought: he had been perfect as he was. So, logically, he had begun to change for the worse. His admirable evenness of temper, optimism, and generosity of spirit had slowly begun to leak away. He had become overweight and unattractive, he had become self-centered and touchy.

Those books were wrong, Jane thought. Pain is bad for the character, just as all misfortunes are: poverty and unemployment and loss of friends and family. It makes you tired and weak; it makes you depressed and anxious and fearful. Nobody says this, nobody is supposed to say it, but it is true. Even Jane herself, who was only forty and healthy and strong and attractive, would one day be old and tired and ugly and probably self-centered and touchy as well.

"Ja-ane." Alan's voice was tense.

"Yes?" She stopped washing lettuce and hurried to the sitting room.

"Could you possibly get me the bottle of Valium from my toilet kit, and some cold grapefruit juice to wash it down?"

"Yes, of course." Jane ran upstairs and down, filled a glass with grapefruit juice in the kitchen, and added two ice cubes.

"Thank you." Alan drank. "Yes, that's good," he said, smiling at her. But then, as he lifted the glass again, his arm struck the arm of the sofa, and the rest of the grapefruit juice spilled onto the coffee table and the carpet. "Oh, fuck!" he shouted in a sudden rage. "I didn't need that."

"Don't worry, I'll take care of it." Jane picked up the glass and ice cubes, ran to the kitchen, and returned carrying a pan of warm water and detergent and a sponge.

"Aw, shit, look at the mess," Alan growled.

"Don't worry, it's nothing," she assured him.

"It's the drugs, they interfere with my coordination."

"Yes, of course," Jane said as she knelt by the sofa, mopping up the juice, then soaking the carpet with water and detergent, while thinking that she too did not need this, but that at least it hadn't been grape juice.

"I wish I could help—"

"It's all right, really. It's nothing." She went to the kitchen, dumped the dirty water, rinsed the sponge and brush, and filled the pan again with clean warm water. Back in the sitting room she scrubbed the suds off the carpet and patted it dry with a wad of paper towels, then returned to the kitchen again and washed everything out.

"Ja-ane," Alan called. "When you're finished, could you possibly bring me another glass of grapefruit juice?"

"Yes, just a minute." She put the pan in the drying rack.

"Okay. Here you are," she said a few moments later, aware of forcing her voice into a pleasant neutrality.

"Thanks. You're so very good to me, darling." Alan smiled at her briefly, sighed, and drank.

"You're so very welcome," she said. The words sounded flat in her mouth, but he did not appear to notice.

"I'm so lucky to have you here. It makes all the difference."

Between what and what? Jane thought, but did not say.

"It's those goddamn stairs in Mahoney Hall. They get me every time." Alan's office was on the top floor of the high-ceilinged architecture building, which had no elevator.

"I know. It'll be easier next month when you move into the Center." Last term Alan had been appointed as one of the two Faculty Fellows of the Matthew Unger Center for the Humanities, familiarly known as the Much, and sometimes as the Too Much. This was an endowed facility for visiting scholars and artists housed in a handsome Victorian mansion just off campus. Jane, for the last five years, had been its administrative director. The idea that Alan should become a Fellow had not been her idea, and the appointment had made her anxious, in case people should think so. But it had also made her grateful and pleased. For a whole year Alan would be relieved of teaching, which had become harder and harder for him. He would have peace and quiet and no stairs to climb and be able to finish his new book.

"I hope so," Alan said in the voice of one who doubts this.

"I'm sure it will."

No answer. "I'm going out to the garden now," she said. "Is there anything else I can get you?"

"No thanks. Well, if you see the *Times* around anywhere."

"Of course. I think it's in the dining room."

Back in the kitchen at last, washing the last of the lettuce, Jane waited a couple of minutes to see if any further requests would follow, then took up her basket and almost fled from the house.

It's not right, it's not how the story was supposed to turn out, she thought as she knelt in the garden pulling long, sticky, scratchy pale-green strings of bindweed out of the strawberry bed. That was stupid, it was silly and romantic: but Jane had once been romantic, though almost nobody who knew her now would have suspected this. At work she appeared practical, rational, and calm. Nobody would have guessed that twenty years ago, long after she knew the phrase to be foolish, she had clung to the belief that one day her prince would come, and that he would appear at the University. That was partly why she had stayed so long in an entry-level job at what her father always called "the big store at the top of the hill."

Most of Jane's many relatives, including those who also worked at the University—running offices and laboratories and lunchrooms, keeping up the grounds, or repairing office machines—had wondered at her decision. They believed that the faculty, on the whole, consisted of incompetent ninnies. Only Jane's mother, who was also somewhat of a closet romantic and considered a wedding the high point of a woman's life, saw it differently. "It doesn't pay much," she admitted. "But maybe you'll marry one of those professors."

Jane did not say so, but it was what she hoped for too. And as it turned out, not in vain. At twenty-four, when many of her friends were already married, she remained single. Because she was lively and pretty, with curly reddish brown hair and the look of a small friendly Welsh terrier, she had many suitors. Though some of them were attractive and likable and ambitious and already becoming successful, none of them, in her view, were princes. Somewhat discouraged, but refusing to compromise, she continued working at Corinth University, now at a more responsible job in the Entomology Department, all of whose unmarried male faculty, according to her fellow staff members, resembled different species of bugs.

Then, miraculously, Jane's prince appeared. He was an expert on architectural history, called in to consult on the possible preservation or demolition of the Biological Sciences Building. Alan Mackenzie was only thirty-six, but already an associate professor, and he even looked like a prince. According to one of his colleagues whom Jane met later, his friendly but slightly formal manners, his pale-brown wavy hair, and his classical musculature suggested the ideal Renaissance courtier. He came from the romantic state of California, and his attitude toward the world was curious, skeptical, and easygoing. And, unlike a couple of instructors whom Jane had briefly dated, he did not condescend to her because she had gone to a local branch of the state university.

In time, her prince had become a king: a wholly admirable and lovable man, a world-renowned expert on eighteenth-century architecture, and the holder of an endowed chair at Corinth University. Meanwhile, Jane had continued to work at increasingly interesting and well-paid University jobs. For more than sixteen years she had been lucky and happy.

And now all that was over. She sighed heavily and slumped into a crouching position against a bale of straw mulch. Over the last fifteen months, her admired and beloved king had turned into a kind of shabby, whiny beggar. Like the tax inspector, the FBI man, and the hitchhiker that he had reminded her of earlier that morning, he always wanted something, something she didn't always want to give and he didn't always need. No, no, I mustn't think that way, Jane told herself, digging into the earth and pulling up not only bindweed but, by accident, a long pale-red runner of next year's strawberries. But it was too late—the idea had already appeared in her mind and was sitting there heavily, as if glued in place.

A dirty wave of guilt and self-hatred washed over her. How can I mind doing things for Alan or think such mean, selfish thoughts, when I am well and he is in such pain—when I promised always to love him and cherish him, for better and worse, in sickness and in health?

Maybe the most awful thing about it all was that she wasn't a good person anymore. All her life, ever since she was a seven-year-old at Sunday school, it had been Jane's secret plan to be good. Already in second grade she had known that she wasn't remarkable in any way—not exceptionally intelligent or gifted or strong or beautiful. Well, all right then, she had decided, she would be good. Not heroically good: just reasonably decent, honest, fair, and kind. A good girl, a good woman, a good wife. She had never confided this ambition to anyone—to do so would have been to invite ridicule and possibly retribution. But for most of her life she had managed pretty well, though of course there had been lapses. When she went to church with her parents on Christmas and Easter, she usually felt that God (if he existed) understood and pardoned her failings. Now she felt that he was angry with her, even scornful.

Until last May it had mostly been easy to be good—maybe too easy. Occasionally in the past Jane had felt her virtue untested. When Alan first became ill she had almost welcomed it as an opportunity. She had been lucky in life; now she would be the patient and reasonable and loving spouse of an admirable man who had hurt his back and was therefore sometimes impatient and unreasonable and unloving, but would soon be well. It was a test of her virtue, and for many months one that she passed nearly every day. Sometimes people saw her taking and passing this test, and told her that she was wonderful.

And it had been true, for a while. For months Jane had been wonderful to Alan, and Alan had been grateful. But now she was tired of being wonderful, and Alan, she suspected, was tired of being grateful. As time passed, her virtue had failed. Like an old dish towel, it had begun to wear thin, developed holes and creases and stains, and she had begun to turn into a mean, grudging, angry person.

Often in the past, when Jane felt low, she would go out to the garden, and soon her sprits would rise. This year, though, it had been planted too late because of Alan's operation, and neglected because of all she had to do for him. Though the beans and squash and lettuce were fresh and full and beautiful in the warm sunlight, and the green tomatoes had begun to turn a splendid sunny red, there were bare patches where things had died from lack of water, and weeds everywhere.

Time would continue to pass, but Alan would not get well. He no longer expected to get well, and Jane—though she constantly assured him otherwise—no longer expected it either. His illness would continue to wind itself around them greedily, choking their marriage just as the bindweed was choking her strawberries. They would never get rid of it.

TWO

Some days were better, Alan Mackenzie thought as he lay on the sofa. Some days were worse. All were bad. None were good. Always the pain was there. Alan imagined it as a lizard about ten inches long, its sharp scales mottled red and brown as if with blood and shit. It was there inside his back, gripping his spine with its dry twisted legs and claws, moving its jaw to bite and flicking its forked tongue. He knew what the lizard looked like because he had seen it sixteen months ago in New Mexico. It was spring vacation and he was viewing churches for his current project, a history of religious architecture in America. He was alone: after twenty minutes at the church, Jane had gone to sit in a nearby coffee shop and read the paper.

Alan was around the far side of the building, taking photographs with a heavy camera especially designed for architectural photography. It was a bright but slightly overcast day, ideal for this purpose, and he was happy with the way things were going and with the last set of prints he had collected. He snapped a couple of pictures; then he climbed onto a pile of stones to get a better view, and stepped on something that hissed and shifted. He shouted and leaped back, thinking *Snake,* stumbled, and dropped his camera with a crack that broke the lens.

But what he had stepped on wasn't a snake, only a big ugly reddish brown lizard with twisted claws. Strangely, it did not scuttle off, but stood and looked at him. Its bulgy black eyes were hard, and its long jaw moved, as if it were saying something. What? Alan couldn't tell then, but he knew now: *I see you,* the lizard was saying. *I know you. And you will know me.*

As it turned out, that church in Santa Fe was the last one Alan successfully photographed. He had had other trips planned for the summer, and in June he'd actually set out to look at a monastery on the Hudson; but after half an hour he had to stop the car. For the rest of the way Jane drove, while he lay crumpled on the back seat, moaning under his breath from time to time and half sitting up to drink lukewarm bottled water and swallow painkillers. Compared to him Jane was a slow and timid driver, and by the time they got to their destination he was in such agony that he could hardly hold his new and even heavier camera. It was no surprise that those pictures came out blurred and useless.

After that disastrous trip Alan had canceled the others. Jane was visibly relieved. She hated distance driving, and couldn't bear to see him suffer, she often said. And besides, he knew, though she politely did not say, she couldn't bear how difficult and impossible he was when he was suffering.

Alan knew he was difficult and impossible, and was becoming more and more so. He also knew that as time went on his pain and self-absorption, his depression and anxiety, were driving his wife further and further from him. She never said this, never even hinted it, but he assumed that she was angry and full of despair, just as he was angry and full of despair. And the fact that she would not admit this somehow made him even angrier, at her dishonesty.

He was almost sure that Jane didn't love him as he was now, how could she, how could anyone? But month after month she had remained kind and patient and helpful, assuring him that she still cared for him, that they had a wonderful marriage, and this was, as she put it, "just a rough spot." Alan knew he should feel gratitude; he did feel gratitude. But he felt this gratitude as a weight, increasing every day, tipping the balance further

If she did really still love him it was worse, because he wasn't sure he loved her. This was now even literally true; it was more than a month since they had last gone through the awkward, self-conscious, often painful process that had taken the place of what used to be one of their happiest and most carefree activities.

Often he woke in the middle of the night and lay moaning and shifting, trying not to wake Jane. At the same time, like a nasty child, he hated her for being asleep and not in pain, and sometimes, meanly and shamelessly, he would moan louder and toss about, trying to wake her, so that she could be aware of how miserable he was. Sometimes he would succeed; more often, ashamed, he would get up, take another pill, and move to the guest room downstairs.

There, as he drifted in and out of an ugly sort of half sleep, he would think of the lizard behind the church, and say to himself that it had been a demon. Not the Devil himself, of course, but a minor member of his company, like those little monsters that appear in the corners of paintings by Bosch, sometimes carrying a pitchfork or a butcher knife. It would be natural that such creatures should hang about outside large old churches, seeking someone to tempt and torture and destroy.

It had taken the demon lizard over a month to follow Alan across the country from Santa Fe to Corinth, but it had not come alone. It had been accompanied or trailed by a gaggle of smaller demons; or, in medical language, complications and side effects. The primary and almost unbearable pain in his lower back was now from time to time accompanied by migratory pains in his left hip, groin, leg, and foot. The strain of trying to find a comfortable position to lie in produced lesser aches in his upper back, neck, and shoulder. The opiates and analgesics he took caused insomnia, headaches, and constipation, which could only be relieved by further drugs with their own side effects—among them indigestion, cramps, and mental confusion. The electronic contraption that blocked maybe twenty percent of the pain produced patches of ugly red rash where the electrodes were attached with a glue to which he was apparently allergic.

Of course, Alan didn't believe in demons. He had lost his faith years ago, and anyhow the faith he had lost, or maybe only misplaced, the Scotch Presbyterian faith he had been brought up in, didn't include demons. But sometimes as he lay awake in the spare room, he visualized the lizard and the little accompanying evil creatures that were causing the side effects. The constipation, for instance, he saw as a mud turtle that had taken up residence in his bowels, and the rash was an invasion of invisible red ants.

Meanwhile, he was falling apart both physically and professionally. Because he was no longer able to play tennis or squash or swim or go to the gym, he had gained weight and lost muscle tone. And because it was agonizing for him to sit in a chair for more than five minutes, he had been unable to work on his book—and in any case, he hadn't visited and photographed more than half the buildings he wanted to include. In his current depressed condition, he felt revulsion from the book, because even if it were completed and published, so few would know or care. Most people now had no interest in the architecture of the past: they liked or at least were used to the featureless or pretentious modern buildings, slabs and rectangles of plaster and glass and metal, that were everywhere now. Alan had grown up among constructions like that in California. But when he was twelve his father, a professor of engineering, had taken the family on a summer vacation to New England. The houses and churches and public buildings he saw there, with their classical beauty, simplicity, order, and harmony of design, had been a revelation to Alan—had in the end determined his life's work.

His love of Colonial architecture had even played a part in his marriage. When he met Jane, it was not only her good looks and lively charm that attracted him, but her intelligent and sympathetic appreciation of his plans for the building in which she worked, and her honesty and straightforwardness. Compared to her, most of the women he had known in California seemed noisy, frantic, self-centered, and overdecorated. Like the architecture he admired, she suggested order, harmony, and tradition. She was also, he discovered with joy, quietly passionate in private, and a thoughtful reader and critic of his writing.

Alan had already published four books on architecture, though the only one that anyone ever seemed to have read, the only one that was still in print, was a short guide to architectural follies in Great Britain. Small royalty checks for this title continued to arrive regularly, and according to his publisher, it was popular with tourists. But it had done little to add to his scholarly reputation; most of his colleagues, he knew, considered it amusing but trivial.

In his opinion, they were wrong. The study of architectural follies—those imitation Greek temples, artificial ruins, shell grottoes, miniature pyramids, and prospect towers that rich landowners had constructed on their estates from the seventeenth century to the present day—was fascinating and rewarding. In some ways, these follies gave him more aesthetic pleasure and said more about architectural and social history than most conventional structures. When he was in college, majoring in art and thinking of becoming a landscape artist, Alan had often included such constructions in his drawings and paintings. More recently, before he became ill, he had erected two such follies on his own property in Corinth: first a small triumphal arch based on the one in Washington Square, and then a former henhouse partly converted into a ruined late-nineteenth-century neo-Gothic chapel. Even with the help of his graduate students, building these follies had not been easy, but it had been deeply satisfying.

Now Alan could hardly bear to look at these constructions: he was far too aware of the irony involved. Building them himself had been folly, and worse than folly, a kind of hubris—a refusal to accept that he was over fifty years old and unable any longer to move heavy stones and raise roof beams without strain. It was related to the folly and hubris of his insisting on playing volleyball on a hot day, and then reaching for an impressive long shot, when his back already ached from carrying a pile of slates for the roof of his chapel earlier in the day. Building a ruin, he himself had become a ruin, and one that received no respect. In the past, aging men, like aging buildings, were admired as rare and marvelous survivors of time and weather: they appeared often in romantic painting and poetry. But since the twentieth century, which produced so many human and architectural ruins, they have not been seen as picturesque, but rather as ugly and even frightening.

Alan had never revealed any of these thoughts to Jane or anyone. As much as possible, he concealed his anxiety and depression. If Jane wanted to know how he was feeling, he would tell her, but mostly he said nothing. When other people asked how he was, he was noncommittal. He had memorized several banal phrases for this purpose. "Oh, I'm getting along," he would say. "Hanging in there." Such phrases made most of them think he wasn't as badly off as he really was and probably made others think he was malingering. Even on the rare occasions when he admitted the truth, most people didn't listen. Nobody wants to hear bad news, he had discovered, except for certain ghouls who feed on the misery of others. He hadn't known who these people were before, because they operated under disguise, pretending to be normal human beings. But once you were ill, they came out of the woodwork, like woodworms, white and flabby and rapacious. "You must be very discouraged," they said. Or, "Of course, most back trouble never really goes away." Or "You look awful. I guess you're not getting much sleep, huh?"

When he heard remarks like this Alan was consumed with rage, and it wasn't just their authors he was angry at, but everyone who was well, including Jane. In fact, the only people he felt comfortable with now or really enjoyed talking to were other semi-invalids, especially those with back trouble. It had been amazing for him to discover how many such people there were. It was almost like a secret society: non-members might know of its existence, but only members understood its power and importance, and only they knew what went on at meetings. They didn't keep their illness a secret, but

among outsiders they mentioned it only rarely, and spoke of it care-
lessly and dismissively. Only in private did they admit the extent of
their suffering, compare symptoms and diagnoses and treatments
and side effects, rate doctors and hospitals, and sometimes exchange
prescription drugs.

Alan had become particularly close to two local members of the
society of back-pain sufferers, both of them people who would have
been of little interest to him in the past. Both had been ill longer
than he had: he therefore looked up to them and listened to them
with respect, just as those who had joined later looked up to him.
One was a semi-retired veterinarian called Bernie Kotelchuck, a
big, hearty, red-faced elderly man who wore loud plaid shirts.
Bernie was the veteran of nearly a decade of back trouble and of
three operations—two diskectomies and a fusion—the last of which
had been about sixty percent successful. Because of these experi-
ences, and his medical knowledge, he was respected by everyone in
the back-pain society. In Bernie's opinion, Alan might profit from
surgical intervention, but the longer he could wait, the better his
chances. Right now, any operation was risky, but progress was being
made, and in a hundred years there was sure to be a cure. Whereas a
hundred years ago the kindest thing would have been to shoot both
him and Alan to put them out of their misery, as Bernie had once
shot a beloved Labrador retriever that had been hit by a car.

According to Bernie, what Alan should do now was get a recliner. He had one himself at home: a huge, hideously vulgar gray
pebbled leather object that Bernie's wife had christened The Hip-
popotamus and banished to his study. Maybe one day, when he had
given up all hope of recovery and all aesthetic sense, Alan would
have to buy something like this, but as yet he had refused to do so.

Alan's other new back-pain friend was a shy, wispy, forty-five-
year-old teacher of freshman writing for foreign students at Corinth
named Gilly Murphy. Gilly was a Buddhist and a vegetarian; she had
long pale hair and wore long trailing flowery skirts and had had
back trouble for over two years. When she was at her worst, she

couldn't even walk. So far, she had treated her pain with chiropractics, meditation, exercise, acupuncture and acupressure, and a kind of hands-off massage technique called Reiki. She also consumed large quantities of herbs and seaweed, which she was eager to share with Alan. As a result of all this, she claimed, she had experienced brief periods of complete relief. Probably it was mostly nonsense, but he had to admit that meditation sometimes did reduce the pain temporarily, and that Gilly's fragrantly flowery but subtly bitter herbal tea sometimes helped him to sleep.

In Bernie's view, there was no reason for him or Alan to feel specially afflicted by fate. "We've had it too good all our lives, so when something like this happens we feel insulted and injured. In most other parts of the world, they'd think we were damn lucky to have survived." Both he and Gilly believed that in fact there were many more sick people than well people anywhere, even in a relatively healthy environment like Hopkins County. "The thing is," Bernie had explained, "people who are sick are in the hospital, or at home, where you can't see them. And those who don't stay home, the ones you might meet in the course of a day, even if they admit to a cold or a headache, a lot of them don't let on if they're chronically ill. Course, it's different for me. Because I'm a vet, a lot of people want to tell me all about it, and they want me to suggest a treatment. I tell them, unless you're a horse or a cow or a dog, nothing doing. I don't want to lose my license."

Gilly, though from a different perspective, concurred in this view of a world mostly composed of the ill. A lot of the people she met, especially her students, she said, were victims of an imbalance between body and mind. Her classes at Corinth University were largely remedial, and her students tended to be either athletes, recruited for their physical rather than their intellectual prowess, or those for whom English was a second or third language, who had had to study night and day to pass their courses. The former group suffered from overemphasis on the body, the latter from mental strain and lack of sleep and exercise.

Levering himself painfully off the sofa, Alan shuffled into the downstairs bathroom, where he peed and took half of another pill. Then he rolled up his shirtsleeves to inspect his latest symptom, a red, itchy rash on his forearms. Either Gilly or Bernie, he seemed to remember, had once complained of something like this. Maybe whichever one it was could recommend some kind of cream, or a good dermatologist. He returned to the kitchen, poured himself a glass of orange juice, and tore open a virgin bag of potato chips. If Jane were there she would give him her silent better-watch-your-weight look, but (he glanced out the kitchen window to check) she was still in the garden. And anyhow, so what? Eating, as Bernie had once remarked, was one of the few pleasures left when you had back trouble, and (unlike alcohol) wasn't dangerous in combination with drugs.

Trailing crumbs, Alan passed through the dining room, taking the portable phone off its base, returned to the sofa, and began to dial. When neither of his new friends answered, he uttered a curse that was almost a sob. Hearing this unpleasant, shameful noise, a kind of darkness of self-disgust came over him. How had he gotten to this place in his life, where he was consumed with rage and despair because he couldn't whine about his rash to other invalids, people he wouldn't have even cared to know two years ago?

Alan had always had many friends, maybe he still did, but he didn't want to see any of them. Once it became clear that his back wasn't going to get better soon, they had begun to treat him in an awkward uneasy manner, as if he had joined a cult or been convicted of some embarrassing felony. It reminded him of a book he had read in college, Samuel Butler's *Erewhon,* set in an anti-utopia where illness was a crime. Back then, Alan had assumed that was either a joke or a bid for more understanding of criminal offenders. Now he knew it was no more than the truth. To be briefly ill was merely a misdemeanor, like exceeding the speed limit or lifting a monogrammed towel from a hotel. People didn't approve, but the slip was soon forgiven if not forgotten. Chronic illness made you into a chronic offender: even your best friends didn't treat you the same as they once had. They were solicitous, but formal and uneasy, glad to see you but gladder to leave. Eventually even your own family was affected. "Danielle and the kids are bored with the whole thing of my back," Bernie had once said. "They don't want to hear about it anymore."

Jane isn't bored, Alan thought. She still cares, she wants to help. But there had been something strange in the way she had looked at him this morning out in the driveway, just for a second, almost as if she didn't recognize him. And again later, when she brought him the icepacks, the same sort of look. As if she were seeing him from a great distance, and maybe not liking what she saw.

Only eleven in the morning, and he was exhausted. If he could read, it might distract him, but the *Times* had somehow fallen to the floor in disarray. He felt about with his hand, but could reach only the business section, which reminded him of the declining economy and the many medical bills he continued to receive for amounts not covered by his insurance. Meanwhile, he realized that the blue icepacks Jane had brought had softened and turned lukewarm and useless. Alan pulled them out from behind him with an impatient, agonizing wrench, and threw them on the floor. Then he lay heavily back, trying to decide if it was worth it to get up, carry the icepacks into the kitchen, put them into the freezer, remove the inferior white icepack, return to the sofa, and lie down again. All these actions would hurt, possibly more than the ice would help.

Maybe in a few minutes he would have the energy. Or maybe Jane would come in and he could ask her to do it. Meanwhile, he lay there, and the lizard continued to chew on his back.

THREE

On a hot late August afternoon at the Matthew Unger Center for the Humanities, things were not going well. Five professors were scheduled to move in the day after tomorrow; but that morning a large piece of ceiling had fallen in the kitchen, filling much of the ground floor with dust and debris.

Jane had not been very surprised by this event. One of the things she knew by now was that for anyone in an administrative position, probably right up to the dean of the Arts College and the provost and president of the University, the question is always, "What is going to go wrong today, and how will I deal with it?" As her husband Alan had said of his own department chairmanship, "You take the job because you have ideas about how things could be better, and then you spend most of your time keeping them from getting worse." Over the past few years she had learned to anticipate and even in a way to appreciate problems and their repair.

Jane usually got to the Center just after lunch. During the morning she was at her other job on campus, where she was the administrative secretary of the Humanities Council. There, in Knight Hall, she collected and issued announcements of lectures and conferences and prizes, scheduled campus events and conferences, interviewed students for work-study jobs, and sent out bulletins and e-mails.

There were problems at Knight Hall too, but they tended to be smaller. Files were lost, mistakes were made in memos and bulletins, students did not go to their assigned jobs, and computers broke down.

But at the Center there was almost always, or seemed to be, a major crisis. For one thing, her assistant there, a young skim-milk blonde called Susie Burdett, was the sort of person to whom problems naturally seem to come, eager to cause alarm and worry. Susie almost appeared to enjoy reporting to Jane, for instance, that the copier had broken down again. When Jane asked if she had called Technical Services, the answer was always no. "I thought you might want to look at it first," Susie would say, clasping her plump pink hands, whose nails were painted a different color every day.

Today Susie's nails were a shimmery yellow-green, coordinating peculiarly well with her long blond hair, which always had a slightly greenish tinge from the chlorine in the college pool. Now her green nails held a wad of pink tissues to Susie's nose, which quivered with a series of sneezes. The dust from the accident, she explained, had brought on an allergic reaction.

Jane followed her to the kitchen, where they contemplated a gaping hole in the ceiling near the sink that exposed broken plaster, wires, and pipes, and a corresponding heap of debris on the floor below. "It was a couple of hours ago," Susie explained, sneezing again. "I was in the office and I heard this awful noise, sort of like thunder, only indoors. The cleaners heard it too, so we all rushed in."

"I see. You didn't ask them to sweep up while they were here?"

"Uh-uh." Susie sneezed again. "They wanted to, but I was scared. I thought, maybe there's asbestos in that stuff. And maybe more of the ceiling is going to come down anytime. Like even now." She gave Jane a panicky Chicken Little look and backed toward the door.

"I suppose it could," Jane said. "Well, Buildings and Grounds should be able to tell us that. Let's get out of here for now." She shut the kitchen door firmly.

Sneezing violently, Susie followed her through the dining room into the wide, oak-paneled central hall. "I think maybe I ought to leave before my allergy gets worse," she said when she could speak again.

"Yes, maybe that's a good idea. It's nearly four anyhow," Jane told her. "I'll call B and G, unless you did that already."

Susie, sneezing more quietly and pathetically now, shook her head.

"Really," Jane said, and might have said more, except that she had heard in her own voice a new, unpleasant tone that she recognized. Though she was still managing, just barely, to be patient and kind with Alan, she had ceased to be an automatically nice person. Often now it was as if all her suppressed impatient unkindness was in danger of slopping over into the rest of her life, onto innocent people like Susie.

She returned to the office and made the call, stressing the word "asbestos." The B and G people usually went home at four o'clock, but the voice on the other end promised to try and send somebody over that afternoon to inspect the damage.

"Better not go in there again," the voice ordered Jane, who, once she had hung up, immediately disobeyed. The consequences of the accident were beginning to appear in her mind, and she needed a cup of tea.

Jane was not sorry to have gotten rid of Susie, who would certainly have gone on sneezing, and also been made anxious by this disobedience. She only wished that she could get rid of Susie permanently. Though she liked her assistant personally, she deeply regretted having assigned her this job. She had been misled by Susie's many good qualities: she was cheerful, accurate, and reliable; she was also quite pretty, something the Humanities Council had felt desirable in someone who would sit at the desk in the front hall of the Center and meet the public. When Susie had worked in the big Arts and Sciences office in Knight Hall it had not been apparent that she attracted problems, or that she was fearful of taking any initiative in solving them. She had been sociable and outgoing, and had many friends. But that had turned out to be a problem in itself. Susie had been happy in Knight Hall with her friends; the promotion in rank and raise in pay had not made their loss up to her, and she was lonely and unhappy at the Center. Moreover, recently she had quarreled with her boyfriend and become allergic to a wide range of substances. Jane had promised her a transfer back to Knight Hall as soon as a suitable job turned up, but so far there had been nothing that paid as well as this.

Carrying her tea in a mug with the Corinth crest on it, Jane returned to the Center office, a small sunny room with a white marble fireplace and blue Morris wallpaper, formerly the back parlor of the mansion. Built in the 1890s, this was a substantial brick house picturesquely covered in Virginia creeper, with an imposing entrance, bulging bay windows, and heavy dark Victorian furniture. Its large downstairs rooms were elaborately decorated and in continual demand for official lunches, dinners, receptions, and lectures. Permission to use these rooms was nominally in the gift of the Humanities Council; essentially Jane made the decisions, which added considerably to the respect she received from the various departments in the Arts College.

The standard procedure of the Matthew Unger Humanities Center was to invite a diverse group of Fellows, from different universities and fields, and to unite them by designating a yearly theme, thus encouraging interdisciplinary dialogue. This year the theme was "Structures of Faith," and, as usual, there were three outside Fellows: a sociologist from India and Yale, an economist from Bosnia and the University of Ohio, and the famous writer Delia Delaney, the author of *Womenfaith* (spiritual essays), *Dreamworks* (poetry), and *Moon Tales* (modern fairy stories). There were also two Faculty Fellows: Jane's husband Alan and a young literary theorist from Comparative Literature called Selma Schmidt. All of their projects had some relationship to the economic, social, or artistic aspects of religion.

Jane had already assigned the Fellows offices according to rank and reputation: Matthew Unger's very large former bedroom had gone to Delia Delaney; and his wife's only slightly smaller bedroom across the hall to Alan. The sociologist and the economist would occupy the other big rooms on the second floor, while Selma Schmidt would have to make do with a former sewing room next to the supply cupboard.

According to one of the senior administrators in Knight Hall, five Fellows automatically meant trouble, since about one professor out of five was always a real kook or a bastard or both. To Jane these statistics seemed exaggerated. The Fellows were usually very agreeable and accomplished people, well liked by their colleagues. Once in a while, of course, one of them was a disagreeable person whose colleagues wanted him or her out of the way for a while, so they could have a holiday from this person's obnoxious behavior. It was true that each year at the Center somebody became a problem, but this was not always their own fault. Last winter, for instance, a well-known naturalist called Wilkie Walker, whom everybody liked, had slipped on the front steps one icy day and broken his leg.

Jane finished her tea and sat waiting for the man from Buildings and Grounds. Susie's anxiety about future falls of plaster, she had realized, would probably be shared by B and G, which like all administrative offices was ever mindful of possible legal liability. It was very probable that once they saw the kitchen they would want to close it until a full structural inspection could be made. That could take a week or two, and meanwhile the room couldn't be used, which meant that any University event involving more than minimal refreshments would have to be moved or rescheduled, including the Labor Day reception for incoming Fellows. For a moment Jane contemplated trying to convince them simply to cover the hole with a piece of drywall until it could be repaired; but a picture immediately came into her mind of heavy chunks of plaster and dust and drywall falling upon a group of catering students from the Hotel School, some of whom might be seriously injured or turn out to be the offspring of lawyers. Sighing, she took out the schedule for

September and began to make a list of the people in various University departments whom she would have to phone on Monday, causing them irritation and inconvenience.

It was hot and stuffy in the Matthew Unger Center, which, unlike Knight Hall, was not air-conditioned. As time passed, Jane remembered that she had promised to stop at the drugstore on her way home and pick up a prescription and some grapefruit juice for Alan. She became more and more impatient to leave, and doubtful that anyone from Buildings and Grounds would appear. But shortly before five she heard the front door open, and a strong-looking man in his fifties, in jeans and a blue denim work shirt, carrying a clipboard, came in. He had curly dark hair and a friendly smile.

"Mrs. Mackenzie?" he said. "I'm Henry Hull."

"Oh, good." She smiled back "You've come about the ceiling."

"The ceiling?" He gazed vaguely upward.

"Not here, in the kitchen. Come on, I'll show you." She headed for the back hall, thinking that as a rule the guys from B and G were much better looking than the average professor. "There."

"Wow. It looks like a big piece of plaster has come down," he said.

"Yes." Clearly, though attractive, he was a little slow on the uptake. "So what do you think?"

"It doesn't seem too bad. I guess you should call Buildings and Grounds, or whatever."

"But you are Buildings and Grounds," Jane said, her voice fading from irritation to uncertainty.

"No. I'm Henry Hull," he repeated. This time, a vague feeling of having heard the name somewhere came over Jane.

"Delia Delaney's husband."

"Oh. I'm sorry. I didn't remember."

"That's all right. Nobody does." He smiled very slightly.

I suppose not, Jane thought, and for the first time she considered that it might not always be wonderful to be married to a famous person. She tried to remember what she knew about Delia Delaney's husband—not much compared to the masses of information the Center had received on his wife. All she could recall was that he was an editor at a small publishing company, but worked mostly at home.

"Well, how do you do?" Embarrassed, but determined to be polite, she held out her hand. After a second of hesitation, Henry took it; his grip was warm and hard, like that of the Buildings and Grounds employee she had believed him to be. "So how is everything going? Are you comfortable in the Vogelmans' house?" One of Jane's regular jobs at the Center was to find sabbatical rentals for the Visiting Fellows.

"Oh, very. Nothing but comfortable." Henry Hull smiled ambiguously. "You've seen it?"

"Oh yes." The Vogelmans' house was one of the largest on the hill; it was totally modern, with four bedrooms, three baths, a two-car garage, a large deck, and central air-conditioning. Since Henry did not comment further but only smiled, she added, "Is something wrong?"

"Not essentially. But it's a bit disconcerting, don't you think, all those dead gray and brown birds?"

It was true, Jane remembered, that in the dining room and study of the house there were a number of cases containing stuffed birds. "Professor Vogelman and his wife are ornithologists," she said.

"Yeah, I know."

"I think they've actually discovered a new species, or maybe it's what's called a variant."

"But they look so unhappy—the birds, I mean. They sit in their glass cases, on their brown and gray twigs, and look at you while you eat dinner. Some seem angry, but most are just miserable."

In spite of herself, Jane giggled. "I know what you mean," she said. "I wouldn't really want them in my house. But maybe you could move the cases," she said.

"Not a hope. They're built into the walls. I looked."

"Or put something over them?"

"But we'd know the birds were still there, underneath."

"You'd forget after a while."

"Maybe." He looked grave: for a moment she wondered if perhaps the whole thing wasn't a joke. "I'd forget, but Delia wouldn't. No, the only solution is never to use the dining room."

"Or the study."

"That's all right. I'll be working in the study: I can get along with the birds."

Jane returned his smile. Her wish to leave for home had wholly vanished. "Would you like a cup of tea?"

"No thanks. I've really just come to look at the office for Delia."

Jane, who knew that the upstairs wouldn't be cleaned until tomorrow, would normally have said that the Center wasn't open yet. But now she hesitated, not wanting to seem rude or unfriendly. "Couldn't she come herself?"

"No, she has a migraine. Is the office upstairs?"

Already he was moving toward the hall. Jane reluctantly followed.

"This won't take much time," Henry assured her, beginning to ascend the wide red-carpeted staircase two steps at a time. Though his build was solid, he seemed agile.

"If you'll show me. . . . This one?" He walked into the former master bedroom, which had a bay window with views to the south and west. "It's a good big space," he said thoughtfully "She'll like that."

"I hope so." Jane spoke with confidence: all the past Fellows to whom she had assigned this office had been appreciative and grateful.

"It's very bright," he added after a moment.

"Yes, you get wonderful light here. Even in the winter." She paused, registering something negative in his intonation. "You mean it's too bright for you?"

"Not for me, but maybe for Delia." He smiled almost conspiratorially, and Jane smiled back. "Bright light sometimes brings on one of her attacks."

"There are blinds," Jane said. "And drapes she can pull." Going

to one of the west-facing windows, through which the August sun
poured like thick, hot honey, she demonstrated.

"Yes, that might help." Henry made a note on his clipboard; then
he began to circle the room, opening the drawers of the big leather-
topped oak desk, trying out the desk chair and the easy chair by the
bay window, lifting the phone, and turning the desk lamp off and
on. "There's a connection to the University computer system?"

"Oh yes, right here."

He leaned and peered behind the desk, as if he did not quite believe her.

"That's good. And do you have a surge protector?"

"She won't need one. We're already wired for power outages, it
was in the brochure we sent you," Jane said, beginning to feel impatient.

"Great." Henry smiled at Jane again, but this time with less effect. "I think we may have to move the desk," he said. "Delia works
best when she has a view."

You may have to move the desk, not me, Jane thought but did
not say.

"Well, it's a pretty good space," he said. "I think she could be
happy here. But she'll need a sofa."

"A sofa?" Jane said, not encouragingly.

"Yeah, you see, when a migraine's coming on Delia mostly gets
an aura. Then if she can take her pill and lie down in a darkened
room, sometimes that will head it off."

"Does she get migraines often?" As far as Jane could recall, nothing in any of Delia Delaney's glowing, even fulsome letters of recommendation had mentioned this.

"It varies," Henry said vaguely. He ran a hand along the pink
marble mantel, over which hung a large antique sepia photograph
of the University quadrangle, glanced at the dust that had collected
on his fingers because the rooms hadn't been cleaned for a month,
but made no comment.

Jane sighed almost audibly. Very possibly, Delia Delaney was going to be this year's problem Fellow. "And how long do her migraines last?"

"Oh, that varies too. Sometimes only a few hours, sometimes up to two days."

"That's too bad," Jane said. "I hope she won't have them on Tuesdays and Thursdays." In exchange for a generous salary, free secretarial service, free campus parking, and what most of them considered luxury accommodations, all the Fellows were expected to hold office hours and make themselves available to students and faculty with a special interest in their subject. They were also expected to attend the two public lectures or readings each of them would give, and the informal weekly lunches to which selected members of the faculty would be invited.

"Unfortunately, they're not scheduled in advance." Henry sat casually on the edge of the leather-topped oak desk, which had once belonged to Matthew Unger himself. "I'm sure she'll come in when she can."

"It's important, you know," Jane said, beginning to be irritated by his manner, which somehow suggested that his wife was doing Corinth University a favor instead of the reverse. "Really."

"Really?" He raised one eyebrow slightly.

"Yes, it is. You know, a few years ago we had a Fellow who only showed up once a week to get his mail and use the copy machine. It turned out that most of the time he was in New York. He didn't understand that if he wanted to collect his paycheck he had to be in residence, the way it said in the contract he signed."

"So what happened?" Henry smiled as if this cautionary tale were a joke.

"Oh, well. Eventually he understood," Jane said in what she hoped was a meaningful way. "I'm afraid I have to leave now," she added. "If you have any more questions you can call me here tomorrow afternoon."

"Yes. Thank you." Henry Hull's tone was subdued; finally he seemed to have gotten the message. He followed Jane out into the wide, elegant upstairs hall, where the big stained-glass window over the entrance cast a confetti of color on the flourishing indoor plants and the pale Chinese carpet. He glanced out at the view, then into the office opposite his wife's, which looked north and west.

"Oh, look! There's a sofa in here," he said with an air of happy discovery. "It should be easy to move it into Delia's office. Or," he added, walking into the room, "why not just switch rooms? The light's not so glaring here too, that would be better for her." He pointed toward the bay window, where a magnificent copper beech tempered the hot afternoon sun.

"I'm sorry," Jane said in a not-sorry tone of voice, "but the offices have already been assigned."

"Yeah, but nobody's moved in yet."

Jane did not reply. A vision had come to her of Alan lying on the sofa at home in pain, waiting for his prescription, while she was chatting, almost flirting, with a stranger. You may be attractive, she thought, looking at Henry, but I'm not going to give your wife Alan's office, and I'm not going to give her Alan's sofa. "Anyhow," she said, "the professor who's using this room needs a sofa." Then, realizing that inevitably Alan's identity would come out, she added rather lamely, "It's my husband, he has a serious back condition and he can really only work lying down."

"Oh, that's too bad," Henry said. "Your husband?" He smiled in a way that Jane somehow did not like.

"Yes. Alan Mackenzie. He's an architectural historian."

"Ah?" Henry spoke as if this were news to him. Clearly, he had not read any of the material Jane had sent.

"Yes." Jane had an impulse to elaborate on this information, mentioning Alan's fame as a teacher, the books he had published, the awards he had won; but something told her that none of this would impress Henry Hull much. Instead she looked at her watch meaningfully. "I really must close up the building now," she said, and headed for the stairs.

"Okay, sorry."

They descended the stairs in silence.

"Hey, look," Henry said, stopping and glancing into the down-stairs rooms as they passed. "This place is full of sofas." In fact, there were four sofas in the principal rooms, including a picturesque but horsehair-hard little Victorian one with mahogany arms and back carved with lumpy wooden fruit. "I bet somebody could arrange for Delia to have one of them."

He's going to go over my head if I don't stop him, Jane thought, and a feeling near to rage came over her. "I'll see what I can do," she said, giving the horsehair sofa a quick meaningful look, and Henry a cool smile.

"Thanks so much." His smile, in contrast, was warm and friendly.

Jane collected her handbag from the office and led him outside. She rounded the building to the parking lot, with Henry Hull fol-lowing her, and stood by her car. "So, I'll see you again, probably," she said, uneasily aware that this was something she wanted.

"I'm sure you will." He smiled again; then, without warning, put his hand on her bare shoulder, causing a tremor to run down her arm. "You're very pretty, you know that?" he said.

Jane, who in a sense knew this, but had not actually considered the matter for some time, since it was no longer relevant to her life, did not answer. Don't you try to sweet-talk me, she thought; and without speaking, she got into the car, slammed the door, and started up the engine.

FOUR

On Labor Day, in the big bedroom that he now only occasionally shared with his wife, Alan Mackenzie stood at the window looking down over his back lawn, which sloped gently toward the woods and the silvery lake beyond. Usually empty, today the scene would soon be crowded. Students from the University Catering Service, whose truck was parked in Alan's driveway, had just set up two long folding tables and were covering them with white cloths. Next they carried in a large cut-glass punch bowl, plastic plates and glasses, buckets of ice, and bins of soda and juice bottles. Then came plates of cheese and vegetables covered in plastic wrap, and containers of crackers and dips. One of the students, as she crossed the bristly grass that had just been cut that morning, stumbled in her high heels and fell, dropping a bowl of potato chips. Alan winced; every accident now reminded him of his own accident, his own disability and constant pain. Was the girl hurt, would she too soon become a wretched invalid? Apparently not. She rose, stooped gracefully to pick up the bowl, and hurried on, leaving a spray of yellow chips like broken flowers on the grass.

"How're you doing?" Jane said, coming into the room behind him. She was wearing faded jeans and a T-shirt, and looked a little worn.

"Not too great," Alan replied, half turning around. "I've got that pain in my shoulder again."

"Oh, I'm so sorry."

"I don't think those goddamn exercises have helped at all; in fact I think they've made it worse." He rotated his arm, wincing.

"Maybe you should stop doing them, then."

"I've got to do something. I can't go on like this, I can hardly type anymore. I probably never should have gone to that new physical therapist. She seemed so eager to help, but I didn't trust her from the start. I'm not sure she even understood my X-rays."

"It could be."

"I told her there was a bone spur, but I don't think she really listened. I should have waited until the other woman got back from vacation, the one I saw before. Or at least until I talked to the doctor again."

Jane, who was standing in the walk-in closet changing her clothes, did not reply. Probably she too hadn't really been listening, he thought. More and more often, she didn't listen to him, or didn't listen carefully. In a way he didn't blame her: what he had to say was usually unpleasant and often monotonous. But in a way he did blame her. Impatient, troubled, he moved toward her.

"What I want to know is, am I ever going to get better," he demanded loudly and suddenly. "What do you think?"

"I—I don't know," Jane stuttered, clearly frightened by his tone, clutching a white silk slip against her naked body.

"Yes, but what do you think, honestly?" he insisted, moving nearer.

"I don't know, how could I know?" she said. "I mean, most people do; that's—that's what everyone says."

"And some people don't get better. I'm sorry," he added, realizing that Jane had burst into tears. "I didn't mean to scare you." He put his arm around her, touching her smooth bare back for the first time in weeks. "Of course you can't know. Come on. Stop crying. Get dressed and go on down to your party."

"It's not just my party, it's yours too," Jane said, her sobs beginning to subside.

"Whatever." Alan gave a sigh and moved toward the window. "I still don't see why you had to have it here, though," he said presently, looking down again at the lawn, over which the caterers were now distributing white plastic chairs.

"But we talked about it already, we agreed," Jane said, now in almost a normal tone of voice. "We're having it here so you don't have to spend any more time socializing than is comfortable for you. You can come in and lie down whenever you feel tired."

"I feel tired already," said Alan. "I always feel tired."

"You only need to put in an appearance—speak to the people on the Council, meet the other new Fellows—" Jane, now wearing a tan shirtwaist dress and low-heeled white sandals, came to look out of the window beside him. "Do you think the tables are too close together?" she asked.

He made no comment.

"And why are they setting the chairs in rows? We're not having a lecture. I told them already—I've got to go down. Come whenever you can."

Alan did not move. In fact, he understood very well why the Matthew Unger Center reception was being held at his house: it was not for his convenience, but because Jane was determined that he should appear at it, demonstrating proper gratitude for his faculty fellowship. She knew that if the party had taken place anywhere else he would probably have refused to come, or would have wanted to be driven home early. Or, possibly, he would have gotten drunk. Alcohol cut his pain, though only briefly, and if he drank enough to make any real difference he would begin to feel dizzy and sick and behave badly.

Alan was only minimally grateful for his fellowship. For one thing, he was convinced that it had been Jane's idea, though she denied this. In the eagerness of his colleagues to recommend him he saw mainly self-interest, for it meant that they would not have to fill in when he was too ill to meet a class, and would not have to see or hear about his pain and disability. On the other hand, he was grateful that he would not have to see them so often and experience their condescending pity.

Alan Mackenzie was a proud man, and in the past his pride had been of the sort known as "proper," meaning that it had been well grounded in fact. It was grounded, for example, in his professional success, his health and good looks and athletic prowess; his attractive, affectionate, and intelligent wife; and his beautiful hundred-and-fifty-year-old house with its view of the lake. He had never called attention to these advantages—rather, he often spoke freely and humorously of his disadvantages: his lack of skill at golf, his failure to graduate from Yale with honors. Nevertheless, one or two envious friends and colleagues had sometimes mockingly referred to him as The Mackenzie, as if he were a Scottish clan chieftain. Now, of course, it was no longer necessary for him to deflect envy, since his friends and colleagues pitied rather than envied him.

The move to the Unger Center last week had been difficult. Jane and a team from Buildings and Grounds had packed and transported Alan's books and papers, his computer and printer, and the drafting table he now used as a desk because he could not sit down to work. But he had had to select what was to be moved and organize the packing and unpacking. Presently, becoming impatient with the process, he had joined in, and had wrenched his shoulder again.

And even after everything was in place at the Center Alan hadn't been able to get down to work. It was really too soon to start his book on religious architecture in America: his research wasn't complete. Nearly half the buildings he wanted to discuss hadn't been photographed right, and until he got well they never would be. If he ever got well. "But you can write up the material you have, can't you?" Jane had asked. She didn't understand that it didn't work that way. The ideas and the research had to come first, then the outline, and then finally the writing.

Alan had always been interested in religion, once maybe too interested for his own good. But his main feeling now was relief that
he had gotten over his early beliefs at college. If he still had faith he
would have had to consider the spiritual meaning of the last sixteen
months of severe, unrelenting pain. Was he being punished, and if
so, for what? His life had not been blameless, but he had never been
guilty of murder or plagiarism, never cheated on his taxes. He had
not stolen anything since sixth grade, and it was years since he had
committed adultery. On the other hand, he had not been so good
that God would have been tempted to test his faith as he had Job's.

Outside, the lawn was beginning to fill with guests, among
whom presumably were the four other Fellows, whom Alan had not
yet met. Sighing, he took up his cane and went down to join them.
I'll give it half an hour, Jane will have to be satisfied with that, he
decided, clenching his teeth as he descended the staircase, one agonizing step at a time.

Twenty-five minutes later he had drunk two glasses of semi-
alcoholic pink grapefruit punch, which only dulled the pain slightly.
He had eaten too much Brie and crackers, spoken to the five members of the Humanities Council and three of their wives, and met
three of the four other Fellows. Only Delia Delaney, this year's star,
was missing, and already her absence was beginning to be unfavor-
ably commented on. From time to time Alan had observed Jane
looking at him, her expression a mixture of encouragement and
concern, and given her a small, ironic nod or wave. *See? I'm doing
what you wanted me to do, okay?* it conveyed.

His back hurt worse and worse. He was about to excuse himself,
and had turned to set down his empty plastic wineglass, when he
saw an extraordinarily beautiful woman approaching. She was tall
and fair, with masses of heavy red-gold hair, elaborately arranged in
a series of braids and puffs and tendrils in the manner of Botticelli's
Simonetta, whom she strongly resembled.

"You must be Alan Mackenzie, who's won all those prizes," she
said. Her voice was low, vibrating, breathy, with a warm Southern

accent; her gauzy white dress was cut low, revealing full rose-pink breasts.

"So they tell me," he admitted. It was true that two of his books, both now out of print, had been given awards.

"I'm Delia Delaney." She smiled and looked up at him,

Of course, Alan almost said. He had seen a black and white photo somewhere, but it hadn't revealed Delia's spectacular coloring, including the satiny rose-flushed skin and the silver-gray eyes that matched her lacy shawl.

"I'm so happy to be here." She sighed as if with actual happiness. "And now I want to see your famous folly, I've heard so much about it."

"That's it, over there." Alan pointed to where, beyond the last curve of the flower bed, a gray stone arch was partly visible. "Help yourself."

"But I want you to show it to me." Delia put a warm hand on his arm.

Phrases of polite but honest refusal passed through Alan's mind. *I'm sorry, but I have a bad back, I can't walk that far. I was just about to go lie down.* But pride and good manners and Delia's touch on his arm outweighed them, and he allowed himself to be led painfully down the lawn toward the miniature triumphal arch he had constructed three years ago to celebrate the publication of *British Ruins and Follies.* He had to admit that it still looked good—maybe even better now that ivy covered one side of the arch and a velvety dark-green moss had spread over the lowest stones.

"But I know it!" Delia exclaimed, laughing. "It's the arch in Washington Square, isn't that right?"

"Yeah," Alan agreed. "About one-quarter the size, of course."

"It's wonderful," she breathed.

"Thank you."

"Most people don't recognize it." And they don't always think it's wonderful, either, he remembered. Jane, for instance, did not think so. When he had first shown her the drawings, she had seen them as a mildly entertaining joke, but once she realized that he was actually going to build the thing in their back yard she was clearly puzzled and dismayed, though she had never openly said so.

"I knew it at once," Delia said. "My best friend in school moved to New York when I was about seven, and she sent me a postcard of that arch. I had it up on my wall at home for the longest time. I used to imagine I was a princess going to my coronation, and I would drive through Washington Square and under the arch in my golden coach." She looked up at Alan with an uneven smile, as if she were about to weep. Then, blinking her long-lashed gray eyes, she glanced down.

"Oh, look at all these delicious little white flowers growing in the grass," she said. "What are they called?"

"I haven't any idea," Alan admitted. "Jane would know. My wife. Have you met her?"

"Oh yes," Delia said, smiling, and somehow this time her smile conveyed the idea that this had not been an especially exciting meeting.

"She could tell you their Latin name."

"I don't want to know their Latin name," Delia said. "It's bad enough knowing that my Latin name is *Homo sapiens*. I try to forget that sort of thing as fast as I can." She began to walk around the arch, admiring it from all angles, trailing her gauzy skirts and silver net shawl in the long flowery grass. Alan, steadying himself with his cane, followed.

"Marvelous," she murmured. "Are there any others? Someone told me there was at least one other."

Alan hesitated. There was another folly, the ruined chapel, but except for Jane and the graduate students who had helped him, almost nobody had seen it. He had wanted to present it formally, as a completed project, and had often refused to allow spectators. "Well, there is one," he admitted, not wanting to lie. "But I can't show it to anyone yet, it's not finished. I hurt my back, and then—"

"I must see it," she interrupted.

"Not now."

"Please." Delia gave him an almost absurdly seductive smile.

"It wouldn't be right. I'm sure you don't publish your stories before they're finished."

"Please." She pouted like a hurt child; her soft mauve-red lower lip trembled. "I'll only be here in Corinth for a few months; I may never have another chance."

"Well. All right," Alan heard himself say. He led the way farther down the lawn, past two old apple trees and a tall, thorny mass of blackberry bushes that were now turning a dark, smoky red. "There you are." He indicated a long shingled building with a low tower. Only part of the roof and two and a half walls were standing, the latter overgrown with a tangle of climbing roses. "I didn't build the original structure," he said. "It was the chicken house when this was a farm."

"But now it's a ruined church," Delia said. "A miniature Tintern Abbey."

"Yeah."

She looked him full in the face, her silver eyes wide. "Amazing. You're a real artist."

"Thank you." No, it's not so bad, he thought, looking at the three miniature Victorian Gothic window frames he had installed along the side wall. Even if I never write another book, I can be proud of this.

"I want to walk around it."

"All right." Alan turned toward the blackberry bushes, but Delia did not follow.

"No, no!" she cried. "We mustn't go that way, that's widdershins."

"What?" He stopped.

"Widdershins, against the sun. You must never walk widdershins around a church."

"Really? Why not?"

"What they say back home is, the Devil will carry you off. Or you could just disappear. It's a superstition, of course. But you never know." She laughed lightly.

"But this isn't a real church," Alan said. "It's an abandoned chicken house. It's not consecrated or anything."

"Maybe. But I don't want to do it anyhow." She turned resolutely in the other direction, and Alan, shaking his head, followed her. Clearly, Delia Delaney was a flake. At the same time, though he was not and had never been superstitious, the memory came to him of the church in New Mexico where he had seen the lizard, and he recalled that he had in fact walked around it in what Delia Delaney, if she hadn't just been joking, would consider the dangerous direction.

Completing the circuit, Delia stepped over a heap of grass into the center of the building. " 'Bare ruined choirs where late the sweet birds sang,' " she quoted, looking around.

"Well yes, I suppose so. Or clucked. After all, they were chickens." He followed her, and they stood where the altar would have been—its absence, or presence, suggested by a hummock of stones, grass, and tangled dark-green creeper.

"I don't recognize the original—is there one?"

"Yes, partly." Alan had the sense that he was recklessly giving away secrets. "Thyme Chapel, on campus. It's Victorian Gothic, built about 1880."

"Oh. I haven't seen that yet. I really haven't seen anything on campus but the library and the Center. But your chapel is perfect anyhow."

"It's not finished, you know. I wanted to build up that third wall a bit more. And maybe fill in some of the windows with stained glass."

"Yes, I can see it," Delia breathed. "All purple and gold and cobalt blue, with swirling iridescent Tiffany flowers."

"That's sort of what I planned. There's several like that in the campus chapel. But these would be original designs."

"With the Holy Ghost as a white chicken."

"That's an idea." Alan laughed. She's witty as well as beautiful, he thought.

"I love the wild roses."

"I can't claim credit for that. They were always here. I think they were just waiting until the chickens left."

"You're lucky. And will there be more follies?"

"I don't know. Not now. I once thought I might do the Plaza fountain, or an Italian Renaissance bridge over there by the brook." He gestured widely and unwisely with his sore arm, and winced. "But then my back went out—" For almost fifteen minutes, Alan realized, he had forgotten that he was in pain.

"And after that?"

"Oh, I had plans for a lot more—drawings and site elevations and everything. But now—" As if he had deliberately recalled it, a spasm struck him: the lizard dug its claws deep into his spine. Suppressing an ugly moan, Alan turned aside, staring out toward the distant lake. He didn't want to leave Delia, but he needed more codeine and he needed it now. "Listen, I'm sorry, but I've got to go back to the house," he told her.

Slowly, leaning on his cane and breathing hard, not looking at Delia in the stupid hope that she would not look at him and see his ugly grimaces of pain, Alan made his way through the old apple trees. There were lumpy, unsprayed pale-green apples among the branches, and here and there he could see a spray of chrome yellow, predicting autumn. Delia, silent now, followed, her gauzy white skirts trailing in the long grass. As he started up the slope of the lawn, he saw Jane break away from a group of people and come toward him.

"I thought you'd gone inside," she said. "Are you all right?"

"All right," Alan lied, grinding his teeth against the pain. "I was showing Delia the ruin." In this last word he heard another lie, one of omission—the omission of a single letter, the letter s. Unfortunately, he realized at once, it was a lie that would instantly be exposed.

"Yes, it's just delightful." Delia laughed lightly. She said no more, but it was clear to Alan that she had heard his lie and recognized it, and that she had deliberately decided not to mention the ruined chapel. He looked at this smiling, innocent-seeming woman with some astonishment. They had only met fifteen minutes ago, and already they were in a conspiracy.

Jane's own smile faded. "It's not a joke, you know," she said, clearly trying to keep her voice pleasant. "It's a historical reproduction. It took months to build, you have no idea how hard Alan and his students worked."

"Oh, I can imagine." Delia laughed again and rearranged her shimmering fishnet shawl.

"Alan's published a book about ruins and follies, you know."

"Yes, Ah've seen it." Delia's Southern accent seemed to deepen, and she smiled even more pleasantly than before.

Jane did not reply. Even in the increasing grip of his pain, it was clear to Alan that there was not and probably never would be any meeting of minds between Delia and his wife, who had already complained to him about the difficulty the former's demands were causing at the Center. An awkward silence began, but it was luckily broken by the arrival of several other guests, all apparently eager to meet Delia, and one who seemed to know her well already.

"Hello there, darling," this man said, putting a heavy arm around Delia's creamy bare shoulders. (Did Alan imagine it, or did she flinch slightly?) "How's it going?"

"Just wonderfully. . . . This is my husband, Henry Hull," she told Alan. "Alan Mackenzie."

Alan registered the presence of a muscular person in a checked shirt who was several inches shorter than him. "How do you do," he said resentfully.

"Hi," Henry Hull said, as if identifying some neutral object. He took Alan's cool, long-fingered hand in his broad sweaty one and gave it a painful shake. "You have the office across the hall from Delia's at the Center," he remarked.

"That's right." Suddenly the implications of this fact became clear to Alan. He would see Delia again; he would have plenty of chances to see her again. For the first time in several minutes, he smiled. "If you'll excuse me," he said, "I'm afraid I have to go back to the house now."

FIVE

In a downtown coffee shop, Jane Mackenzie was having her regular beginning-of-term lunch with the chairman of the Humanities Council, a bachelor professor of music in his sixties called Bill Laird. There were several more convenient places on campus, but since the purpose of this lunch was to exchange confidential information, Bill had always ruled them out.

"So how are you?" he asked, leaning forward over the little glass-topped table. Today he was wearing a pink and white candy-striped shirt that brought out the natural pink and whiteness of his face and hair, and his bright blue eyes were alight with interest.

"Fine, thanks." Jane gave the standard response with what sounded to her like forced enthusiasm.

"And how's Alan?"

"He's doing all right," Jane lied. "About the same, really," she amended. Though the move to the Unger Center had relieved her husband of the need to climb stairs and teach courses, it had not relieved his constant pain—even though he had begun doing some exercises again.

"Working, I hope?"

"Oh yes." This was not so much a lie as a hopeful assumption. Jane had no idea whether Alan was working in his office at the

Center—but, after all, what else could he be doing there all day long?

"And how's everything else at the Center?"

"Not bad. There's always a few problems at the start." Jane smiled a bit tightly—she liked and trusted Bill Laird, but she didn't want to begin with a complaint.

"Of course there are. For instance?" Bill stirred two packets of brown sugar into his iced tea and smiled with an equal sweetness.

"Well, there's a big hole in the kitchen ceiling; I sent you an e-mail about that."

"Oh yes. Luckily there was no asbestos involved. . . . Thank you, darling, that looks wonderful," he told the waitress, contemplating a red pepper and mushroom omelet.

"No, that was a relief. But it means Buildings and Grounds won't fix the ceiling until next month. And the copier's not working right, as usual." This machine was an ongoing problem: Vinnie Miner, a professor of children's literature who had now retired and moved to England, had named it the Copy Monster. It would have been retired too, even sooner than Vinnie Miner, but it was sneaky. It never broke down completely, and for days or even weeks at a time it gave no trouble. It had been Vinnie's theory that whenever replacing the copier was discussed at a council meeting the machine somehow knew about it and behaved better for a while.

"As usual," Bill agreed.

"And then yesterday Delia Delaney kidnapped one of the Emerson Room sofas."

"Really?" Bill laughed. "Why would she do that?"

"Because it turns out she has migraine headaches, and when they come on she needs to lie down. Her husband told me about it before Delia moved in, and I arranged for her to have the little horsehair sofa from the front hall. But then yesterday morning Delia apparently decided that wouldn't do, and without waiting to ask me or anyone she somehow persuaded two of the other Fellows and a custodian to take it back downstairs and carry up one of the big red velvet sofas from the Emerson Room. It wouldn't fit in the elevator, so they dragged it up the front stairs somehow, and it got stuck, and they cracked one of the banisters in half."

"Really!" Bill repeated. It was clear that he was amused rather than distressed.

"Delia's going to be difficult, I'm afraid. Or else she'll get other people to be difficult for her. Just yesterday her husband came around again with two down pillows and a special reading lamp for her office. I mean, doesn't he have anything better to do?"

"I shouldn't think so," Bill said. "Delia described him in one of her letters as a freelance editor, whatever that means, and I heard somewhere that he published a couple of books of poetry once."

"Really," Jane said. For some reason that she had not bothered to analyze, not only Henry Hull himself, but the idea of Henry, made her feel edgy. "I can't decide what to do about the sofas," she added, contemplating a tuna fish salad sandwich with indifference. "I mean, I could call B and G and get them moved back."

"Oh, I don't think so," Bill said. "I think you should just ask for someone to mend the banisters."

"But it wasn't right what Delia did. It was so rude. She didn't even leave me a note, I had to hear about it from Susie." Under the table Jane clenched her small tanned hands into fists.

"Of course she should have asked you," Bill said soothingly. "But we have to think of the reputation of the Center. If we cross Delia Delaney there could be trouble."

"How could there be trouble? She'll still have a sofa."

"Not the one she wants." Bill smiled. "You've got to realize, Janey, that woman is armed and dangerous."

"Armed?" For a moment Jane saw Delia taking a pistol out of her big tapestry handbag and pointing it, and she felt a sharp imaginary pain in her chest. "You think she might have a gun?"

"I suppose it's possible." Bill laughed again—clearly he did not suppose this. "But she's armed with her celebrity. And her computer. If she felt like it she could write an article for the *New York Times*—"

"Delia doesn't use a computer," Jane interrupted, embarrassed at her brief panic. "She writes by hand with an old-fashioned pen and ink."

"Even worse. She could stab us with a goose feather. She could tell the world how cold and uptight and full of regulations we are. When she was suffering we wouldn't even let her lie down." Bill looked at Jane. "I'm surprised you should even think of trying to take a sofa away from someone like Delia Delaney. You're an experienced administrator, and she's this year's star."

"I suppose you're right. But she gets my goat sometimes."

"Your goat?" Bill smiled. "That's an odd phrase. You don't have a goat, do you?"

"Nobody has a goat," Jane said impatiently.

"Well, not many people at the University do, I expect. But all the same, why a goat?"

"I have no idea," Jane said. She was used to Bill Laird's fascination with language, but did not share it. "But you know, sometimes I wonder how long I can bear this job."

"Come on. You know you love it, really."

"Well. I suppose so. At least I used to. But this year—"

"Think of it this way. Every autumn fate brings the Center a new collection of entertaining characters, and then, before we can get tired of them, it takes them away."

"Except I'm already tired of one of them," Jane said. "You know, usually I like all the Fellows. But there's something about Delia—I don't know how to describe it—It's not as if she's pretending to be someone she isn't, like that professor who came to the Linguistics conference last year, who said he'd graduated from Oxford and had published two books that didn't exist. With Delia, it's like she's pretending all the time to be who she is." Jane sighed.

"I know what you mean. But that's part of what makes her

interesting, you know. Delia's a phenomenon. Great beauty and great egotism—that's a winning combination. And that wonderful mezzo Southern voice. I can't decide who it is she reminds me of—it's not Joan Sutherland, in spite of the height and the hair." Every other year, Bill gave a famous lecture course on the opera. "Is it Cecelia Bartoli?"

Jane, who had never heard this name, shrugged.

"She's a real diva, though. I haven't seen anything like that close up for years. I expect a lot of people will fall madly in love with her."

"Are you going to fall madly in love with her?"

"Heavens, no." Bill laughed. "But I admit I'm intrigued. It'll be fun to watch her in action. I wish I could have been there when she got them to move the sofa."

"I don't think it'll be fun for me," Jane said, giving up on her sandwich and pushing it aside.

"Well, maybe not," Bill admitted. "But never mind, she won't be here long."

"She'll be here until the end of next May," Jane sighed.

"I don't think so."

"But she has to be. She signed the contract, like all the other Fellows."

"I doubt she'll stay the course," Bill said. "The Corinth winter will drive her away if nothing else does. She's a summer creature, you can see that by looking at her. Like me. The minute the first flakes fall I want to be in Key West."

"You really think she'd walk out on the Center?"

"I'd bet on it. Would you like a little dessert?"

"No thanks." Jane smiled, hoping Bill was right, then frowned. "But if she does go, what will we do?"

"Oh, we'll sigh with regret, and with relief, and plow the rest of her stipend back into the endowment, and buy you a new top-of-the-line copier."

"That'd be nice." For the first time that day, Jane laughed spontaneously.

"Any other problems?"

"No; everything looks good. Even Susie seems happy: she's not so lonely now that the Fellows are there."

Back at the Center, Susie, wearing a white T-shirt and tight pink cotton slacks—too tight, in Jane's opinion—was reading *People* magazine.

"Hi," she said. Then, lowering her voice and gesturing with her head toward what had once been the long drawing room of the mansion—it still contained its original Victorian furniture and pictures, but was now called the Emerson Room and used for lectures and receptions—"Mrs. U is here."

"I'll go speak to her," Jane said with a certain amount of apprehension. Lily Unger, the widow of the man after whom the Unger Center was named, was not only still alive but often in evidence. Though it had been six years since her husband died, and four since she and her three Persian cats had moved into the former carriage house, she still apparently considered the main building her property. When she was in town, she often wandered over to "see what is going on," as she put it. Without calling ahead to announce a visit, she would tour the rooms downstairs, and any upstairs office whose door was open. In the past, this had caused problems. "I looked up from the computer, and there was this little old lady in a hat standing in the middle of the room. She'd walked right in, as if it was her own house," one Fellow had protested last year. "Well, it was her own house for fifty years," Jane had told him.

If Mrs. Unger had nothing better to do on Tuesday afternoons she often attended the Fellows' lectures, and if they displeased her, she complained. "I don't think Matthew would have cared for that," was a frequent comment. Jane never answered back. It was necessary to treat Mrs. Unger with great courtesy, since she still owned two-thirds of her husband's former property, more than an acre of lawn and garden only two blocks from campus. There was almost no department at Corinth University that did not want to get its hands on this land, the carriage house, and the financial portfolio that Lily Unger, who had no children, had inherited.

Mrs. Unger, who unlike her husband was nobody's fool, had remained cool to the many chairmen and deans who had urged her to make them a gift of her property and move into an assisted living facility, and she was even more scornful of the people from the Development Office.

"They must think I'm going soft in the head," she had once remarked to Jane, to whom, perhaps as a fellow townie, she had taken a liking. "I know perfectly well that as long as I own the property the University will be nice to me. But once I sign it over to them, it's finished. Poor old Nat Greene, I warned him, hold on to those fields out by the University orchards if you want to keep their respect and your parking permit, but he didn't listen to me. He gave them the land and they gave him the ceremonial dinner, and the brass plaque, and a lot of pretty thank-you letters on thick cream-colored embossed paper from everyone in Knight Hall, and then they forgot about him, more or less.

"I've made my will," she had added, "but don't you tell anyone that, Janey. I want to keep them guessing. That makes it more fun. I want them to think I could change my mind anytime. I could leave the property to the Metropolitan Opera or the Republican Party or a home for orphan cats. Last time I saw that smarmy young woman from Development, at a concert in Bailey Hall it was, I couldn't stop myself from telling her how I'd been thinking that something should be done for all those AIDS orphans in Africa. She practically turned green."

"Oh, I see the new letterhead has come." Jane indicated a stack of boxes on Susie's desk. "If you're not busy, you might distribute some to all the Fellows."

"Okay." Susie rose without complaint and left the office. Though incapable of initiative, she was always accommodating.

For a moment, Jane sat on, gathering her resources; then she headed for the Emerson Room.

"Oh, hello there, Janey," Lily Unger said. She was a small, plump elderly woman with curly white hair and big brown eyes, wearing a flowered silk dress, matching pumps, and an interfering expression. "What on earth has happened to the other red sofa?"

"It's been moved upstairs temporarily," Jane said, thinking that she should have known this question would be asked. Alterations in the structure or furnishings of the mansion always concerned and often annoyed Lily Unger. "One of the Fellows has migraine headaches, she needs to lie down sometimes."

"You mean Delia Delaney."

"Umhm."

"It would have to be her. From what I've seen of Selma Schmidt, she never lies down. Wound up tight, like a clock spring." Lily Unger always took an interest in the current year's Fellows. If she liked them, she sometimes invited them to lunch and even attempted to read their books. "She looks frustrated. Not married, is she?"

"No." Jane neglected to add that Selma was a lesbian feminist, two words that had formerly aroused Lily Unger to rage.

"I'm not surprised. Most men like a wife to be more restful." Mrs. Unger smiled. It was clear that in her time she had been able to be, or at least to appear, restful. "Delia Delaney's married, though."

"Oh yes."

"Been married three times, I hear."

"I don't think it's that many," Jane said. "Two, maybe."

"Three." Mrs. Unger spoke with authority.

"Really? Where did you hear that?" Lily Unger sometimes proffered information of this sort, which often later turned out to be correct.

"Oh, here and there." It was typical of Lily not to reveal her sources. "I've got nothing against it, if she can stand the strain. This current one is good-looking, anyhow. But I'm afraid he's a tame man."

"Really." Jane's conscious opinion of Henry was not wholly favorable, but this statement annoyed her. "How do you mean?"

"You know, like those tigers in the circus. You often see women who look like Delia there. Same hair, same sort of figure. It's amazing what they can do with a whip and a little gilt chair. But of course it's not so easy to tame something that size. Eventually those beasts can rebel and maul you, I saw it happen once—" Lily broke off as, from overhead there came a sound somewhere between a squeak and a scream. "Heavens, what was that?"

"I don't know." For a moment, Jane's mind remained occupied by a vision of Henry Hull transformed into a tiger and snarling on a stool in a circus ring, with Delia Delaney, in spangles and tights, cracking a whip at him.

"Jane, I have to talk to you!" Susie cried, rushing into the Emerson Room; her face was damp and flushed.

"Yes, what is it?" Jane lowered her voice; but Lily Unger, exercising her self-assumed proprietary privileges, followed them into the hall.

"It's that Professor Amir," Susie gasped, choking back a sob. "He sort of just grabbed me."

"Oh, I'm sorry. That's awful. Where did he grab you?"

"Right there in his office. I brought him the letterhead, like you told me, and he said could I put it on his desk, and so I did, and he said something in a funny language, and then he sort of grabbed me and kissed me." Susie indicated a blur of pink lipstick around her mouth and began to cry.

"I'm so sorry," Jane repeated.

"I never did feel comfortable around him from the start," Susie gasped. "He always looks so sort of sad and starving."

"I know what you mean," Jane admitted. It was true that Professor Charlie Amir had a hungry look. His wife had gone back to Europe to visit her family, so that he was alone in Corinth for the time being, and Jane had sometimes wondered if he was getting enough to eat. "Don't worry, he won't bother you again. We'll talk to him."

"I can't talk to him," Susie said with a sob.

"You don't have to. I'll do it, and if that doesn't work, Bill Laird will. We'll tell him that if he tries anything like that again he'll be really sorry. Now why don't you go and wash your face, and then maybe you could type up a report of what happened, just like you told me. After that you can go home, if you like."

"No thanks," Susie choked down a final sob. "I feel better now."

"It was that skinny one with the beard, wasn't it?" Lily Unger said after Susie had gone. "Comes from somewhere in Eastern Europe, doesn't he? They aren't brought up to respect women over there, not like here in America."

"I'm sure some of them are," Jane said.

"But this one wasn't."

"No, I guess not." Jane frowned as she began to consider the possible consequences of this fact.

"Of course you have to speak to him," Lily Unger continued. "But I do think there's too much fuss made about this so-called sexual harassment these days. When I was first working, back in the forties, there were guys like that in every office. It was an occupational hazard, sure, but nobody got hysterical about it. When you first started the job the other girls warned you. 'Don't go into Mr. Smithers's office alone,' I remember Margie, the office manager, telling me on my first day at the bank. 'He can't keep his hands to himself. Make some excuse if you can, and if you can't, stay on the other side of the desk,' that's what she told me. 'And if he tries anything, scream.' Creeps like that, they're not going to rape anyone. They don't want to cause a commotion, all they want is to cop a feel. A little noise and they back off."

"I hope so," Jane said. "I guess I'd better go talk to him now, if you'll excuse me."

"Would you like me to come too?"

"No thanks," Jane said, though at the same time it occurred to her that Mrs. Unger's disapproval might be more effective than her own. "Not yet, anyhow."

"Well, just let me know if I can help," Lily Unger said, giving Jane a disappointed glance as she left the room and headed toward the stairs.

In the upstairs hall Jane hesitated, looking toward Charlie Amir's office and trying to plan what she would say. Charlie was the youngest Fellow, only in his early thirties, but he had already distinguished himself as an economist. Born in Bosnia, he had somehow managed to attend London University, and his growing reputation had won him fellowships to Oxford and a tenure-track appointment at the University of Ohio. His current interest was in the economics of the Catholic Church, and he was writing a book about the church as a landowner in Central Europe, from a Marxist revisionist point of view.

In person Charlie seemed pleasant and rather shy, but two letters of recommendation had called him brilliant, which meant that his mind probably worked faster than hers did. Jane told herself that she must speak slowly and not make any mistakes, in case the matter ended up in the office of the University ombudsman, an apparently neutral but frighteningly powerful person. But what should she say?

She looked toward the door of Alan's office, which was shut. But he was there, she knew: she could tell him what had happened, and receive his sympathy and advice. As a former department chairman he had dealt with similar cases. But two things stopped her: first, the closed door, which in their private code meant that the person inside could only be disturbed in an emergency; and second, the fact that since he had developed back trouble her husband did not always seem able to offer either sympathy or advice.

Well, but this was an emergency, sort of, Jane told herself. Approaching Alan's door, she knocked lightly. When there was no answer she quietly turned the handle. There was nobody at the desk, but something like a bundle of clothes with wires coming out of it lay on the sofa. It was Alan, she realized, curled in a semi-fetal position with his back to her. Wires were running out of his ears and attached to a tape-playing device. Another set of wires ran from his lower back to a black electronic box that was supposed to block pain signals. In the last few months since he got this box Alan had spent more and more time like this, lying on a bed or a sofa and listening to music or to books on tape. When interrupted he was always disoriented and sometimes irritated.

As silently as possible, Jane closed the door.

The door of Charlie Amir's office was open, and he was sitting at his desk rolling a yellow pencil about nervously.

"Professor Amir—"

"I know why you've come," he interrupted. "I am very sorry, I am acting very wrongly." Charlie Amir was a pleasant-faced young man, with curly light-brown hair and a short curly beard. Ordinarily his English was excellent, but Jane had noticed already that in a crisis (the breakdown of the copier, for instance) it began to fail.

"You've upset Susie very much."

"Yes, yes," he agreed.

"We can't have that sort of thing here, you know," she continued. "This isn't Bosnia."

"I do nothing like that in Bosnia, never anywhere, I swear by God," Charlie protested. "I am very sorry, Mrs. Mackenzie, I have so much strain now. You know my wife, she went home this summer to see her family, and she was to come back now, to join me?"

"Yes, I know," Jane said.

"But now she says on the telephone that she did not get a permit. Why does she say that, when already she has a permit?"

"I don't know," Jane said weakly.

"I know what you are thinking, you are thinking maybe she does not want to return to America."

"No, I—"

"I am thinking this too. She is never happy here. And she has many friends who say to her two years ago, when I get the job in Ohio, do not go, America is an evil country. Her mother says this also, continuously."

"I'm sorry," Jane said.

"I don't feel so good then, you know. It is always in my mind. So I do wrong, and I am very sorry, and also about the steps."

"Steps? What steps?"

"Yesterday, when we were moving up the sofa, a pole of the steps was broken, by me. And I acted wrongly, I didn't admit—I was afraid to lose my fellowship. But I told Susie this afternoon, she should give me the bill, and I will pay, but please not to tell anyone. And she is so kind, she says never mind, they will fix it anyhow, no need to pay. So I don't know what happened, but I looked at her, and I wanted to embrace her, to thank her. I did not mean any harm."

"Maybe not," Jane said. "But you've upset Susie, and it's got to stop. I won't say anything more about it to anyone. But I have to tell you, there will be a report. And if there are any more incidents there could be an official inquiry, and sometimes this is a very unpleasant process."

Charlie Amir visibly flinched and looked stricken, and Jane realized that in his country of origin her statement would probably have suggested something far harsher than a reprimand from the ombudsman or even the loss of a fellowship. "You threaten me," he said bleakly.

"No, no. I only warn you," Jane hastened to say, so rapidly that she found herself adopting Professor Amir's diction. "Really."

"I understand. I will be careful. Also I will apologize to Susie."

"That's a good idea. But maybe it might be better if you just wrote her a note."

"You think?"

Jane nodded.

"Very well, I will do that." For the first time, Professor Amir seemed to relax. "I am sorry that I have disturbed her, you know, she is so pretty and soft and kind. She is like the peaches in my country."

And I'm not, Jane thought as she left the office. Well, too bad. Somebody has to have some backbone around here. But why does it have to be me? Why do I always have to do everything? An uneasy echo sounded in her head, of something Lily Unger had said, what? Yes, that Henry Hull did everything. But it wasn't the same, Jane thought, because Delia didn't need everything done, she wasn't really ill.

But the result was the same. She was always tense and tired lately, probably because she had so much more work at home. Not only all the usual cooking and cleaning and shopping and errands, but everything Alan used to do: the dishes and the laundry and the household repairs, taking the newspapers and bottles and cans and trash out, dragging the garbage cans and recycling bins up the steep driveway to the road and then down again. And rewiring lamps and hanging the new shower curtain, putting up the storm windows, raking the leaves, unblocking the sink, changing the furnace filters, and replacing bulbs in ceiling fixtures. For a long while she had seen it as temporary. She had kept telling herself that for a while she would have to do these things, but then it would be over.

Because it wasn't fair now, it wasn't right. Though healthy, compared to Alan Jane was small and slight, barely five-foot-two. In the past one of the many things she had loved and admired about her husband was his height and strength: the easy, casual way he could lift heavy boxes of books and open bottles and reach things on top shelves. But last spring, when Alan went to have his operation, Jane had had to carry everything and drag both their suitcases and lift them onto the X-ray machine, while Alan just stood there, leaning on his cane and looking off into the distance as if he weren't involved and had never even met her. He had probably been embarrassed; she recognized that. But the bottom line was that she had had to do everything on that trip and she still had to do everything, and though she shouldn't, she resented it, and sometimes even showed this, and she was slowly but steadily turning into a mean, resentful person.

SIX

Outside Alan's window at the Unger Center the sky was a bland blue, the maples a cheerful chrome yellow, and none of the people passing along the sidewalk were running or screaming. There was no sign that since last Tuesday the University, the town, and the nation had been in a state of shock. Over three thousand people had died in the World Trade Center, and as Susie Burdett, in the Center office downstairs, had put it, weeping, nowhere seemed nice and safe anymore.

Alan had agreed with her, without adding that for him this was not new—that nowhere had seemed nice and safe to him for the last eighteen months. Ever since the lizard moved into his back the world had been full of hazards: noisy gangs of students that might knock him over in the hallways; cars that might hit him as he slowly and painfully, leaning on his cane, made his way from the parking lot to his office; chairs and beds that were agony to sit or lie in; irregularities in the natural landscape that might trip him up and make his pain worse.

Alan had always thought of the World Trade Center as a rather banal structure; if in the past he had been asked whether it should be torn down for aesthetic reasons, he might have said yes. But its sudden destruction had affected him like a physical blow. Last Tuesday, alerted by a phone call from a colleague, he had stood in his sitting room watching a TV replay of that horrible and unbelievable event. As the first plane hit, he felt a sudden, much sharper pain in his back, exactly as if his spine were the inner armature of a skyscraper into which something had just crashed. He gasped for air, felt dizzy, and had to lie down on the sofa.

The president of the University and his colleagues in Knight Hall, predictably, had announced to what they sometimes called the Corinth Community (thus including both town and gown) that life and classes must go on—indeed that to cause them to go on was everyone's patriotic and academic duty. Alan's particular duty, apparently, as the senior Faculty Fellow at the Center, was to deliver his lecture on religious architecture, titled "Houses of God" and scheduled for that afternoon. In the light of the morning's events it seemed totally irrelevant to him, and he had e-mailed the chairman of the Humanities Council, Bill Laird, to say so. Bill had e-mailed him back, agreeing and suggesting they reschedule the talk for the following week, at the same time quietly deploring the president's speech.

It was the first, but not the only intimation Alan had had in the last week that the public and larger disaster had somehow made his private one seem petty and egocentric. It was as if it were willfully selfish of him to have a bad back at a time like this, and he ought to shape up and forget about it. No one had said this directly, but Alan imagined he could see it in people's faces, for example in the face of Delia Delaney.

It had been stupid of him to think that Delia was as interested in him as he was in her. In the past he had been her equal: and at the party on Labor Day she had seemed to see him this way still, to recognize that they were two of a kind, both of them unique and superior beings. Afterward he had been inspired to take out his drawings of architectural follies and work on them, and also to restart his exercise program.

But in fact Delia's warmth and encouragement had probably

been merely charm and good manners. Even before the disaster he had seen almost nothing more of her. Her door at the Center was usually shut, with a DO NOT DISTURB sign, presumably stolen from some hotel, on the doorknob. Once the door had been open and he had paused in it to say hello, but Delia was on the phone and merely smiled and fanned the air with one smooth white arm, in the gesture of someone waving away distraction. If he had been her equal, she would not have done that. But he was not her equal anymore: he was a semi-invalid has-been, while she was still beautiful and famous and well. Since then, his impulse to work had gradually faded. When he had looked at his drawings this morning they seemed mere piles of scribbled irrelevant paper, and his mind was empty and dark.

Next week Alan would have to give his useless postponed lecture, to which probably almost no one would come. If he could have canceled it he would have done so. Religious architecture no longer interested him, and he was sure it would interest his students and colleagues even less. Jane had tried to convince him that this was not true, but her effort, though no doubt well-intentioned, had ended yesterday in one of the most unpleasant conversations they had ever had.

In fact, things had been bad between them from the afternoon of September 11, when Jane was unbearably late picking him up, because she was consoling a campus acquaintance whose brother-in-law worked in the World Trade Center. She had let Alan stand there for half an hour in front of the building, in increasingly severe pain, so that finally he had to lie down on the dusty grass next to the driveway. When he asked why she hadn't at least called him, Jane replied that she had tried, twice, but nobody had answered the phone. (She was probably telling the truth, he admitted now. The Fellows had been asked to answer after four rings, in case Susie was away from her desk, but Alan suspected that they did not always do so, and in fact he himself never did so. For a while Selma Schmidt had taken on this task, but then she had rebelled. "I am not a switchboard operator," she had protested, "but because I am a female the rest of you assume that is my job.")

"Even so," Alan had told Jane, "you could have driven around to the Center and told me you'd be late. You know it just about kills me to stand up for more than fifteen minutes at a time."

"I'm awfully sorry," Jane had said, with an unusually cool smile. "But you know, darling, you aren't dead, and Becca's sister's husband probably is."

Well, the way I feel now, I wish I were dead instead of him, Alan had thought, but did not say.

At supper the night before last, when he spoke again of canceling his lecture or at least postponing it further, Jane had pointed out that the posters had already gone up, and said she agreed with Bill Laird that the lecture should be given as soon as possible, and that it would help to raise morale at the Center and on campus. Alan had said that was ridiculous; that essentially his topic, and he, were irrelevant in the present situation. She was treating him as if he were a small child, he said, she was fibbing to make him feel better.

Jane, setting down her mug of Sunburst C herb tea, had wearily and indignantly denied this, and in turn suggested that in the present situation it was important not to give in to defeatism and self-pity. Alan had then, against his better judgment, suggested that considering recent world events, people who thought like her were either fools or hypocrites. He had accused these theoretical people of a blinkered optimism, and cast doubt on their ability to see the world as it really was. Jane had choked up with tears, shoved her half-eaten slice of apple pie away, and run out of the house into the vegetable garden, where for the next half hour she vindictively pulled up carrots in the gathering dusk. Later that evening they had exchanged formal apologies, but the phrases "defeatism and self-pity" and "fools or hypocrites" continued to reverberate through the house like the distant echoes of an ugly gong, and communication between them had remained tense ever since.

Over the past year Alan had in fact sometimes found Jane's optimism foolish or hypocritical, though at times comforting. Now it seemed almost disgusting. He also found himself and his continued existence disgusting. Thousands of strong, healthy, productive people had died in the disaster, while he, an aging unproductive invalid, survived. He suspected that rules had been bent and letters written to get him this fellowship, to provide him with a generous income and a beautiful place to work, but the beauty meant nothing to him and he was not working. Also, every day when he entered or left the Center he was reminded of the irony involved. Five years ago, when he had been consulted about the remodeling of the Unger mansion, he had been impatient at learning of the handicap access requirements for all new university construction. He had grumbled about the need to install a ramp to the back door and an elevator that spoiled the classically Victorian lines of the hall. The jealous gods, who were clearly on the side of the handicapped (after all, Hephaestus, patron of architects, was lame himself), had heard him, and now Alan used this authorized equipment every day.

As, gazing out the window of his office and groaning from time to time with pain, he revolved these unpleasant thoughts and memories, there was a knock on his half-closed door.

"Yes?" He turned. Delia Delaney stood there in a gauzy lavender dress and sandals, with her hair in a long braid. "Oh, hello."

"Please, you've got to help me," she said in a tremulous half whisper. "I need to hide somewhere."

"You need to hide?" Alan repeated. "From what?"

"It's this awful reporter from the local newspaper. He's pursuing me for a statement about the World Trade Center." She put a soft white trembling hand on his arm. "Please, can I stay here, just for a little while?"

"Well—yes, all right."

"Oh, thank you." Delia came into the room and shut the door behind her, letting out a deep soft sigh that smelled of oranges. "He's downstairs right now. I can't bear to see him. Besides, he's brought a photographer, and I look frightful today."

This last statement was, if not a lie, a delusion. With her thick golden braid, from which gilt tendrils like sparks escaped in every direction, her flushed face, and her wide, pale gray eyes, Delia looked like a frightened but beautiful schoolgirl.

"That's them now," she whispered, gesturing toward the hall, from which steps and loud voices could be heard, followed by knocking and shouts:

"Ms. Delaney? Ms. Delaney? Are you in there?"

"Please, could you lock your door?" Delia whispered.

"Okay." As quietly as he could manage, Alan crossed the room and turned the key.

"Oh, thank you." She gave a warm, breathy sigh.

"You know, you could have locked your own door," he whispered.

"No, I couldn't. I couldn't have borne it to be in there while they were yelling and pounding."

Out in the hall, there was more loud, half-audible conversation, and then the sound of steps receding. "They're going away," Alan whispered.

"Maybe. Or maybe they think I'm in the washroom, and they're going to wait downstairs for me to come out. Please don't make me leave now." She looked up at Alan, her silver eyes swimming with unshed silver tears. Why, she's terrified, he thought.

"Of course not," he said.

"He's hateful, that reporter. You haven't seen him, he's a great big ugly young man like a rhinoceros, with heavy legs and feet, he frightens me so."

"I think I have seen him," Alan said. "Isn't he called Tom something?"

"How should I know? But it's not fair, this is the second time he's come after me." She gazed up at Alan with a blurry, frightened smile. "Yesterday he tramped right into my room with his big rhinoceros feet, when my mind was full of all those people falling through the air, the size of flies, with the smoke pouring out above them and around them, the air full of flies that were human beings.

I almost told him that, but thank God I stopped myself. Instead I said I was too upset to talk. So then he asked if he could come back today. I didn't say no, I was afraid to make him angry. But I'm not going to speak to him. There's nothing I can say that won't either sound stupid or get me into trouble."

"How could it get you into trouble?"

"You can always get into trouble if you give an original answer to a journalist." Delia sighed, and subsided onto the upholstered window seat with a flutter of lavender gauze. "They're looking for that; they want shock and scandal. It's especially dangerous to have an aesthetic take on any disaster. Even if you're as horrified as everyone else, they'll make you sound callous."

"I know what you mean," Alan said. "When I talked to the guy from the paper he kept asking me what I thought of the World Trade Center as an architect. The truth is I didn't think much. It was a boring design, you know, architecturally uninteresting and out of proportion with its environment. But I definitely didn't say that. The architecture is not the point, I said. The point is that over three thousand people are dead. I could tell it wasn't what he wanted."

"No," Delia agreed. "I expect he wanted you to say that the World Trade Center was a tragic loss to American architecture."

"Maybe. Anyhow he kept after me and kept after me, and finally I told him that it was a significant structure, one that could only have appeared at this time in history and in this country."

"Perfect." Delia laughed lightly. "I wish I had your presence of mind."

Across the hall, a ringing began. "That's your phone, I think," Alan said.

"I'm not going to answer it. It will be the rhinoceros again, or some other awful animal."

The ringing stopped; then it commenced again in Alan's office.

"If they're asking for me, don't say I'm here. Please." She gave him a frightened smile.

"All right," Alan agreed. "Hello. . . . What? . . . Just a moment, let me go and look. . . . No, she's not in her office." Again, he realized, he had somehow become involved in a conspiracy with Delia Delaney.

"Thank you," Delia said. "That was very convincing. And the absolute truth, too. Very neat." She gave a silvery laugh.

"Shh, he's probably still downstairs."

"But maybe he'll go away now." Delia stood up and moved toward the window, swaying slightly toward Alan, so close that he felt the warmth of her bare arm against his. Together they looked down through the golden, windblown leaves of the big maple. "Yep, there he goes."

"It's the same guy that came to see me," Alan said as two heavy figures crossed the lawn. "Very persistent, he was."

"Yes. Awful. I hate journalists, but you have to be polite to them, or they'll destroy you. Well." Her voice changed as she moved away, and it was as if a cold wind were blowing on him.

She's used me, now she's going to leave, Alan thought. He felt an irrational disappointment and loss; and became aware again of the clawing pain in his back.

Delia crossed the room, paused by the door, and then turned. "You're speaking next week," she said. "I'm going to come and hear you."

"Why?" Alan asked coldly.

"Why not?"

"Are you interested in religious architecture?"

"I could be interested," Delia said, smiling.

He shrugged. "I'm not sure I am anymore, since last Tuesday. Who can care about religious architecture, or any architecture, after what happened to those towers?"

"They always reminded me of the sign for Gemini," Delia said. "Communication, speed, restlessness, short journeys. You're not a Gemini, are you?"

"No." Alan, who despised astrology, volunteered no further information. The idea came to him that Delia was spacey as well as beautiful. "You don't really believe that stuff, do you?"

"Oh, but I do." Delia laughed lightly. "I believe it every Friday from two to three p.m."

"Really."

"It's always fun trying on different faiths. Expands the mind. If you were a Gemini, for instance, you would have liked the World Trade Center better. You'd think of it as a kind of temple of commerce and communication." She laughed again.

"A form of religious architecture." Alan smiled, reassured as to her basic good sense. "You know, I have thought something like that. That you could see skyscrapers as the capitalist equivalent of church steeples. The visible connection of business to its god."

"In that case, the World Trade Center must have been the temple to a twin god," Delia said.

"Castor and Pollux, then, probably. They were violent gods, in charge of the city of Rome and thunder and storms."

"I thought they were supposed to protect travelers. But I guess they didn't always."

"Apparently not this time," Alan said. "Too bad I can't say that in my lecture."

"You can't say it right out." Delia gave him a sideways look. "But you could suggest it."

"Yes. Maybe I could." He smiled, realizing the possibilities.

"So I'll look forward to your talk." She turned the knob, but the door, being locked, did not open.

"Sorry, I'll get that." He crossed the room. Again he stood so close to Delia that he could see all the separate sparkling gilt tendrils that escaped from her braid, and breathe her scent of orange peel.

"Thank you for taking me in," she half whispered, putting her soft white hand on his arm. Then suddenly she stood on tiptoe and kissed him. The sensation was light but very hot, as if a burning butterfly had brushed his cheek. Before Alan could react, Delia was gone.

He did not try to go after her. Instead he turned back toward the drafting table he now used as a stand-up desk, and the draft of his lecture. This morning it had lain there dead, but now the sheets of paper seemed to glow gently, and new sentences had begun to appear in his mind.

SEVEN

The automatic door of the supermarket shut behind her with its rubbery swish, and Jane was surrounded by a blast of clammy air, at least twenty degrees colder than the golden autumn outside. In her sleeveless flowered cotton dress she felt chilled almost at once, and also angry. Not only at the store, but at her husband Alan, whose pathetic request, as usual disguised as a question, had separated her from what might be one of the last warm Saturdays in her garden.

"Are you going to the grocery this morning?" he had asked as she headed for the back door, carrying her garden basket and a trowel. "Because if you are, I need a bag of prunes and a couple bottles of prune juice. And if you have the time, I'd like a box of Fleet Enemas from the drugstore." Yes, he had admitted, he was constipated again, in fact very constipated, and yes, he was very uncomfortable.

Naturally Jane had said that she was going to the grocery and would have time to stop at the drugstore. She had put down her basket and taken off her gardening hat and gloves, and hastened to make this statement true.

When Alan was in pain, which was still almost always, his needs took precedence over hers. That was natural and inevitable, but it was also annoying. But it was useless and also mean to give in to her annoyance, to let it ruin her day and also Alan's if she wasn't careful. I must try to be a good person, even if I'm really not, she reminded herself, as she often did now. He is in constant and awful pain, and I am not in pain.

Anyhow the current annoyance was nearly over. She'd already been to the drugstore and in twenty minutes she'd be back in her garden, picking ripe tomatoes and cutting some of her basil for pesto and covering the rest in case there was an early frost tonight. But making pesto was selfish, since Alan now wouldn't eat anything that obviously contained garlic. Since his illness began he had also declared a distaste for cucumbers, cabbage, spinach, artichokes, and zucchini (this last was a special nuisance since at this time of year Jane's garden, like that of everyone she knew, was oversupplied with that vegetable). Once Alan had been happy to eat all these things, and also the wild dandelion greens, sorrel, purslane, and chives that she loved to gather and add to salads and soup. Now he would not even touch the splendid watercress that grew in the stream near their house. He had also recently asked Jane not to bake or buy any cookies, cakes, or ice cream, because he wanted to lose some weight. She had complied, though she sometimes concealed a chocolate bar in the drawer of her desk. Meanwhile, Alan, as if reverting to childhood, had begun to crave high-calorie snacks. When he couldn't sleep at night he would go down to the pantry and graze; next morning a whole bag of potato chips or peanuts or dried coconut would be gone.

What made all this worse was that it was so out of character. In the past Alan had never done anything of the sort, no more than he had ever hung around the house most of the day or constantly called for her help or wanted to know where she was going to be at every moment. Often now when she looked at the man lying on her sofa or bed or in her bathtub she almost did not recognize him. That isn't Alan Mackenzie, she would involuntarily think: it's some pale, fat, weak, greedy, demanding person—someone like the shabby, threatening stranger she thought she'd seen coming down the drive on that bad morning in August.

The supermarket was more or less empty, but as Jane reached the end of one aisle and hastened up the next, she saw a man in a bright yellow shirt, jeans, and sandals frowning in front of a display of lettuce. Jane noticed first that he was very attractive, and then, less happily, that he was Henry Hull, Delia's husband.

"Well, hello," he greeted her.

"Oh, hi, how are you?" she replied neutrally.

"Discouraged. Look at this lettuce, it's pathetic." Henry held up a bunch of yellow-green leaves that drooped from his square brown hand in a sickly manner. "And the tomatoes. Hard as rocks and such a peculiar color, like dried tomato soup. Even the carrots are rubbery and withered. I don't get it. Here we are in the middle of farm country, you'd think they'd have something better."

"Yes, but nobody buys vegetables at the grocery, not at this time of year," Jane said. "If you don't have a garden yourself, you go to the Farmers' Market. They have wonderful tomatoes there now."

"Oh? I must look into that. Where is this market?"

"It's downtown, near the lake."

"Downtown?" Henry said in a vague manner.

"Yes, you take Route 13, that's just up the road, and then . . ." Jane paused. "I was planning to go there today anyhow, for apples and honey."

"They have apples and honey?"

"Oh yes. They have lots of things. . . . If you can wait until I'm finished shopping, I'll show you," Jane was surprised to hear herself say.

"That's very kind." Henry also sounded surprised but pleased. "And I'll get rid of all this pathetic stuff." He began to restore the vegetables to a bare space on the slanting counter; then to create a face from them. The lettuce became limp, disheveled green hair, the pale tomatoes two bulging eyes, one of the carrots a nose, and another a mouth.

"It doesn't look happy," Jane said, laughing, though at the same time glancing around uneasily for the produce manager.

"No, why should it? Ashamed of itself, that's how it should look."

"Yes," she agreed.

"He's unhappy because you don't love him," Henry suggested. He replaced the carrot with a limp zucchini, giving the face a mournful, longing expression.

"He can't expect me to love him," Jane said, laughing again, almost giddily.

"But he does. We all do." He gave her a quick stare.

"No, you mustn't," she replied awkwardly, and turned away toward the front of the store.

"I have to drop some things off at my house, it won't take long," she said as they left the grocery, with Henry pushing the cart. He would have seen the prunes and prune juice as she went through the checkout, and drawn conclusions, she thought, though she had attempted to muddle the message with a bag of brown sugar and some crackers. *It's my husband who is constipated, not me,* she had suddenly wanted to say, though this would have been disloyal and also vulgar.

As she drove home to deliver Alan's groceries and enema, and then down to the Farmers' Market, followed by Henry's SUV, Jane's mind was troubled. It was over eighteen months since she'd had the kind of conversation she'd just had in the grocery, and she was out of practice, she told herself. In the past, she'd enjoyed flirting lightly and easily with Alan's friends. But since his back trouble all that had stopped. You don't flirt when your husband is seriously ill—nor, if you are a man, do you flirt with the wife of a seriously ill friend.

Those old encounters weren't supposed to and didn't ever go anywhere; they were meant only to prove to both parties that they were amusing and attractive. But Henry wasn't Alan's friend, and there was something about the glance he had given her in the grocery— But maybe, no, probably, she was imagining it, because it had been so long.

———

An hour later Henry and Jane were sitting at a picnic table between the Farmers' Market and the lake, under a big willow tree that trailed its bright delicate yellow leaves (which, Jane noticed, exactly matched his shirt) in the water. They were drinking fresh cold apple cider, and beside Henry was a large new split-wood basket full of vegetables and fruit and homemade bread and honey and goat cheese and free-range brown eggs. Jane had prevented him from buying any zucchini or tomatoes, promising to donate some of the excess from her garden. It had turned out, as Lily claimed, that he did most of the shopping and cooking for himself and Delia.

"Hey," he said. "I'm so lucky I ran into you."

"Mm." Maybe Henry was lucky, Jane thought, but what was she? Why had she volunteered to take him to the Farmers' Market instead of just giving him directions and going home? Why was she here by the lake at noon instead of making lunch for Alan and finding out if he was feeling better and if there was anything else he needed? Guilty was what she was, and selfish and careless.

"So how is everything going?" she asked politely, to break the silence and distract herself from these familiar self-accusations.

"All right. Delia's having one of her migraines, though."

"Oh, that's too bad," Jane said, struck by the use of the possessive, as if the migraines were Delia's personal property. "I'm very sorry," she added, conscious that she was not especially sorry. The more she saw of Delia Delaney, the less she cared for her. When Delia wasn't demanding some special service or equipment, she was interfering with things at the Center in other ways. A few days ago, for instance, she had taken, or rather openly stolen, a whole ream of expensive pale-green paper (normally used only for posters and announcements) from the supply cupboard. Also, after Susie had received a polite written apology from Charlie Amir, which should have closed last month's unfortunate incident, Delia had completely spoiled its effect. She had done this by telling Susie that the bunch of roses that accompanied the note conveyed a message in the Victorian Language of Flowers: dark-red roses, appropriately, meant Bashful

Shame, but the ferns that came with them signified Fascination. "He's ashamed of what he did, but he's also fascinated by you, Susie," Delia had said, laughing. "When he kissed you, he couldn't help himself."

When Jane remarked that it was very unlikely that a Bosnian economist would be acquainted with this code, Delia had contradicted her. The Language of Flowers was still known all over Europe, she claimed. Anyhow, she had added, segueing into a vatic Jungian mode, these ancient symbolic meanings were innate. Even if Charlie hadn't known what the flowers meant, they expressed what he subconsciously wanted to convey. It was meant as a joke, probably, but for the rest of the afternoon Susie had remained in a dreamy, inefficient daze. "Nobody ever sent me so many roses before," she kept saying.

"It's weird, you know," Henry remarked, as if to himself. "When she's having a migraine it's as if Delia's a different person. Sometimes I almost don't recognize her."

"Yes, it's—" Jane said involuntarily, then checked herself, hoping she had given nothing away. "Does Delia have migraines often?" she asked, aware that she had allowed a silence to fall.

"Fairly often." Henry took a slow drink of cider. "They come on when she's under stress, or when she doesn't get what she wants. That's my theory, anyhow." He smiled briefly and without mirth.

"Really. And what does she want?"

"Oh, the usual things that people want. Fame, love, money."

"Really," Jane repeated. "But doesn't she already have those things?"

"Not completely. Reviews often make her ill, for instance. Last night it was a piece in the *Times Literary Supplement*. It was favorable, mostly, but it called her the American Angela Carter. Delia said the implication was that she was a weak transatlantic copy. And it wasn't fair either, because Angela's tales all came out of European folklore, while most of hers are inspired by Southern popular traditions and ghost stories and American Indian legends. 'The English are so sneaky and devious,' she kept saying. 'They destroy you with a thousand little needle-pricks. I can feel them now in my head.'"

"And she got a migraine just from that?" Jane asked incredulously. "But she's had so many, many good reviews, and articles and letters—I know, I've seen her folder."

"Yeah, but you see, Delia doesn't feel safe unless the applause is complete. She needs for everyone in the world to love her. And usually they do."

"Yes; I've noticed," Jane said. Bill Laird's prediction had come true, she thought. Both Mrs. Unger and Susie admired Delia immensely now, and all the Fellows except Alan seemed to have a crush on her, including Selma Schmidt.

"But it's never enough, you see," Henry said. "There's always a few people here and there who don't love Delia, however hard she tries. However brilliant and charming she is, they just won't." He paused to take another swallow of cider. "People like you, for instance."

"Oh, I never said—I didn't mean—" Jane protested.

"Of course not. But I can always tell. And so can she, usually. 'Jane Mackenzie doesn't like me,' she said, just the other day. 'How can I get her to like me?'"

No way, Jane thought, but said nothing. She looked at Henry and noticed that he was smiling, almost laughing. It amuses him that I don't like Delia, she realized. Maybe it even pleases him.

"It's not always fun being famous," Henry said. "But somehow people want it."

"I don't see why," Jane said with distaste. "All those people looking at you and talking about you all the time and printing your name in the papers."

"You might like it," Henry said. "You never know till you try."

"No, I wouldn't. I was sort of famous here in Corinth once, for a week or so, and it was just hateful."

"Ah? How did that happen?" He smiled and leaned toward her.

"Well, it was kind of a mistake. My picture was in the local paper because I was buying a big stack of books at the library book sale. I didn't even know they'd taken it, but it was on the front page. Everybody in town saw it, and they all said different intrusive things, even people I hardly know. They said how I must read so much I would hardly have time for anything else, or that my hair was untidy. The pharmacist in the drugstore told me I needed a haircut, and this woman in Benefits in Knight Hall said I looked very worried and unhappy; but I wasn't unhappy at all. I only looked that way because the books were heavy and slipping." She flushed, embarrassed. Why am I running off at the mouth like this? she thought. I hardly know this person.

"I think I know what you mean," Henry said, and waited for her to go on, and for some reason, maybe because he was listening so carefully, she did.

"You see, if I hadn't been in the paper nobody would have dared to tell me I looked unhappy or needed a haircut, they would have known it was none of their business. Nobody asked them to have an opinion, but they somehow thought it was their right, because I was in the paper. I don't know how famous people can stand it. I mean, it's no wonder Delia gets headaches."

"No, perhaps not." Henry was silent for a moment, looking out over the long, shimmering lake, and then back at Jane. "I wanted to be famous once, you know," he said. "Before I saw it up close." He shrugged and turned, glancing around at the group of musicians on the dock who were playing a ragged but cheerful bluegrass number. "This is a great place," he said finally. "I think I'm going to come here every Saturday."

"Why not?" Jane frowned. Before Alan hurt his back, they used to visit the market together. He would carry the basket, and often they would run into friends and acquaintances. Today Jane hadn't seen anyone she knew well enough to speak to at length, but she had been uncomfortably aware that one of the technicians in her dentist's office, and an elderly couple who often came to chamber music concerts in Bailey Hall, must have noticed that a strange man was accompanying her.

"You know, it kind of reminds me of home," Henry added.

"Oh? Where is home?"

"Well. It's in Ontario. Or was."

"In Canada."

"Uh-huh."

"You're a Canadian."

Henry sighed. "God. The way you say that."

"What?"

He laughed. "Oh, it's not just you. Everyone down here says it that way. With a kind of bored, dying fall."

"I didn't," Jane protested.

"Yes, you did. To an American, a Canadian is something like— like this cabbage." He lifted it from his basket. "Organic, healthy, solid, reliable, boring."

In spite of herself, Jane laughed.

"Why are you laughing? It's no joke to be Canadian."

"I didn't say all that, you did. Anyhow I don't think of Canadi- ans as cabbages."

"Ah. So what do you think of them as?"

"I don't think of them as anything," Jane said, half amused and half uncomfortable.

"Exactly. You don't think of us at all. That's our tragedy." Henry grinned and took a final gulp of cider. "You don't know how it is for us up there. We're always looking south. Aware that beyond the boundary there's another world: brighter, richer, full of abundance and adventure. It's like being poor relations or hired help. We're stuck up in the cold attic, and you're all down below where it's warm and there's always a party going on."

"Is that why you came to America?" Jane asked. The idea of a whole nation—or at least of Henry Hull—longing for her life, and envying it, seemed both childish and cheering.

"Well." Henry paused and looked up the lake, where a little breeze was now stirring the water. "I suppose so. At least partly."

"And you found what you wanted?"

"Hell, no." He laughed. "I should have known. See, back home I was just a guy like other guys, but the minute I got here I was a Canadian. As soon as anyone heard where I came from, the organic cabbage was all they saw."

"But you didn't go back," Jane said.

"No. I just stopped telling people where I was from."

Jane looked at him, meeting his smile. "You told me," she said.

"Yeah, I did. I don't know," Henry said. "I guess I feel safe with you." He put his large square hand on hers in a friendly manner.

But I don't feel safe with you, Jane thought. She tried to move her hand, but found it impossible.

"You're not like most Americans," Henry said meditatively. "With most Americans I never feel safe. You're kind of like a Canadian," he added, smiling now.

"Really." She found the strength to pull her hand away. "Is that a compliment or an insult?"

"What do you think?" Henry continued to smile.

"I think it's a bit of both," Jane said as evenly as she could manage. "I must get back now," she added, standing up. "Alan—"

"Yeah. How is Alan?"

"Not too well today, actually."

"It's rough, back trouble," Henry said. "Or so I hear."

"Yes." Jane picked up her own basket. "It's not easy for him."

"Or for you either," Henry suggested. He looked up at her, not smiling now. "It's no joke, being a caregiver, right?"

"Well, no, not always," Jane admitted, a little surprised. "But of course it's much worse for him. I mean, he's in terrible pain a lot of the time. I don't have any right to complain."

"Sure you do. And so do I." Henry stood up. He was not as tall as Alan, but darker and broader, and unmistakably strong and in good health. "It's what you do that counts, not what you say. Or what you feel."

"Well. Maybe." In spite of herself, Jane smiled; but she also took a step away.

"I think we should meet often and complain to each other." Henry put his warm broad hand on her bare arm, pulling her back toward him for a disturbing moment. "What about lunch someday next week?"

"Oh, I don't know," Jane said, shifting from one foot to another.

"I'll call you. We caregivers have got to stick together."

EIGHT

At the Unger Center for the Humanities, Alan lay on a dusty green plush sofa in a position that decreased but did not eliminate the gnawing pain in his back. For a few hours this morning he had been able to work through the pain, but then it had become too exhausting.

Still, he had accomplished something. He had written three pages on the semiotics of American religious architecture, with representative examples. Catholic churches in this country, he had proposed, tended to have sturdy, even stocky brick or stone bell towers, or at least towers capable of containing bells. It was usually possible, though not always easy, to climb them. The standard Episcopal or Presbyterian church tower was narrower and often taller, and more difficult of ascent. And in the newer and more radical denominations, the steeple tended to become thinner and thinner, so that eventually it was sometimes reduced to a mere symbolic white wood or shiny aluminum spike, a kind of exaggerated lightning rod. Was this development, perhaps, related to a conception of the Holy Spirit as no longer a benevolent dove that might roost on or nest in a tower, but instead more like a bolt of electricity that could and sometimes did strike worshippers down, so that they fell to the ground and babbled in tongues?

For the last week or so things had been looking up a little. Alan's back was not well, nothing even approaching well; but at last it was no worse than before his operation. Possibly this had something to do with his new office, with its sofa and the drafting table; possibly he was just managing the drugs better, so that he got some relief without headache, constipation, confusion, and all the other nasty side effects. Or, possibly, his recent attempts to resume an exercise regime were paying off. Encouraged by his friend Bernie, Alan had begun going for walks, and even (with the help of a charity transportation service called Gadabout) visited the YMCA pool, where he swam for twenty minutes and did uncomfortable water exercises.

The lizard, though slightly less active, was still there in his back; but the lecture on church architecture had gone well, and the questions and comments from the audience had suggested several new lines of inquiry. Delia had been there as she had promised, though her congratulations afterward were irritatingly cut short by the arrival of Selma Schmidt. Selma, who like all the other Fellows seemed to have a kind of adolescent crush on Delia, had come up to pant and gush not over his talk, but over Delia's latest story, actually pushing him aside in her haste.

Ultimately, though, the interruption hadn't mattered, because the following day Delia had come to Alan's office to repeat her praise both for his lecture and for the artificial follies on his property. Moved by her enthusiasm, Alan had shown her, first, his watercolor rendering of the ruined chapel as it would look when completed, and then his drawings for several other possible projects. Delia's reaction—impressed, amused—had been gratifying.

"Yes—this is the real thing," she had declared finally. "Have you shown it anywhere yet?" Alan had shaken his head. "You must have sent slides to your gallery, at least."

"No," he had admitted. "I don't have slides, and I don't have a gallery. I did these drawings for myself. For the fun of it."

"But you should have a show." Delia opened her great gray eyes even wider. "Everyone should see this work. You mustn't be selfish."

"I don't know." He smiled. "It might be dangerous, you know. All these destroyed buildings, especially now. If they went on view somebody might report me to Homeland Security."

Delia laughed. "I suppose anything is possible," she said.

"But seriously, you know, some people might be angry." He was quoting Jane now. When she had helped him move his drawings to the Center she had suggested that this wasn't a good time to leave them lying about. "There's some things you can't make fun of," she had warned.

"No, no, no," Delia interrupted, tossing back her heavy shock of golden hair. "You've got it all backwards. What's happened makes your drawings more serious; it gives them a kind of visionary, prophetic quality. You see these monuments as simultaneously beautiful and endangered. I wonder—I have a friend in New York who runs a gallery. I think he might be interested. Would you let me contact him?"

"Well—" Half doubting, wholly charmed, Alan had arranged to have photographs made of half a dozen drawings and the two follies on his property, and Delia had sent them off.

Or so she had said. But since then, nothing. Over two weeks had passed and Alan had hardly seen her again, and never alone, until twenty minutes ago, when she had hastened by his office with her face averted, not responding to his greeting. Probably she was avoiding him. Either she hadn't heard anything from the gallery, or his slides had been rejected and she was reluctant to tell him so. That had been Jane's opinion when he mentioned the matter to her. She didn't like to say this, she told Alan, but she would be surprised if anything came of Delia Delaney's proposal. Yes, of course Delia had encouraged him, Jane said; it was the sort of thing she did. Already she had encouraged and then disappointed several people at the University.

When Alan said he found this hard to believe, Jane gave examples. "She promised to go to lunch with Lily Unger and some of her friends, and then canceled at the last moment, said she had a headache. She's persuaded Susie that Charlie Amir is in love with her, which of course he's not. And she flatters all the Fellows and anyone else who turns up and promises to read their books or manuscripts, but then she never does, and when people try to reach her she isn't there. She's already missed one of our weekly lunches and walked out of the other two early. If you ask me, she's here to collect her salary and do as little as possible."

It was clear to Alan that Jane had it in for Delia; he just didn't know why. It was unlikely that she should be jealous—that had never been her nature, and anyhow he was in no condition to be unfaithful. He had never shown any enthusiasm for Delia's writing, and when Jane had recently referred to her most famous book as "pretentious imitation fairy tales," he hadn't protested. But it wasn't just that Jane didn't like Delia—she also didn't like his follies and ruins, especially now.

She had been doubtful about this project from the start, and now her doubts had increased. In her opinion, Alan would probably do best to keep that side of his work quiet for a while. There were a lot of people, especially in New York, who would be upset if they saw paintings like his. When Alan suggested that they might be seen as ironic and amusing, Jane wasn't convinced. "There are some things you can't make fun of," she had repeated.

In spite of Jane, Alan was still sure—well, almost sure—that Delia really had liked his work and that she had tried to interest the gallery in New York. He considered going across the hall and saying that if her friend didn't want it, it wasn't her fault, and he was grateful anyhow. He didn't want to become another pathetic claimant on Delia's warmth and generosity of spirit. Everyone at the Center now continually vied for her time and attention, and it was embarrassing the way Susie and Mrs. Unger and the other Fellows and visitors and guests crowded around her in the hall and at lectures and at the weekly lunch meeting, maneuvering to sit next to her, smiling and staring and posturing and complimenting and, almost always, asking for favors. No wonder that sometimes at lunch she would excuse herself early and flee half fed to her office. Still, he had waited long enough.

Sitting and then standing slowly, with pain and difficulty, he went to look across the hall. Delia's tall paneled door, as usual, was shut. He knew now that often she did not open it when someone knocked, and only rarely answered her phone. He himself had never knocked or phoned: he did not want to be one of the intrusive people who at all hours of the day attempted to invade Delia's privacy and interrupt her creative work.

Yet as he started back, Alan heard a strange and disturbing sound: like someone breathing hard, gasping or wailing. At first he thought it was the autumn wind in the tall white pine tree outside his window; but the sounds weren't coming from there. When he turned again to Delia's door, which was in fact not quite shut, he could hear them more clearly. Someone inside was half sighing, half sobbing.

"Delia?" he called softly. There was no answer. Slowly, Alan pushed the door open a few inches.

At first the room seemed empty: the heavy dark-red velvet drapes were drawn, allowing only a few slashes of late September sunlight to carve up the gloom, and there was no one at the desk. Then he saw something like a bundle of crumpled white washing huddled on the sofa. Delia Delaney was lying there, staring at him silently.

Or was that really Delia? She seemed somehow wan and limp, more clothes than body; it was as if all her life had gone into the great bush of red-gold hair.

"Go away, would you, please?" she said in a half-drowned voice.

"I'm sorry." He began to back out of the room.

"Wait. Who is it? Alan? Is that you?"

"Yes. What's the matter? Are you all right?"

"No. I'm getting a migraine. Or I should say, a migraine is getting me." She gave a thin imitation of a laugh.

"I'm sorry," he repeated. "Shall I go away?"

"Yes—no. I've just taken something for it. It works about half the time if I take it soon enough, but it always makes me a little dizzy, a little drunk." She laughed lightly, sadly. "If I'm lucky it'll kick in after ten, fifteen minutes. I'd like to pass out until then, but I won't. Come and talk to me, distract me." Her voice was low, tremulous.

"I— All right." Alan crossed the darkened room and stood beside the sofa. Pale and ill as Delia looked, with great blue-violet smudges under her eyes, she was still voluptuously beautiful.

"Tell me a story. No. Sing to me."

"I don't know . . ." Clumsily and painfully, he lowered himself onto a nearby chair. "Okay, I'll try."

Alan had a light but true tenor voice, and a small repertory of old tunes and hymns, learned from one of his aunts. He chose at random.

> *Down in the valley,*
> *The valley so low,*
> *Hang your head over,*
> *Hear the wind blow.*

"That's nice," Delia murmured, closing her eyes and stretching out on the sofa, so that most of a bare round white leg became visible, lit at the thigh by a thin stripe of sunlight.

> *Build me a castle*
> *Forty feet high,*
> *So I can see her*
> *As she goes by.*

Allan paused, thinking that his unconscious had somehow directed his choice: that the Unger Center, with its brickwork parapets, was the nearest thing to a castle on campus; also that, counting the cupola, it was about forty feet high. Am I in love with her too, like everyone else? he asked himself.

"Please, go on," Delia whispered plaintively, and he complied.

> *If you don't love me,*
> *Love whom you please.*
> *Throw your arms 'round me,*
> *Give my heart ease.*

Maybe I just want to fuck her, that's what the song says, he thought. Yeah, that certainly. But to make a move, even if it was welcomed, would precipitate a shameful disaster. It was months since he'd been able to perform normally; fear and pain and the fear of greater pain had always blocked him.

"Don't stop," Delia begged, and Alan searched his memory for the innocent tunes his mother had sung to him when he was a small child.

> *Lavender's blue, dilly dilly,*
> *Lavender's green.*
> *When I am king, dilly dilly,*
> *You shall be queen.*

He broke off, embarrassed by this second message from his unconscious, then went on through the remaining verses, stumbling over the last one:

> *Some to make hay, dilly dilly,*
> *Some to cut corn,*
> *While you and I, dilly dilly,*
> *Keep ourselves warm.*

"That's so nice," Delia murmured, opening her silver-gray eyes, now rimmed with long wet dark lashes. "You know, I used to be called Dilly when I was little."

"Really." Coincidence was still working against him, Alan thought. Or for him. "How are you feeling?" he asked.

"A bit better, you know. I think maybe the pill's going to work this time. Or maybe it's your singing. You have a wonderful voice, so soothing." She reached out one soft white hand to touch his.

"Thank you." I must get out of here before I do something stupid, Alan thought. Aware again of his pain, he rose agonizingly to his feet, leaning on the arm of the sofa.

"Don't go yet." Delia smiled at him through the gloom. Already she looked less ill: a rosy flush had come into her face. As she pushed herself up slowly, her blouse slipped down to half reveal one pale, rounded breast in a border of crumpled white lace. "Come on. Sit down again."

"I can't—my back," Alan said. "It hurts like hell if I sit for more than a few minutes."

"Ah." Unlike everyone else he knew, Delia did not express sympathy. "So what do you take for it?" she asked.

"Different things." Then, not wanting to seem rude, he added, "Codeine mostly. And alcohol."

"Does that work for you?"

"Well, sometimes. But if I mix them or take too much I get a splitting headache. Not a migraine like yours, at least from what I've heard, but a kind of steady hammering pressure."

"I've had that. It's agony. Vodka is a help, but what I really like is morphine, only it's so hard to get here."

Alan looked at Delia with some surprise, realizing that they were having exactly the same sort of conversation that he often had with his back-pain pals. She's an invalid too, he thought, feeling for the first time a rush of warmth that wasn't admiration or lust. "I know," he said. "It really works for me too."

"I went to see this silly little woman at the University Health Center, and she started whining about how it wasn't medically advisable. That's so stupid. My doctor in New York says you can't get addicted to morphine if you only take it for serious pain."

"Mine says the same thing. Would you like to go and see him? I'll give you the name."

"Not now, thanks. I'm going down to New York soon, I can get a new prescription then. I could have brought more with me, but I know it's a mistake to block all my pain. Even if I could."

"How do you mean, a mistake?" Alan asked. "Hell, if I could block all mine without side effects, I'd do it like a shot."

"It's cowardly. I know my migraines come for a purpose. They're bringing me something I need."

"Really?"

"But you must feel that too, about your pain. It's there for a reason. I mean, don't you feel sometimes, when you lie there suffering, that images or messages are coming to you, ones you'd never find otherwise? I know some of my best stories began as those strange kind of half-dreams, half-hallucinations I have late at night, or just before dawn, when I'm totally exhausted with a migraine. Isn't it like that for you too?"

"Sometimes," Alan admitted, remembering that the idea of turning the Plaza Fountain into a picturesque ruin had in fact occurred to him as he lay awake in agony one black rainy night last summer.

"When my aura starts, there's no way of knowing what will come. Sometimes there are visions, sometimes nightmares, sometimes just blackness, oblivion."

"There's times I could use some oblivion."

"Yes, but we can't choose. In the end you have to accept your affliction as a gift. You have to ask, what is it trying to tell you, to give you? What has it saved you from, what has it brought you?"

"I hadn't thought of it like that," Alan said. It's brought me Delia Delaney, he thought suddenly. If my back were well, she wouldn't be speaking to me so intimately.

She leaned toward him, her eyes hypnotically wide. "Inspiration comes from a dark, distant place, and it can't come without pain. When I feel a migraine starting, it's as if I can see these great black things flying towards me over the hills and over the city, half-bird and half-bat, with their claws out and their beaks open. Coming to hurt me and help me."

"Mine is just a big ugly reddish brown lizard," Alan said. "Only it's always there, in my back." He laughed awkwardly; he had never mentioned the lizard to anyone, not even Jane.

"But you can numb it with alcohol and drugs," Delia suggested. "Stupefy it."

"Oh yes. And then I'm numb and stupid too."

"Yes." Delia nodded. "I know all about that. Your life becomes a blur, a sort of sodden, mean half-life. There's some pain still, but nothing to show for it."

"No," Alan said. "And then you keep thinking stupid things. Like, It's not fair. Why should I have this pain, and not other people? I mean, well, for instance"—he laughed awkwardly—"Jane and your husband aren't attacked by bats and lizards."

"But they're not creative people," Delia said. She sat forward on the sofa and ran both hands through her tangled hair, combing it out into a great skein of red-gold silk.

"Are you feeling better?"

"Yes," she said tentatively. "Yes, it's gone. All gone. I'm just a little dizzy." She stood up, putting one hand on Alan's arm to steady herself. The crumpled white washing resolved itself into a gauzy low-necked blouse and a long pale flowered and ruffled skirt above bare white feet.

"Oh, lord," she added as if to herself. "Look at that, what a disaster." She held out one hand, and Alan, touching Delia deliberately for the first time, took it. Delia did not pull away, but let her hand lie in his own, trembling slightly, cool and soft, with white rounded fingers, each of which ended in a long sharp silver-pink talon. It was like holding an exotic marine creature, he thought, some pale starfish or sea anemone.

"I don't see any disaster," he said.

"It's the polish. It's all chipping."

Alan bent closer; it was true that here and there the talons of the anemone were speckled with flakes of a darker rose. "It looks fine to me," he told her. "But I don't see—" he added, struck by this for the first time, "I mean, how can you do anything with nails that long?"

"What sort of anything do you mean?" Delia asked, smiling oddly.

"I don't know. Cook, clean, shop, sew—the things women do."

"But I don't do those things anymore." She gave a little laugh and slid her hand softly away. "I especially don't do them, and my nails are a sign that I don't."

Alan looked from Delia's hands, now clasped in a double underwater flower, to her smiling face. "Even so, isn't it hard for you to work—to type on a computer?"

"But I don't. That's the point," she murmured, smiling up at him.

"But then, how can you write?"

"Oh, I can write. I always write by hand anyhow." She turned toward her desk, which, Alan realized now, was empty of electronic devices. It held only a vase of flowers, a stack of pale-green paper, and a flowered china mug full of pens. "It's the natural way—has been for thousands of years."

"Yeah, but—" Alan said, mesmerized.

"I despise the idea of being separated from my words by a machine. I want them to flow directly from my mind down my arm into my hand and out onto the paper in one uninterrupted motion." Delia demonstrated, stroking her bare rosy arm, long fingers, pointed seashell nails, and an imaginary sheet of paper in one slow, graceful gesture. "Just the way you do when you're drawing, you know."

"Uh—yeah." You're so beautiful, he thought.

"For me, writing is a sensual act. Well, you must know. It's like that for most artists, isn't it?" Delia turned slightly away, glancing out of the window as if she saw a procession of artists passing.

"Yeah, you're probably right," he agreed, swerving around toward her, his mind blurred by a surge of pain and the impulse toward another sort of sensual act.

"I'm sure I am," Delia said, stepping away as if she had intuited what he was planning. Her voice had strengthened and lost its murmuring, confiding tone.

"I—you—" Alan uttered inarticulately, putting one hand on the pain in his back.

Delia did not reply. She felt about on the carpet for her shoes, slipped her feet into them, and moved toward her desk.

"You know, I think I'd like to work now," she said.

"Okay. I'll let you." Alan heard a hurt, resentful overtone in his voice. A few moments ago he had felt closer to Delia than to anyone in the world; now she was speaking to him like a polite stranger. Or an impolite one. "Well, so long," he added, attempting an equal unconcern.

"Mm." Delia sat down at her desk, drawing a sheet of pale-green paper toward her and picking up a pen. "Oh, I forgot to tell you," she added casually, glancing up. "I heard from Jacky Herbert yesterday. He really likes your paintings."

"He likes them?" Alan felt suddenly out of breath

"Mm," she said after a pause. "He wants to meet you." Again she turned away,

"He wants to meet me when?"

This time Delia did not even seem to hear. Alan stood for a moment staring at her bare flushed arms and her thick sheaf of hair. As he took a step toward the door, one of the slices of dust-filled sunlight that escaped from between the heavy velvet curtains slashed and suddenly blinded him. Stumbling with suddenly renewed pain, he left the room.

NINE

In a campus coffee shop known as the Red Bear, Jane and Henry Hull were having lunch. It was heavily cloudy outside the window, and damp yellow leaves splattered the lawns, but Jane's spirits were not cloudy or damp. More and more she looked forward to these lunches, which occurred more and more often. They no longer made her uneasy, since all this time Henry had never made the move she had guiltily desired and dreaded. Clearly she was safe with him: all he wanted was a friend, a friend who also had an invalid spouse.

Mainly they spoke of ordinary subjects—local and national news events, films they had seen, their own histories. Jane now knew that Henry had at one time or another been a waiter, an advertising executive, a counselor of troubled adolescent boys, a taxi driver, and a high school teacher. At present he was a freelance editor. "What that means is, somebody who knows something but can't write, puts together a book," he had explained. "It's on weather forecasting, or city planning, or Colonial history, or whatever. The information is all there, and there are readers who want it—but the prose is clumsy and the organization is confused. So they send the manuscript to me. And the worse it is, the longer it takes, the more they pay."

As a result of his profession, Henry knew a lot about some unusual subjects. "When I take on a project I sometimes think, Oh,
this won't be very interesting, but I always get hooked. Did you
know, for instance, that you can tell whether the moon is waxing or
waning by whether its horns point east or west?"

"I did, actually," Jane had admitted. "You need to know that if
you have a garden, because you have to plant aboveground crops
when the moon is waxing, and root crops when it's waning."

"You really believe that?" Henry said, smiling.

"I don't know; but I planted my carrots at the wrong time this
year, because of Alan's operation, and they're not very good—pale
and kind of tasteless. That's why I didn't bring you any." Jane had
continued giving Henry her excess vegetables, and he in return (in
spite of her protests that the vegetables were free) insisted on paying
for their lunches.

She had learned that Henry had two grown children by an earlier marriage, both successful yuppies. "I love them, and they love
me, but they're more serious and grown-up than I am by now. Their
attitude is, what crazy thing is Dad going to do next? The trouble is,
I don't usually know the answer myself." Jane, in turn, had confided
that she and Alan hadn't really wanted children.

"Really?" Henry said.

"Well, no. That's not exactly so," she amended. "We wanted
them, but we didn't want to adopt. Alan didn't think he could ever
feel the same about a child that wasn't his."

"Ah." Henry gave her a steady look. "And could you?"

"I—" Jane swallowed. "I thought maybe I could," she admitted.
"But it's not right to have children that one parent won't ever love."

"I suppose not," Henry said slowly. "You know what's so remarkable about you?" he added. "You always try to say what's true,
not what will make you look good or please the person you're
speaking to."

Yes, maybe, she had thought. But that's partly because you're the
person I'm speaking to.

For Jane, the most important subject of their conversation was what Henry had proposed that day by the lake: the problems of being a caregiver. Theoretically she could have spoken of this to her women friends, and in the past she had tried to do so. But their first question was always, "How is Alan doing?" Often it did not occur to them to ask how she was doing. After all, she was perfectly healthy. Only her mother had ever suggested that Jane's role might not be an easy one. "Yes, it can be hard," she had told Jane. "You just have to do your duty the best you can." It was her mother's standard solution to the problems of life, but one that had begun to work less and less well for Jane.

Even with Henry she had resisted the topic at first. "Really, I shouldn't complain," she had said. "It seems so disloyal."

"Of course you should complain," Henry had replied. "Besides, if you don't, I can't either."

"Well." She smiled.

"Do you think I'm disloyal?"

"No. Not really." In Jane's opinion, it was quite reasonable to complain about Delia Delaney, a deeply self-centered person whose headaches were, if not wholly fraudulent, certainly manipulative. But Henry never said anything negative about Alan, and she had therefore resolved to refrain from criticizing his wife, though sometimes she almost slipped.

"We both need to let off steam," Henry said. "It's better and safer this way. If we don't, it's going to explode and burn someone."

"I guess you're right," Jane said. She imagined a cloud of scalding hot steam bursting from his mouth and engulfing Delia. How she would scream, she thought.

"Absolutely."

Jane had not protested again, though sometimes she would take an awkward step back after revealing the latest problem: today, Alan's sluggishness about doing the exercises that had been prescribed for his back. "He keeps putting them off, and then when he finally starts he groans so, you can hear it all over the house. He wants me to come running and tell him that he must stop if it's hurting so much, and bring him a glass of grapefruit juice and his icepacks."

"It's like that with Delia too. Misery loves company. I used to think that meant that miserable people love to be with other miserable people. That could be true too, sometimes. But lately I think it mostly means that they need for us to be there and see them suffer, and be miserable too."

"Well, yes. Sometimes it seems that way," Jane admitted. "Like last Sunday I was going to have lunch with a friend. I'd told Alan about it the day before, but when I said I was leaving he acted as if I hadn't. 'Oh, do you really have to?' he said. I felt terrible, because I knew he had had a bad night and was in awful pain. And of course I didn't *have* to go. I just wanted to."

"And did you go?"

"Yes, eventually, but I maybe shouldn't have." Jane sighed.

"If you'd stayed, would Alan have felt better?"

"Maybe. At least I could have made him lunch. Well, I did make him lunch, and left it in the fridge, but it's not the same."

"Uh-huh. They want us there when they want us there. And then when they don't, they don't."

"Alan always wants me there," Jane said. "But then he's in pain all the time, not just now and then."

"At least you always know what to expect," Henry said. "I can never tell from one day to the next whether Delia will get a sick headache and everything will have to be canceled. She'll be dressing to go out to dinner, and suddenly she'll collapse and throw up, and I have to get on the phone to make excuses, and then go mop up the bathroom."

"I thought she could tell when a headache was coming on," Jane said.

"Not always." Henry looked at her. "You think maybe her migraines aren't real, but you're wrong."

"I didn't say that—"

"But you thought it, I can tell. And it's not true. When one hits,

Delia's in agony. She wouldn't ever choose to lie for twenty-four hours in a dark room; she loves life too much."

"Mm," Jane said, ashamed but only partly convinced. The headaches may be real, she thought, but Delia uses them. Did that mean that Alan too used his pain? That he deliberately— But at that disloyal thought she felt a pang of acid guilt like heartburn.

"Her life hasn't been easy," Henry told her. "Bad things happened to her when she was a kid. Her parents were both drunks, and she saw things no kid should see."

"Um," Jane said, remembering Delia's story "A Woman Made of Fire," one of her most famous works. The language of this tale was so poetic and allusive that it had been hard for Jane to figure out what happened. But it seemed to be about a beautiful princess who is vaguely but horribly attacked in the forest at dusk by a man or monster with a burning torch. As a result she is both damaged and metamorphosed, burnt and transfigured. Afterward she goes to live alone in a tower by the sea. Her hair grows very long, and many men come to court her. They stand on the shore and call up to her, they sing and play musical instruments and recite poetry. She looks out of the window, but never lets down her long burnt-gold hair to them.

According to Lily Unger, this tale was supposed to be based on a traumatic event in Delia's early adolescence, and the burning torch was really a flashlight. "When she was fifteen, sixteen, Delia was kind of a freak," Lily had explained to Jane. "The other kids thought she acted superior, put on airs. She wore strange clothes, and she used to go out and walk in the woods after supper, talking to herself. So one evening some boys followed her into the woods, four or five of them."

"Yes, I've heard that," Jane said now.

"She was damaged," Henry said. "It was a long time ago, but nothing can make it up to her."

"But you try," Jane suggested.

"Yeah. Sometimes." Henry shrugged.

"It's different for Alan," she said. "His life has been pretty easy. Until he got ill, I mean. And it could be so much worse—I mean, he doesn't have a fatal disease or anything like that."

"Neither does Delia. But in a way that makes it harder. I remember when my father was terminally ill. Of course he was miserable, and my mother was totally wiped out. But they both knew that one day, maybe quite soon, it would all be over. For us, it could go on the rest of our lives."

"Yes," Jane admitted. "I'm afraid of that sometimes."

Henry stirred his tea slowly. "I figure there's no point in looking too far into the future. What we have to do is enjoy the world as much as we can right now. It doesn't do anyone any good for us to give up things and be miserable."

"I don't know." Jane laughed unhappily. "I mean, I've thought sometimes maybe it does. If Alan sees me enjoying myself he might feel worse because of the contrast."

"Maybe," Henry said. "But I don't think it works that way. At least not with Delia. She wants me to be strong and well and happy, otherwise I might not be able to take care of her, or I might not want to. She doesn't want me to get worn down or fed up. That's odd. Why isn't it 'worn up' and 'fed down'?"

"I have no idea." Jane laughed. "You sound like Bill Laird. He's always looking sideways at words, turning them around in his mind."

"I used to do a lot of that," Henry said. He sat back and pushed his empty plate away. "You get in the habit."

"Oh yes?" Jane looked at him, admiring his thick eyebrows, high color, and thoughtful meditative expression. "You mean when you were in advertising."

"Yeah, and when I was a poet."

"You were a poet? I never knew that."

"I don't admit to it very often. But I was. It was a long time ago, but I even won an award for it, and I published two books. They were mostly white space, though, because I was a minimalist."

"Really? So why did you stop?"

"I didn't exactly stop. My poems got shorter and shorter, and then they just sort of disappeared, and it was all white space." He smiled and ran one hand around the collar of his denim shirt, as if it had suddenly become too tight.

"I'm sorry," Jane told him. "But maybe you'll start again sometime."

"That's what Delia always used to say. She got quite angry with me when I wouldn't even try."

"But that's not fair," Jane exclaimed in spite of her previous resolve. "It's not the sort of thing you can just decide to do."

"Depends on how you look at it." He shrugged. "Wouldn't you like me better if I were a poet?"

"No, why should I?" She laughed.

"Delia would." His face darkened; he looked away from her, out of the window, which was beginning to blur with rain.

"Well, I like you just fine the way you are," Jane said, feeling a rush of distaste for Henry's wife. At least Alan never wants me to be something else, something I can't be, she thought.

Henry turned back; he looked at her, then slowly smiled. "And I like you just fine the way you are," he said, less casually.

Jane caught her breath; for a moment the whole room blurred like the rain-washed quadrangle outside. Something is happening, she thought. Alarmed, she tried to block it.

"I'm afraid Delia has the same sort of idea about Alan," she said rapidly. "She's convinced him he's an artist; and now she's convinced some friend of hers who owns a gallery in New York to show his pictures of ruins."

"Yeah, she told me about that."

"Of course Alan was very excited when he heard the news. Over the moon, he said himself. He didn't say anything about his back for nearly a whole day. But I'm worried about the whole thing."

"Worried?" Henry raised his eyebrows.

"You know, what people will think."

"What's that?" He smiled, but Jane did not.

"They'll think Alan's making fun of death and destruction."

"Really? Do you think he is?"

"No, of course not. Alan would never do that. Anyhow he made most of those drawings long before September 11. But most people won't know that. They'll think it's a joke about the World Trade Center, and they'll get angry."

"Is anyone angry at him now?"

"No," Jane admitted. "But not many people have seen his drawings." I'm angry, she realized. Not at the drawings, but at Delia, for charming and bullying her way into Alan's life, making him jump over the moon like the stupid cow in the nursery rhyme, making him forget his pain, when I've been trying to do the same thing for a year and a half without success. It was so wrong, so unfair—It also was something she couldn't complain to Henry about.

"I'd better get back to work," she said instead.

"Okay." He stood up. "Hey, it's really raining," he added as he pushed open the door. "Never mind, I have a big umbrella. Here, take my arm."

Splashing though puddles, Jane and Henry made their way across campus toward the Center, where his car was parked. But though her feet were soon wet, the rest of Jane remained surprisingly dry. This struck her as odd; then she realized that because Henry was shorter than Alan by several inches, his big black umbrella shielded her better. Also he held his arm closer to his side, so that Jane's hand was pressed against his rough tan duffle coat. A shiver ran up her arm toward her shoulder, and farther, and she had to remind herself forcibly that she was suffering from prolonged sexual frustration, and that Henry was just a friend who was married to one of the most beautiful women in Hopkins County.

"I'd like to come in for a moment," he said when they reached the Center.

"Yes, of course." Jane held open the heavy door while he shook out his umbrella. "How's everything?" she asked Susie.

"Very quiet. Nobody's here but Charlie and Selma."

"Yes, I know." Neither Alan nor Delia had come in that day—Delia almost never did on Fridays—and the fifth Fellow, a dignified Yale sociologist in his fifties called Davi Gakar, was on his way to a wedding on Long Island with his family.

"Oh, look at that rain." Susie opened a pink-flowered umbrella. "I'll be back in an hour. Oh, I forgot, Selma wanted me to remind you that she's screening all Delia's calls. Says she's Delia's watchdog."

"Yes, I know," Jane repeated without enthusiasm. Somehow, over the past few weeks, Delia had got everyone at the Center working for her. Selma took her phone messages, Susie typed her manuscripts and letters, Charlie brought her coffee at the weekly lunch, and Davi Gakar passed on his *New York Times* every day. "I expect she'll get tired of it after a while."

"Actually I don't think she will," Henry said as the front door closed behind Susie.

"No, maybe not." Jane recalled the look of doglike devotion that Selma sometimes directed toward Delia. At least Alan isn't working for her, Jane thought.

"Delia understands the use of obligations," Henry said, following Jane into the office and sitting on the edge of her desk. "She knows how to bind people to her with them. When you do something for Delia she's wonderfully grateful. She makes you feel that she couldn't survive without your help, and that you have a big part in her fame and success. But that's not what I wanted to say." He leaned toward Jane and put one hand on her arm. "I w-wanted to say—to tell you—" He stumbled over the words.

Something is happening, Jane thought, I should stop it. But she could not move.

"I— Oh, hell." The telephone had begun to ring.

"Unger Center for the H-Humanities," Jane said, also stuttering a little.

"This is Sergeant Dan Warren at the Hopkins County Public Safety Office."

"Uh, yes?" And now something else is happening, she thought, feeling frightened and confused. Someone has been arrested, someone is dead or injured.

"Who am I speaking to?"

"This is Jane Mackenzie. I'm the administrative director of the Unger Center for the Humanities at Corinth University." Hearing her tense, formal tone, Henry sat back and took his hand off her arm.

"We have an individual here who has been detained by the Airport Security Officer at the county airport. He was trying to board a plane with weapons and contraband materials. Claims he is employed by your organization. Says his name is David Gakar."

"Davi Gakar. Yes, I mean he's a Fellow here, at the Center," Jane said, still shaken but also relieved. "You mean, you're saying they think he was going to hijack an airplane?"

Henry's thick dark eyebrows rose, and he opened his mouth in a mime of astonishment.

"Maybe. He didn't get that far."

"But Professor Gakar is a famous professor from Yale University. He wouldn't—" Jane fell silent. After all, how did she know what Davi Gakar would or wouldn't do?

"He says you can verify his identity."

"Well, yes. Of course I can."

"In that case we'd appreciate it if you would come to the County Security Building as soon as possible."

"Yes, of course. I'll be right there." The phone clattered loudly as she fit it back into its base. "They've arrested Davi Gakar," she told Henry, annoyed to hear the wobble in her voice. "They think he's a terrorist or something."

"Yeah, I gathered."

"I've got to call Bill Laird."

"Yeah." Henry smiled, to her mind inappropriately.

Bill, as usual, was calm and calming. Not to worry, he said: he would get in touch with the University counsel's office and meet her at the Security Building (he called it by its former name, the County

Jail) as soon as he could. She should go there now, and bring Davi
Gakar's file, along with his contract and letters of recommendation.

What is the matter with me? Jane thought as she went through
the necessary actions: getting out the file, asking Charlie to cover the
phone until Susie got back from lunch—carefully not telling him
what the "minor emergency" was. I am a good administrator, she
told herself. I am calm and capable in crises much worse than this
one. When Wilkie Walker slipped on the icy front steps last February and was lying there with his leg twisted under him; when the
fire started in the bathroom wastebasket the year before that, I knew
what to do. But now she was confused; she felt as if she were running a fever, and her heart kept up a fluttering uneven rhythm. It's
because of Henry, she realized, looking at him and quickly looking
away.

"I have to go now," she said.

"I'll drive you." Henry stood up.

The confused thought crossed Jane's mind that this might not be
a good idea. But why not? She did not try to answer her own question, only said, "Thank you."

"I probably won't be of much use, but you never know." He
smiled. "Anyhow, I wouldn't want to miss this."

It's not a TV show, Jane thought, but she said nothing.

They did not speak much on the way to the County Jail. Once
she asked Henry to please not mention to anybody what had happened to Professor Gakar, and he replied, "All right." But most of
the time she was just silently watching the rain soak the windshield
of Henry's SUV and the wipers slosh it away, and wondering alternately whether Davi Gakar was an international terrorist and when
or if Henry would say whatever it was he had started to say at the
Center. She was tensely, annoyingly aware of him beside her, his
rough tan duffle coat, his broad tanned hands on the wheel.

———

In the outer room of the Security Building, Davi Gakar's wife and children were sitting on a long wooden bench. Whenever they came to the Center, they had always seemed happy and casual, and been dressed in casual New England preppie style. They smiled often, showing perfect teeth. Now they all wore formal dress-up clothes and varying unhappy expressions. Davi's wife, a small, sophisticated woman who was a dentist in real life, had on a gilt-embroidered silk sari, heavy gold earrings, and a weary, sour expression. His nine-year-old daughter, in a lace-collared dark-red velvet party dress, looked lost and frightened, while his five-year-old son, in a miniature suit and tie, was restless and bored.

"It's really important that we get to New York this afternoon," Mrs. Gakar said in tones frayed by repetition. "My husband's niece is being married there."

"Yes, I know."

"Davi was extremely upset at the airport. He was in the right, of course, but what he said wasn't useful. Maybe you can talk a little sense into him."

"We'll try," Henry said. Jane, who found Davi Gakar rather formidable, did not have the confidence to echo this promise. Going to the desk, she presented his file, and Sheriff Hanshaw was summoned.

"If you'd come this way, please." Jane and Henry were directed by a female clerk down a corridor to a small ugly room containing six plastic chairs, a table, a very young uniformed policeman, and Davi Gakar, in an elegantly cut three-piece suit and a state of indignation.

"This is totally unreasonable, unforgivable," he declared after being told that he and his family could not yet leave the building. "You have the documents now."

"Please be patient, Professor," the policeman said in a manner that suggested he had said it several times before. "The sheriff is looking at your papers now."

"The staff at the airport are incompetent bunglers," Davi Gakar declared. "They cannot tell a wedding present from a weapon.

Look." He gestured at the table before him, on the white plastic top of which was laid out a heterogeneous collection of objects, as in the memory game Jane had played at children's parties. The centerpiece was a rectangular black leather case lined in royal-blue plush and containing a large carving knife and fork with bone handles. Surrounding it was a debris of shiny silver wrapping paper and ribbon, a child's flute, a pair of nail scissors and a nail file, and a bright-yellow toy bulldozer with a shiny metal scoop.

"The stupidity was amazing," Davi continued. "They imagined that with this equipment my family and I planned to hijack their plane. Presumably, I would attack the pilot with this carving knife and fork. My wife would stab the copilot with her nail scissors, my daughter would poke them with her flute, and my son would hit them with his toy car. That is what they thought, apparently."

The young policeman said nothing, but it was clear from his expression that this was exactly what he did think. Henry, however, laughed, causing Jane to look at him with disapproval.

"Why, I asked them, would an American citizen, born in Forest Hills, New York, wish to attack an American plane? And if I wished to do so, why would I bring my wife and children into danger? I tried to be reasonable. I pointed out that we are not Muslims, we are Hindus, whereas the terrorists of September 11 were Muslims. If they are so determined to arrest someone, I said, why didn't they arrest Charles Amir when he flew to Washington last week? He is a Muslim, and he is not a citizen."

The young policeman, who had been sitting at the table in an attitude of deep boredom, looked up. "Would you repeat that name, please?" he asked.

"Amir, A-M-I— Wait a minute." Davi checked himself. "I am not accusing anyone of anything, I am merely trying to suggest that this sort of profiling is irrational, appalling, and illegal."

"Professor Gakar," Jane said, feeling helpless, "I'm sure this can be resolved—" But Henry interrupted her, turning on Davi.

"Listen," he said. "If you want to get out of here today and get to that wedding, you've got to shut up. These guys don't get academic irony. Didn't you see that sign by the screener in the airport, warning people not to make jokes? You go on like this, you're digging your cell with your own teeth."

"So what do you suggest I should do?" Davi asked scornfully.

"I suggest you should stop complaining and start apologizing for all the trouble you've caused."

"The trouble *I've* caused?" Davi inquired. He frowned, cleared his throat, and looked up at the acoustical tiles as if they were an object of scholarly interest. "You may have a point," he finally said, lowering his gaze. "In certain situations, expediency rules."

Now more people entered the room: the sheriff followed by Bill Laird and an energetic young lawyer from the University counsel's office. It was clear that the balance of the event had shifted. Polite and conciliatory remarks were exchanged by all parties; local and long-distance phone calls were made. The airport manager was consulted, and it was arranged that the Gakars could leave on the next flight to New York, which would depart in about an hour. The carving set and the nail scissors would be transported in checked baggage; the flute and the yellow bulldozer were returned to their owners. Everyone shook hands and smiled, some agreeably and others wearily or ironically. The sheriff bought cans of Pepsi-Cola for the Gakar children from a vending machine, causing them to giggle and gobble, while their mother the dentist suppressed her natural reaction with difficulty. Finally Henry and Jane conveyed the family back to the airport.

"It was really great, what you said to Davi Gakar," Jane told him as they drove away through the rain. "I wouldn't have dared, but it worked."

"For the moment," Henry remarked.

"He was being unreasonable. And why did he insist on putting that carving knife into a carry-on bag?"

"Some people hate to check luggage."

"Then he could have mailed it. Wait, you're going in the wrong direction; this isn't the way to the Center."

"Yeah, I know." Henry turned off the main road onto a wooded lane.

"I have to get back," Jane protested as he stopped the car under a big dripping maple tree whose wet leaves had turned a brilliant gold.

"Not yet." Henry turned off the engine. He moved closer, and kissed her.

"No, you shouldn't," Jane said weakly.

"Yes, I should. We deserve it. You know we do."

"No," Jane murmured, but when Henry moved back she met his mouth with her own. Just this once, she told herself.

Two minutes passed in a silent, deeply satisfying blur; then another car went by, throwing up a heavy spray of water.

"I must get back to the office," Jane said, trembling all over. "Susie will wonder what happened—Bill Laird's probably called too—"

"All right." Henry started the car. "I'll come by the Center later."

"No, please don't. Not now. I can't—it's too much—"

"Okay. But you'll be at the Farmers' Market tomorrow morning, right?"

"Yes, I guess so." I don't have to go, she told her conscience.

"Good." Henry turned back onto the highway. "You don't know how long I've been wanting to do that," he said.

"No," Jane agreed, thinking that it couldn't be as long as she had wanted it. "How long?"

"Since the first time I saw you at the Center, when you were so mean about the sofas."

"Really?" And in spite of herself, she smiled.

TEN

On a late October afternoon, Alan Mackenzie stood at the window of a Manhattan apartment, gazing east across Central Park. Back in Corinth the trees were unsightly and bare; but here they still kept their leaves, and from the tenth floor the view was of a broad sunlit carpet of chrome yellow and ocher and flame-colored chrysanthemums, rippled by a gentle breeze. Indoors, however, there was little to see. This two-room apartment, the occasional pied-à-terre of an acquaintance of Delia Delaney, was furnished in a bleak, minimalist style, all smoky gray mirrors and black leather and chrome.

For Alan, the last twenty-four hours had been strange: alternately exhausting and exhilarating. It was his first trip alone since his illness. Jane had offered to come, but he had refused, partly but not wholly because he knew she disapproved of his purpose and was reluctant to ask for a leave from her job. But without Jane's help he had been burdened with invalid equipment: the cane, the wheeled carry-on, and the clumsy black nylon bag containing his medications, his two icepacks, and the three foam rubber chair pads that he needed to make almost any chair tolerable. Even so he could not sit for more than fifteen minutes without pain, and the flight to New York had been hideous. The seats on the little commuter plane were

narrow and hard, and its wind-buffeted motion made him ill. The
ride to the city in the jolting taxi was even worse, and by the time he
reached his destination he was in agony.

Jim Weisman and Katie Fenn, the friends with whom Alan was
staying near Columbia, were among his oldest and closest. They had
been on sabbatical all last academic year, and had not seen him since
his back trouble. They were clearly disconcerted to find him walking with a cane, and even more when he asked almost at once if he
could put his icepacks in their freezer and lie on their sofa, with a
tapestry pillow under his head and another between his knees. As he
explained his condition, they listened with concern and dismay.
They turned with relief to their own immediate history, describing
with enthusiasm a Fulbright year in Southeast Asia, where Alan
would now probably never go, and New York theater and opera
productions that he would never see.

After half an hour his exhaustion and pain were so great that he
had to retreat to his friends' spare room. For over an hour he lay
there, unable to sleep, listening to their murmured voices. He could
not distinguish the words, but it was clear from the tone that Jim
and Katie were distressed. He realized that he should somehow have
prepared them for the change in his condition and appearance,
which for people back in Corinth had come more gradually.

By the time Alan emerged from the spare room, there had been a
seismic shift in his friends' attitude. They were now warm and solicitous, offering vodka and wine and bourbon, and then chicken curry
and fruit sherbet; but for the rest of the evening they spoke mostly of
the past, recalling their mutual adventures in college and graduate
school and several European countries. Though he joined in, laughing and reminiscing, he became more and more aware that invisibly
his friends had taken a step or two away from him. He had become a
beloved character from their past rather than their present or future.

Alan and Jim were almost exact contemporaries, but he had always been just a little ahead: published sooner, promoted to tenure

sooner, married more successfully (Katie was Jim's second wife). Now it was clear that he had lost this edge. He was no longer ahead of his friends or even parallel with them, but a member of another, inferior species: an invalid. His project for a book on religious architecture was old news, and he could see that they were surprised that it was not yet completed.

Out of superstitious motives, he did not say that he might soon be having a show of his watercolor paintings. Delia had been enthusiastic and optimistic, but she was not part of the New York art world. It was quite possible that she had exaggerated her friend's interest in Alan's work, or that his gallery was only a shabby small-time operation. That at least was what Jane suspected. She had been doubtful about the whole project. ("If that dealer really wants your pictures, why doesn't he come here to see you? He knows you're ill, doesn't he?") Of course, Jane had also been prejudiced against Delia from the beginning, for some reason, and suspicious of her motives. ("She's always flattering people and wanting them to think she has a lot of power and influence.")

Last night Alan had slept badly, in spite or perhaps because of all the wine and bourbon he had drunk and the various pills he had taken. At four a.m. he staggered into the guest bathroom in a state of dizzy, blurred pain and despair. Unlike the bathroom at home, Jim and Katie's was brilliantly lit, and in the mirror he could see himself with hideous clarity as they must have seen him: a sick, worn, overweight, prematurely aging man with a scruffy haircut. That wasn't his fault: for almost a year and a half he had been unable to sit in a barber's chair, and at monthly intervals Jane had climbed on a stool to cut his hair. She had done the best she could; but by New York standards her best was not very good.

As he stood before the mirror a great wash of despair and self-disgust came over Alan. Why am I kidding myself? he thought. My back is not getting better. I am not teaching or working on my book, only wasting time making drawings of imaginary ruins. I am the ruin of a professor, the ruin of a scholar, the ruin of a man. It would be better if I were dead. In a drugged blur of self-hatred he turned to the bathroom window and tried to lift the sash. But the building was old, and the window had warped shut; he could only raise it a couple of inches before he had to give up and lie down on the guest room bed again, giddy and gasping with the effort, wracked and wrecked with pain.

It's a good thing I couldn't get that window open last night, Alan thought now as he stood looking over the field of flowers that was Central Park. I must have been a little crazed from all those drugs. For one thing, Jim and Katie's apartment was on the second floor, and probably he would only have injured himself further, not to mention causing them lifelong remorse. ("What could we have said to make him do that?")

After breakfast Alan had taken a painful taxi ride to the rather grand building on Central Park West where Delia was staying, and waited in the lobby for fifteen increasingly painful minutes. Finally she appeared, strangely transformed. Her mass of hair had been compressed into a chignon from which only a few gold-red tendrils escaped; she was elaborately made up and dressed in fashionable New York black: a long-skirted suit, a black silk blouse, a trailing black lace scarf, and dangerous-looking pointed black high-heeled sandals. She did not apologize for making Alan wait, only gave him a New York air kiss near one cheek.

"I hardly recognized you in that getup," he said as they started across town in another horrible jolting taxi.

"It's protective coloration. I'm having lunch with a new editor; I want to scare him a little."

"I was hoping to have lunch with you myself," Alan said, attempting without total success to keep disappointment and jealousy out of his voice.

"Sorry. Business before pleasure." Even Delia's voice seemed different. Then she turned toward him and gave her familiar low, warm laugh. "You have to dress to distress in this city. And by the way, you should get rid of that tie before Jacky sees it. Artists don't wear ties here, only businessmen."

"You really think—?"

"Absolutely. Anyhow it looks too academic. Jacky doesn't want to meet a professor, he wants to meet a genius. You should really have on jeans and a black sweater."

"Well, all right." Alan laughed. After all, what had he to lose? He pulled off his striped tie, rolled it up, and put it in his pocket.

"Oh, and when you're at the gallery, you should be the strong silent type. Don't talk much. And don't sign anything."

"You're suggesting that Mr. Herbert is a crook," Alan said.

"No, no. Jacky's a very charming, kind man. I adore him."

"Really," Alan said, this time managing to keep the irrational rush of jealousy out of his voice.

"But of course he's also an art dealer. So if he gives you a contract, just say you'd like to show it to your lawyer first."

"In other words, let him know I don't trust him." Alan winced as the taxi jolted over a pothole.

"No, not at all. He'll respect you for it."

Contrary to Jane's suspicions, the gallery, in a Madison Avenue office building, seemed prosperous, and the work on the walls was interesting. And Jacky Herbert was an unlikely object of jealousy, being a heavy, elderly gay man with a shiny pink bald head surrounded by pale gray curls. He was impeccably dressed in a pale gray suit and shiny pink silk tie, and his handshake was fleshy but firm.

After an exchange of compliments and news about mutual friends that Alan could not follow, Jacky expressed his admiration for Alan's art. He would like, he declared, to put four or five of the big drawings into his December group show. Indeed, he had already shared some of the slides with one or two privileged patrons ("I don't like the term 'customers'") and might make a sale even sooner.

"And, the best news!" he enthused in a rumbling near-whisper.

Apparently, one of these patrons might be interested in having Alan design a ruined tower for his Connecticut estate. "All materials and expenses paid, naturally, and the reward (I don't like the term 'fee') would be in the neighborhood of thirty thousand." If Alan could view the site next time he was in the city, the patron would be happy to send a car.

Recalling Delia's advice, Alan spoke very little; indeed, he hardly knew what to say. He allowed that the project might interest him, and, when presented with a contract, mentioned his lawyer.

At the gallery Alan had almost been able to forget his pain. It was only when he and Delia again stood on Madison Avenue that he realized how bad it had become, so that when she suggested they go for a quick cup of coffee before her lunch he had to decline. "I'm very grateful to you," he told her. "Amazed by everything. But I'm not feeling too good. I've got to get a taxi back to Morningside Drive and lie down."

"But that's so far," Delia protested. "Why don't you go to where I'm staying, right across the park? I'll come back there as soon as this stupid lunch is over."

"Well—"

"Look, here's the key."

"Well—thank you."

Once he reached Delia's friend's apartment, Alan had taken a strong painkiller and collapsed on the hard black leather sofa. Half an hour later, when the drugs had begun to work, he realized that he was hungry. He couldn't go out to buy lunch, however, because he had Delia's key, and she would surely be back soon. He explored the minimalist kitchen and found nothing to eat except a box of crackers, a can of anchovies, a bottle of tonic water, and one of gin.

Presumably Delia was having all her meals out. He remembered Jane saying that she didn't cook: her househusband, Henry Hull, took care of all that. The thought was unpleasant to Alan. A woman, he felt, should be able to cook and even enjoy cooking. Also he had never liked the idea that Delia was married to Henry Hull. Henry was a negligible person, a freeloader with no real job, who seemed to have accomplished nothing in over fifty years, and yet somehow projected an ironic, negative attitude toward everything, including his beautiful and gifted wife.

When an hour and a half had passed, Alan began to feel aggrieved. He took the contract Jacky Herbert had given him out of his jacket and discovered that according to it the gallery would get fifty percent of any sales and the exclusive right to market his work. He felt more aggrieved than before. Where the hell was Delia? Was she just going to abandon him here, starving in this minimalist box? He recalled a remark of Jane's, that Delia was a complete egotist, who saw other people only in terms of their relation to herself. It was true that his damaged physical condition, his constant pain, did not appear to register with her as it did with others. Until now Alan had found this strangely soothing. Unlike less self-focused persons, she did not see or treat him as an invalid. Now it had become clear that she also did not consider him as someone who needed lunch.

Well, the hell with her. Angrily he ripped open the box of crackers and the can of anchovies, and made himself a strong gin and tonic. He looked about for something to read to pass the time, but all he could find was a pile of expensive fashion magazines and a few paperback thrillers of the Woman in Peril type, a genre he despised. In his experience, women were seldom in peril.

He lay down on the sofa again. It was harder than ever, and made his back ache worse. Why had he ever come to New York? Or, at least, why hadn't he let Jane come along and take care of him? She had offered to do so, after all, though without much enthusiasm. Alan knew the answer to that one: he had wanted to spend time alone with Delia Delaney, who clearly had no interest in spending time alone with him.

He rose and went into the adjoining room, which was as minimally furnished as the other, but messy rather than bare. A suitcase lay open on the thick gray carpet, spilling multicolored debris. The king-sized bed was a welter of crumpled gray silk sheets and pillows, and clothes, clearly Delia's, were strewn everywhere. They were lacy and silky, colored like a rose garden at dusk: velvety darks, glowing dusty pinks and reds, creamy beiges and whites. It was an entirely different palette from that of Jane's closet, a tidy ranked range of blue and khaki and navy. And even when Jane traveled, her clothes were always hung up or folded in a drawer.

Usually Alan preferred order, though he had sometimes been inconvenienced by Jane's far greater devotion to this principle. Now he had a sudden despairing desire to add to the disorder of this room. He lowered himself painfully onto the unmade bed and buried his head in a pillow that smelled both spicy and sugary. Under his left hand was something slippery—a white satin nightgown, he realized, pulling it toward him and imagining heat rising from it. Probably this is the nearest you'll ever get to Delia, you pathetic fool, he told himself. She might be interested, but if you make a move, she'll find out you can't carry through.

All right, why not? he thought. Holding the satin nightgown against his face, he turned on his side, fighting a short spasm of pain, then dragged down the zipper of his pants. Why not be as near as I ever will be to her, while I can? he thought feverishly.

Half an hour later Alan woke from a blurred sleep, still a little drunk. The apartment was still empty. The hell with her, the hell with everything, he thought. He stood up dizzily, returned to the sitting room, and began to gather his things. But as he did this the doorbell chimed. It was Delia, looking far less urban and formidable than before: more wiry golden tendrils had escaped from her chignon, and her lipstick had been smudged off.

"Oh, I'm so tired," she wailed, heading for the black leather sofa and crumpling onto it. "These awful, awful shoes." She kicked them off.

"Did you frighten your new editor?"

"I hope so." She smiled. "But he's essentially dense. His ideas for the anthology of fairy tales he wants me to edit are so banal, so brainless. It's hard to frighten people like that."

"Did you get a good lunch, at least?" Alan asked, hoping not so much for an answer as for the question, *Did you?*

"Oh, yes. Salmon and snow peas and mango sherbet. First-rate Chablis too. New York has such great restaurants."

"I ate the crackers and anchovies your friend left, it was all I could find. And my back was giving me hell, so I had a couple of drinks."

"Mm." Delia showed no interest in or objection to this fact. As Jane had said more than once, she was completely self-centered. But now it occurred to Alan that for him Delia's egotism, her self-centeredness, was one of her great attractions. She might not notice or sympathize with his pain and disability, but she also never treated him as an invalid, a member of a different, inferior species.

"I adore the city at this time of year," she breathed. She half sat up, pulled off her black jacket, and flung it on the floor, then stretched out on the sofa, extending rounded legs encased in sheer black tights. "It's such a relief to be here, where nobody notices me and I can be anonymous."

"Really?" Alan said, looking down at her—both admiring the view and angry at its effect on him. "I can't believe you wouldn't be noticed anywhere."

"Well, it's true, I am sometimes recognized in New York," Delia admitted, misunderstanding. "But it's not oppressive, the way it's getting to be in Corinth. Ever since those posters went up everywhere, announcing the reading next week."

"Ah?" Alan had seen these posters, which featured a photo of Delia in low-cut white lace, all swirling hair and huge eyes, definitely provocative—though less so than at this moment.

"All of a sudden people know I'm in town, and if they've ever read one of my stories they feel they have the right to call me and bomb me with e-mails and come to the Center any time of the day with books to be signed. And I know it's going to be worse after my reading." She shuddered visibly, causing her black chiffon scarf to flutter and subside.

"Maybe not," Alan said. "Once they've heard and seen you, maybe they'll quiet down."

"I doubt it," Delia said with a movement of her head and wavering glance away that might have been either vanity or fear. "And I'm awfully afraid of the reading too."

"Really? You must have done so many."

"But I'm always terrified beforehand, though I know it's out of my hands. I stand there, and either the spirit descends, or it doesn't. When it doesn't I'm lost, ruined. I hear my voice going on, blah, blah, blah, like some imbecile radio announcer, and I want to die."

"I know what you mean," Alan said, thinking of some unsuccessful lectures of his own.

"But if the spirit descends, I'm like a wild goose. Flying, soaring. I want to keep on forever, to fly out of the window and vanish into the sky." She sighed, first on a rising, then a falling note. "But then it's over. I have to descend to earth. And then comes the awful question period. There's always hunters there, wanting to shoot you down, you know?"

"Yeah," he agreed, remembering some of his own lectures.

"And I'm a sitting goose."

"Duck," Alan corrected automatically. "A sitting duck."

"No. Absolutely not a duck," Delia said coldly. "Don't be such a professor."

"All right. A sitting swan," he suggested. Delia did not reply, but with her head turned away on her long white neck, she did resemble an angry swan.

"And then I have to sign books and go to the reception and meet the audience. They all crowd around like hunting dogs, shoving and barking, wanting to eat me alive. I feel so besieged, so invaded." She laughed nervously. "I can't bear that."

"I know what you mean," Alan said, trying not to stare at the shiny full curves of Delia's thigh, rose-pink under sheer black, where her slit skirt fell apart—or at least not to be caught staring.

"It's already beginning to be like that back in Corinth. I'm more and more afraid to go to the Center." She gazed up at Alan, widening her silver-gray eyes. "You know, if you wanted, you could do something wonderful for me."

"Yeah? What?" Still hungry, Alan was not yet mollified enough to promise anything. Besides, his back hurt.

"You could trade offices with me. That would baffle them." She giggled.

"But if I were in your office, I'd be besieged and invaded."

"No, because we'd keep your name on the door. A lot of them would get confused and go away. And besides, your office is so lovely and shadowy, with that big tree in front of the window. It would be so much better when I have a headache: the light wouldn't cut me like knives the way it does now. Please." Delia raised herself to a sitting position and leaned toward him, dropping her scarf on the floor. Her black silk blouse was also semi-transparent, revealing the flushed pale skin and black lace bra beneath.

"Well . . ." Alan imagined the pain and inconvenience of moving, the loss of his northern light.

"Just for a little while. Till they get discouraged and stop coming." She smiled warmly, pathetically.

"Well—all right."

"Oh, you darling." Impulsively—or with calculation?—Delia sprang to her feet, then reached up and kissed him lightly. "I'm so, so grateful." She sighed and subsided onto the sofa again. "And I'm so, so tired. Did you use up all the gin?"

"No, there's some left. Shall I make you a drink?" he added, when Delia did not move.

"Oh, thank you. Light on the tonic, please."

In the minimal chrome kitchen, Alan made a stiff drink for Delia and another for himself, thinking that it was a long time since he had done this for anyone.

"That okay?"

"Lovely." Delia took a long swallow and lay back. "Much better. If only my feet didn't hurt so. I wonder. Could you possibly rub them a little?"

"Well—all right, sure." Equally excited and uncomfortable, he lowered himself to the edge of the sofa and took one warm high-arched foot in his hands.

"Ahh. That's so nice." Delia sighed and stretched. "Go on. More."

Trying to recall the (ultimately unsuccessful) efforts of a new-age reflexology therapist he had consulted last summer on the advice of his back-pain pal Gilly, Alan smoothed and pressed Delia's broad but graceful feet and stubby round pink-nailed toes, strangely sexy beneath the sheer black hose.

"Yes, lovely," she repeated, stretching luxuriously. "My legs are sore too."

"Okay." Alan began stroking the ankles and full, rounded calves with a slow upward motion.

"Oh yes." Delia sighed. "Could you—a little higher."

"Right you are." He moved to her round rosy knees, then, since she did not protest, beyond.

"Higher," she murmured a few moments later.

"Higher than this?" He looked at Delia, who lay with her eyes closed and her legs spread, breathing slowly and deeply.

"Yes, please."

Alan hesitated. He felt the approach of what seemed like delight but was in fact danger. If this event continued, he would soon be expected to assume a position that would cause agonizing pain in his back, and he would falter and fail.

"But remember what I said," Delia whispered. "I can't bear to be invaded. Never in any way. You understand."

"Yeah," Alan said, and his heart and cock both gave a great leap of relief as he realized what this meant: that if he did as Delia asked she would never find him out. "I understand." He lay down beside her; then, turning toward her with a wrench of pain, kissed her softly. Delia opened her mouth at once, though not her eyes, and gave him a warm, full-lipped kiss.

"But anything else—everything else," she murmured. "Yes. Oh yes."

"That was wonderful," she murmured a little later, opening her long-lashed eyes and stretching.

"Yes," Alan agreed, still a little dizzy with surprise and pleasure—pleasure received as well as given. He ran one hand over the amazing baroque curve of Delia's hip.

"Hey. I scored some codeine from my New York doctor. You want any?"

"No thanks, not now." But then he raised himself on one elbow so he could look down on Delia's flushed face and tangled mermaid hair, and felt a vicious twinge in his lower back. "Well, maybe, if you have a couple extra."

"Sure. In my bag." She gestured at a big soft tapestry carryall on the floor by the door. Alan rose slowly and painfully and brought it to her. It was against the law, he knew, to use someone else's prescription drugs; Jane would have been appalled. Nevertheless, among his back-pain pals this was not uncommon. Gilly had given him many packets of dried herbs (some mildly effective), and he had reciprocated with orthocodone.

"Do you have any grass?" Delia asked, passing over a handful of pills.

"Not here. I didn't want to take it on the plane, after what happened to Davi Gakar. They have dogs now that can smell the stuff, a friend of mine says." Gilly's husband Pedro occasionally gave Alan a joint, the last of which he had—very riskily—shared with Delia in his office, causing them both to have a fit of giggles over one of his latest drawings, a slightly suggestive fountain.

You are a bad influence on me, he thought now, looking at Delia as she lay flushed and disheveled on a black leather sofa on Central Park West. And I am a bad influence on you. And I don't care.

ELEVEN

A few days later, on a misty October afternoon, Jane sat brooding in her office at the Unger Center. The Copy Monster was giving trouble again, the kitchen was full of noise and dust and confusion caused by the men from Buildings and Grounds who had finally come to replace the fallen ceiling, and Susie and the cleaning crew had done no typing or cleaning because they had spent the entire morning moving Delia Delaney into Alan's office and Alan into Delia's, without consulting Jane. "She told me it was all right; she said he'd agreed," Susie had explained.

At first Jane had suspected that Delia had made this up, but Alan (who was at home recovering from a semi-sleepless night) had confirmed it. No, he didn't really mind, he said in a flat, neutral voice, after informing Jane that she had woken him up and that he was in severe pain. But Jane minded: though she tried not to show it, she was furious. Yet again Delia was grabbing whatever she wanted without considering anyone else—without considering the schedule of the Center or Alan's need for peace and northern light.

You are a hopeless ninny, she thought as she looked across the desk at Susie, and Delia is a greedy, selfish egotist. As an administrator it was Jane's job to maintain a cool but friendly attitude toward all the Fellows; but over the past two months she had come to dislike and resent Delia thoroughly. Why should a woman like that not only get more than Jane's yearly salary for sitting in an office for nine months and giving two lectures, but also be married to Henry Hull?

Jane sighed and rested her head against the screen of her computer. She knew that these thoughts were deeply unprofessional; they were also morally wrong, because they were partly based on jealousy. Somehow over the last two months, in spite of all her efforts, she had not only become a resentful unloving wife but was on the edge of becoming an unfaithful one. Already the hot stains of Henry Hull's kisses under the maple tree were on her face and neck, and one, the worst one, just above her left breast, over the heart. And last night, while she lay silently awake after a dream full of flying tropical birds, listening to Alan groan and shift about and pull the covers off her and toward him, she had faced the fact that she was in love with Henry Hull. It wasn't just frustrated desire she felt: it was awe and wonder and a bright dizzy feeling of flying and floating whenever she thought of him.

But what she felt was wrong and awful and disloyal. "I brought you the acorn squash, like I promised, but I can't see you again," she had told him at the Farmers' Market on Saturday, as they stood in front of a display of misshapen organic pumpkins, like huge orange lopsided hearts. "Not like this."

"But you want to," Henry had suggested.

"Yes, but that doesn't matter. It's not right."

A wheeze of cool, foggy air from the hall announced that someone had entered the building. Jane sat up abruptly and composed her expression into one of helpful neutrality. Then she saw that the visitor was Henry, in the same tan duffle coat he had worn two days ago, a coat she now knew the warm, rough texture of intimately. She rose and hurried out into the hall to intercept him.

"Please, I asked you not to come here," she said in a lowered, trembling voice. "You said you wouldn't."

"This is an official visit," Henry replied. "Delia sent me. She's concerned about the room she'll be speaking in next week. She doesn't think it will be big enough."

"I don't see why," Jane told him. "There's over a hundred and fifty seats in Shaw Hall. It's much larger than the room here where the other Fellows have spoken."

"Yeah, maybe." Henry ran one hand through his untidy brown curls in an untidy manner. "But you know, Delia has a lot of fans. It won't be just students. Whenever she reads anywhere lately, these mobs of intense-looking women appear. I think you'd better count on at least three hundred."

"Really," Jane said. Already this reading had become an annoyance to her. The photo that Delia had given her for the publicity release and the poster was, in Jane's opinion, on the edge of unsuitable. Delia's abundant loose hair, low-cut lace blouse, and dreamy, sex-stunned expression suggested the cover of a paperback romance rather than a University lecture. To make matters worse, Selma Schmidt had taken it upon herself to make an extra hundred copies of the poster on hot-pink paper and tack them up all over town. Maybe this would attract a few more listeners; but it seemed very unlikely to Jane that there were three hundred people in Hopkins County who would want to hear Delia's arty, self-conscious poems and tales.

"I promised her you'd fix it." Henry moved nearer to Jane; he touched her hand. She pulled it away, but the place still burnt. "Let's keep her happy, it's so much less trouble."

"I don't know," Jane temporized, reluctant to give Delia anything in addition to what she already had that she didn't deserve. "It's pretty late to find another room, but I'll try." Only not too hard, she thought.

"And I'll see you this Saturday at the Farmers' Market? About ten?"

"All right," she repeated weakly, aware that in fact it was all wrong.

———

"So how's it going?" Henry asked, sitting down next to Jane in a noisy, crowded coffee shop. Outside it was steadily and heavily raining: the bench by the lake where they usually sat was soaked and dark with water.

"Oh, all right." As Jane lifted her cup she was aware that her hand was shaking. All week she had been dreading and desiring this meeting, dreading and desiring what Henry might do or say.

"How's Alan?"

"So-so." She tried to gather her thoughts. "He's been very involved with making drawings for that show in New York. But then yesterday . . ."

"Yeah?"

Jane stared at Henry. How could he be so calm? she thought. It was as if he had taken a six-week step back in time, to a place where nobody felt anything much and all they did was complain politely about their spouses. Of course that was right; it was what they should do. With effort, she tried to take a similar step back. "Well, yesterday he was telling me how he hadn't been able to finish his exercises because of the pain. And I made a mistake, I suggested he might try going for walks instead. Because his doctor said that he should lose some weight, to put less strain on his back. And he got irritated."

"Ah."

"He told me I ought to realize it wasn't as easy as I thought to walk when you were in constant pain and every step you took hurt." Jane spoke almost in a whisper, aware that the people at the tables on either side of them could hear every word.

"Um."

"I said I was sorry, but he's been difficult ever since, he—" Jane realized that Henry wasn't looking at her or even listening to her, only staring out the plate-glass window, where rain streaked down in gray sheets. She felt something like despair. Always before he had sympathized, met her complaints with his own. "So how's Delia?" she asked forlornly.

"All right." He swallowed visibly. "I don't want to talk about her. I want to talk about us. But not here. Isn't there somewhere quieter we can go?"

"I don't know. . . ."

"What about the Center? Don't you have a key?"

"Yes, but so do all the Fellows. Charlie Amir often comes in on Saturday, and so does Selma Schmidt."

Henry laughed shortly. "So what? They aren't going to report us."

"Selma might. She's that type. And she's always looking for some reason to talk to Delia."

"And Delia is always looking for some reason not to talk to her." He set down his half-finished coffee. "Come on, Janey. I'll meet you there."

"It's beautiful up here," Henry said. It was twenty minutes later, and he and Jane had just climbed the narrow, steep stairs to the Victorian cupola above the Unger Center. They had rejected all the other possible places to talk: the kitchen and dining room were still full of ladders and drop cloths and plaster dust; the main downstairs rooms were large and full of echoes, with sliding doors that hadn't been fully closed in years. Charlie Amir was working upstairs, and he would think it strange if he saw them go into someone else's office.

"I know Alan isn't here," Jane had said. "But I keep thinking he could suddenly decide to come in, and call a taxi."

"And I keep thinking Delia could fly in the window on a broom," Henry had remarked, surprising Jane. He never says anything negative about her, and now he's just practically called her a witch, she thought.

"I never knew you could get up into the cupola," he said now, looking out over the tops of the maple trees, through which a few last pale-gold leaves shone, drenched now with rain and shaken with wind.

"Most people don't. But back in Matthew Unger's time they

used to have tea here and watch the storms coming across the lake, Lily told me."

"Yeah, you could do that." He glanced at the padded seats on three sides of the cupola, with their faded, flowered cushions and the little wicker table in the center. "You can see a long way," he added. "Or I guess you could if it wasn't for the rain and the fog."

"Yes, for miles. But Lily Unger doesn't like people to come up here. She says the stairs aren't safe, and it's too full of ghosts."

"Ghosts?"

"Memories, I expect she meant."

"Yeah. A place like this could have that kind of ghosts." Without warning, he turned from the window toward Jane and kissed her lightly, instantly creating one such ghost.

"No-oh," she whispered, and pulled away. "It isn't—we mustn't—"

Henry did not protest. "You're right. We have to talk first," he said, sitting down. "Look, the way it is. I want to be with you, and you want to be with me."

"I never said—" Her voice trembled as she subsided onto a padded bench.

"But it's true, isn't it?"

Jane swallowed. It was one of her principles never to lie to a friend. "Yes, but it doesn't make any difference," she said hurriedly. "We can't be together, because of Alan and Delia. We have to take care of them. We promised, we're married."

"Really? Are you sure?"

"What?" Jane stared at Henry and the rain-smeared glass behind him.

"Are you sure you're married?"

"Yes, of course. What do you mean?" He's going to talk meta-phorically, philosophically, the way some professors do, Jane thought with an irritated sinking feeling. He's never done that before.

"You never can be sure." Henry looked at her with a strange

steady expression in his dark eyes. "I thought I was married, but it turns out I was wrong."

"You're not married to Delia?"

"Apparently not."

"Really? But how? Why?" Jane realized her mouth was hanging open, and shut it. "But that can't be right," she said. "Delia was telling everybody just last week about what a beautiful wedding you had, on a mountainside at sunset in a field of wildflowers, with a string quartet playing Schumann."

"Yeah. We had all that: the music, the flowers, the sunset, the champagne. Everyone said how perfect it was. But it turns out Delia had neglected to get a divorce from her former husband."

"She'd what? Good grief," Jane, stunned, heard herself utter, in her mother's voice, her mother's favorite expletive. "Oh, hell," she amended. "That's awful."

"I thought so. But of course when I found out, she claimed it didn't matter. She'd forgotten all about it, she said. He was the past, and it was gone, blown away. Anyhow our souls and our bodies and our minds were truly married, so who cared about the State of North Carolina? She more or less convinced me at the time. Delia can do that, she can convince anyone of anything. Except you." Henry gave her a brief smile.

"Wow." Jane disregarded the compliment, if it was one. "How did you find out?"

"I saw a letter from her husband's lawyer yesterday. He wants a divorce now, so he can marry again."

"And will Delia agree?"

"I hadn't thought of that. I guess so, if he pays her enough money. He's not a bad guy—teaches at some little college in Ohio."

"So then you could really get married," Jane said without enthusiasm.

Henry did not reply, only shrugged.

"You wouldn't have to have another big wedding. You could just go to the town hall right here."

"Delia wouldn't do that. She'd never agree to get married in an office building. Not her style at all. And what if someone found out? It would ruin her legend."

"Really." Jane looked at Henry. He doesn't like her either, she thought, and felt a rush of joy. But that was wrong, and also pointless. "But if everyone thinks you're married, you should be married," she said. "Otherwise—"

"Otherwise we're living in sin, and we've been living in sin for seven years." Henry laughed harshly. "Is that what you mean?"

"Well, yes. At least, that's how my mother would put it."

"So you think I should marry a woman who's been lying to me for seven years."

"No—I don't know," Jane stuttered.

"But I don't want to get married," he said. "Not to Delia, anyhow. And I don't think she wants it either. I think it's convenient for her to be free. And always has been."

"Convenient?" Jane said, shocked, then convinced. Well, of course Delia didn't just forget she was already married, she thought. Nobody forgets something like that, no matter how poetic and flaky they are.

"In case she should meet someone she liked better."

"But that's awful—that's—" Jane tried to find words.

"Let's not talk about her." Henry moved toward her. "Let's forget about all that for a while." He put one arm about her, then the other. "We're here now."

Yes, but where are we? Jane thought. On top of the Unger Center, in a place battered by wind and surrounded by rain and haunted by ghosts. Confused, she allowed Henry to move even closer. For a long moment she totally lost contact with her conscience. Then, as she felt the cold plate glass of the window against her back, she struggled upright.

"No, no, I can't, I mustn't," she cried with a stifled sob. "You might be free, but I'm not."

Henry scowled, but let her go. "Yeah, but wouldn't you like to be free?" he asked.

"But I can't," Jane wailed, staring past him at the rain-smeared glass, which made her feel as if the whole room were crying. "I can't leave Alan, not when he's so ill. Everyone would hate me. I would hate myself."

"What if he weren't ill? Could you leave him then?"

"I don't know—yes, maybe. But if he weren't ill, if he were the person he was before, I maybe wouldn't want to—I mean—" Jane fell silent, aware that she had said something hurtful. "Or maybe I would, I can't tell. I don't know anything anymore." She swallowed another sob. "Before I met you my life was so simple, and now it's so complicated."

"And before I met you, my life was so complicated, and now it's so simple," Henry said, staring directly at her.

Jane did not speak; all her effort was going into trying not to weep, to explode into a rush of water and wind like the one outside the cupola.

"Tell me something," Henry said presently. "Would you feel any different if you thought you weren't the only person who could take care of Alan? For instance, if you thought he was having an affair?"

"What?" Jane gulped down another sob, and gathered her strength to answer this absurd question. "I don't know, probably, but he isn't. He's not interested in that, not now. Because of the pain, he can't—he doesn't—" She gave a kind of moan, realizing that she had just been deeply disloyal as well as indiscreet. "Oh, I shouldn't have said that, I—" The sobs so long suppressed burst from her, followed by a rush of tears.

"I thought so," Henry said ambiguously. "Please, Janey, don't cry." He put his arms around her again, but lightly this time, and Jane rested her face against the familiar warm, rough tan fabric of his duffle coat. "No, I take that back. Cry if you want to. But it's going to be all right. I promise you, it's going to be all right."

No, it's not, Jane thought. Nothing's going to be all right. Not ever again.

"I can't see you anymore," she said, choking back a sob. "It's got to stop."

On Friday of the following week, Jane was in the supply room, frowning at the Copy Monster, which all day had been refusing to collate or staple. The campus technicians who repair copiers had grown tired of coming to the Unger Center, and when Jane phoned them they would not promise to be there until late next week. As a result, Jane and Susie had been collating and stapling by hand nearly all afternoon. Half an hour ago Susie had run one spike of a heavy-duty staple into her thumb and had to be sent first to the University Health Center and then home.

But the Copy Monster was the least of Jane's troubles today. Though she had refused to see Henry, trying to do the right thing and get things clear in her head, her thoughts had remained uncollated and full of sharp spikes.

When Henry had said that everything would be all right, what he must have meant was that she would agree that they should be together. As he had pointed out, it was what she (or rather the selfish, greedy, bad part of her) wanted. If she gave in to it tomorrow afternoon they would be together, but in a dishonest, sneaky way, in some motel at least an hour from Corinth. Anywhere closer would be dangerous, because Jane, as a local, was known to people who owned or ran or worked in all the local motels. They would have to drive for at least an hour, to some cheap highway motel where they did not ask questions, probably somewhere with a sleazy fake-satin bedspread and plastic glasses wrapped in waxed paper and snow on the television screen. But they wouldn't care about any of that, because they would be together.

Jane scowled, ashamed of her own thoughts. She realized that she was becoming a really terrible person, a person who was imagining how she might commit adultery while her invalid husband was lying at home in pain.

In fact, Alan had not complained quite as much lately about his pain, but this had not made him more pleasant. He was still, or even more, preoccupied, self-centered, demanding, and distant. He had begun to treat Jane as if she were hired help: he no longer always thanked her for anything she did, or apologized for his requests. His mind was fixed more and more on the coming exhibition of his art in New York, and the new job he had taken on of designing a ruined tower for the estate of a foolish Connecticut millionaire. (Jane had not met this millionaire, but in her opinion anybody who would pay thirty thousand dollars plus costs for a pre-ruined tower was a fool.)

In the past, however difficult or distant Alan had been all day, when they got into bed at night he had always turned to her and rested his head in the hollow below her shoulder and told her where and how bad his pain was; often he also asked how she was doing ("Fine," Jane always said) and/or told her he loved her ("Same here," Jane always said). Now he either went to bed at nine or ten, saying that he was exhausted, or stayed up past midnight, saying that he had napped that afternoon and was not sleepy. Often he slept in his study, but if he was in the bedroom he tossed and turned and groaned in his sleep, and sometimes he got up and went downstairs to read and to eat. In the morning Jane would find dirty cups and glasses in the sink and crumpled empty bags of chips or cookies on the kitchen counter.

Clearly, he was not fine, and Jane was not fine, and Henry was not fine. The only person for whom everything was going well was Delia. Her reading had been a huge success: the slightly larger lecture room Jane had found, and hoped would hold over a hundred empty seats, had been full to overflowing. Because of her job Jane had had to be there and listen, and even seem to applaud. Liar, cheat, she had thought as she padded her palms together silently, while Delia, in a long silvery lamé dress and silver sandals, her loosened hair a metallic gold (of course she dyes it, Jane realized), acknowledged the tributes of the audience with a graceful bow and blown kisses.

Jane was familiar with, and even reconciled to, the fact that bad things sometimes happened to good people. This truth had often been mentioned in church during her childhood and youth. It was something that we could not understand but had to accept, their minister, the Reverend Jack, had explained, knowing that God, who loved us, understood it. What we could do was to love and sympathize and offer our help and support to those upon whom affliction had fallen. From these efforts, more love and sympathy and support would come.

In the past, Jane had discovered this to be true. She found it much harder to accept the fact that good things sometimes happened to bad people. In cases like that, there was nothing you could do but smile politely when Delia came into the Center glowing and laughing and preening, and try not to listen when people gushed over her reading or how beautiful she had looked that afternoon or the next day at the trustees' luncheon, at which she had been a featured guest.

As Jane stood brooding with a stapler in one hand, the front doorbell of the Center rang: an unusual occurrence, since most people just walked right in. Since Susie had left, she set the stapler down and descended the stairs. Outside, she found a deliveryman from a local flower shop, with a heavy sheaf of plant material wrapped in shiny paper. Of course, it was for Delia Delaney. There was nothing unusual about this: even before her reading Delia had begun receiving notes and flowers and gifts, and since then it had only become worse. On the other hand, nobody had sent flowers to Jane since she was in the hospital with food poisoning five years ago.

Jane went back into the office and phoned Delia, but there was no answer from upstairs. Probably, while Jane was working in the supply room, she had gone home. Next she tried the office of Selma Schmidt, who would no doubt be delighted to take in Delia's flowers, and indeed would probably welcome the chance to drive them to Delia's house. But again there was no answer.

Jane's impulse was to leave the flowers on the table in the front hall. By the time Delia came in on Monday they would be dead, which would serve her right. She might guess that Jane or someone had just abandoned them, but so what? Nobody had seen her take them in, and it might have been the deliveryman who had left them on the table, where they would lie all weekend, withering slowly and gasping for water.

No. The flowers were innocent in themselves, and it went against all Jane's instincts as a gardener to damage any plant, even by passive neglect. They would have to be saved. Jane unwrapped the shiny white paper in the pantry, exposing a sheaf of almost vulgarly huge gold-fringed chrysanthemums and white autumn lilies nestled in fern, with two packets of plant preservative attached: the gift of someone either besotted or rich or both. She chose a tall pressed-glass antique vase from the cupboard and cut the stems back two inches so that they could take up water. It made a nice display, but Jane wanted it out of her sight.

She carried the flowers upstairs and knocked on Delia's door, then called her name, but there was no answer—clearly, she'd gone home. She opened the door and saw an empty room with light streaming in and Alan's drafting table covered with papers—of course, Alan had changed offices with Delia, she remembered with annoyance—and he, no doubt, was in the library.

The door of Delia's new office across the hall was locked, and she did not answer a knock or call; but Jane had a master key.

Inside, the velvet curtains were drawn, the room full of heavy shadows. The first thing Jane could make out after she pushed the door open was that Delia was still there, lying on the big green sofa. She was in a state of disarray: her hair disheveled, her clothes rumpled. She's having another migraine, Jane thought.

"Oh, I'm sorry, I—I thought you'd gone home," she stammered. "I didn't mean to disturb you, but these flowers came. I didn't want them to die over the weekend, so I put them in water—"

"Yes. Thank you so much," Delia said in a kind of exhausted whisper.

Jane looked around for a place to set the vase down, and saw something strange: the heavy dark-green velvet curtain to the right of the bay window was bulging out oddly, and a pair of large feet, in black socks, protruded from below it. A man was hiding there, she realized. Delia wasn't ill, she was cheating on Henry with somebody. It could be one of the other Fellows, Davi Gakar or Charlie Amir, both of whom had crushes on her. Or it could be somebody else, some stranger who had sneaked into the Center while Jane was in the supply room. In any case it would be best if she did not actually see him or acknowledge that he was there.

"I'll put these on the desk," she said in a strained, artificial voice.

"That's fine," Delia whispered.

But as Jane crossed the room, averting her eyes from the bulging curtain and the feet, she saw a man's jacket lying on the desk chair. It was a jacket that she had seen before: gray tweed with woven leather buttons and a light-gray silky lining like the one she herself had mended only a week ago, with a material that did not quite match. Yes. There was the patch, exactly like on Alan's tweed jacket. Was that possible?

Without stopping to think, wanting only to understand, she turned and pulled back the velvet curtain. There stood her husband, with his shoes off and his denim shirt hanging out.

"Jane, listen, it's not what you think," he croaked.

Jane could not answer: her head was suddenly full of smoke and steam. She had not felt this sort of betrayal since junior high school—and it was the language of junior high school that now rose to her lips.

"You creep!" she cried. "You sneaky, disgusting little creep!" She might have gone on, but was distracted by a sound from across the room: the sound of laughter. She looked around, dizzy and furious, and saw Delia lying in an untidy crush of pale, lacy clothes, convulsed with mirth.

"Don't you laugh at me, you nasty witch!" Jane shouted, enraged, and raised the big vase of flowers, which had now become a convenient weapon. But at the last moment a half-conscious sense of her responsibility as an administrator caused her to pull the flowers and ferns out of their antique cut-glass container (Property of the Unger Center for the Humanities) before she threw them hard at Delia.

Then, stifling a sob of rage and pain, she left the room. In a kind of daze she descended the stairs. She rinsed out the vase and put it back into the cupboard, found her coat and scarf and handbag, left the building, and drove home.

TWELVE

After the door of Delia's office had slammed behind Jane, Alan stepped out from the heavy curtain. "Oh, fuck," he said, as a spasm of pain gripped his lower back.

Delia still lay on the moss-green plush sofa in her rumpled lace skirt and half-open blouse—now covered, as was she, with wet ferns and flowers. She was still laughing, in bursts of amused hiccups.

"So now what?" he asked; but she only released another bubble of hilarity. Was she having hysterics? "Are you all right?"

Delia shrugged, nodded, giggled. Sprawled there among the flowers, she resembled a Pre-Raphaelite painting—Hunt's Ophelia, or a Waterhouse water nymph.

Or maybe she's in shock, he thought, beginning to shove his shirt back into his slacks. "You'd better pull yourself together, honey," he told her. "Jane could come back anytime."

"No, she won't. She was much too embarrassed." Delia sat up, causing foliage to scatter. "Oh, look, here's the card that came with the flowers." She tore it open. *Best wishes from your greatest fan, Wally Hersh*. "Everyone's so unoriginal these days." She sighed and stood up. Then she selected one of the scattered white lilies, tucked it behind her ear, and turned to her reflection in the big mirror over the mantelpiece.

"I don't get it," Alan said, uneasy at this crazy indifference. "You're not bothered by what just happened?"

"Not really." Delia did not glance around. "If Jane was to come back with a shotgun, I'd be bothered. But that's not her style."

"No," he agreed. "She'd never do that. But still—" He heard the sound of a familiar motor and turned to the window, pulling aside the velvet curtain. Below, Jane's Honda wagon was descending the driveway. "You're right; she's leaving. Jesus, my back is killing me."

Delia did not comment. She was now trying the lily tucked into the bosom of her blouse. The effect was striking, but Alan didn't appreciate it fully.

"What the hell is the matter with you?" he said. "Why are you taking this so lightly?"

"Because it's not important." Delia smiled and shook out her hair. She looked beautiful, undeniably, but also somewhat crazy.

"Maybe not for you," he muttered, glancing around for his loafers. As he shoved his feet into them, another spasm of pain sliced through his back. "But what am I supposed to say to Jane when I get home?"

"Just remember that the best defense is a good offense," she replied, not glancing away from the mirror.

"A good offense?"

"You know. Say we're both very hurt and angry. Tell her how rude and intrusive she was, pushing her way into my room without even knocking."

"But she did knock," Alan protested.

"Well, she didn't give me time to answer. Remind her how unprofessional that was. She probably regrets it already. And going into a rage and throwing all these flowers, without stopping to find out what the real situation was. Why, she almost threw that heavy glass vase too. I could have been seriously injured."

"What was the real situation?" Alan asked, amazed.

"Well, obviously—I was having a migraine, and you came in to see if you could do anything for me."

"And why was my shirt hanging out and my shoes off?"

Delia sighed. "Because it was so warm in here. And you took your shoes off because your feet hurt. Use your imagination."

"I don't think she'll believe that," Alan said. "But maybe it's worth a try."

"Of course it is." Delia laughed again. "It's lucky we switched offices; at least you had time to get your pants back on."

Alan did not laugh. "But why was I hiding behind the curtain?"

"Yes, that was a mistake." She smiled. "Well, okay. You knew she'd be surprised to see you. You wanted to protect her, you knew she might not understand. But whatever you do, don't apologize. Make her apologize to you."

Alan looked at Delia with something between admiration and dismay. "You're talking as if we're in the right."

"But we are in the right." She turned away from the mirror. "I was ill, and you were performing an act of mercy."

"Nobody will believe that, not if Jane tells them what she saw. There'll be a scandal."

"So what?" She shrugged.

"You don't care?"

"Why should I? It's right what they say: in the long run, all publicity is good publicity. Scandal is what everyone wants and expects from us: melodrama and farce and comedy and tragedy. Writers and artists who lead conventional, blameless lives, they don't last. Everyone's bored by them." Delia gave a little catlike yawn. "You know, they're rather pretty, Wally Hersh's lilies," she remarked. "Pity to let them die." She began to gather the flowers that lay on the sofa. "They stand for purity and innocence, you know."

"Really." Thinking how inappropriate they were in this case, Alan handed her two long-stemmed lilies that had fallen near him. Close up, they seemed to be made of thick white suede.

"Thank you." She smiled.

"Here's some more." With another twinge of pain, he collected two saucer-sized golden chrysanthemums, but Delia pushed them away.

"No, leave those. Yellow mums mean slighted love."

"You don't believe that."

"Of course I do." She sighed. "Nobody understands the Language of Flowers anymore. And they don't understand that it has power, even if you don't know it."

"Yeah, it looks like you're already slighting Wally Hersh's love," he said, dropping the mums in the wastebasket.

"No; not completely." Delia giggled and stooped to gather more lilies and pose with them. In spite of what had recently happened, she seemed quite calm, and fully absorbed in this task.

"Well," Alan said, after watching for a few moments, baffled. "It doesn't look like Jane's going to give me a ride home. I'd better go call a taxi. Do you want a lift?"

"No thanks. Henry will pick me up."

"I don't suppose you're going to tell him what happened."

For the first time since Jane had left, Delia looked at Alan directly. "Are you mad?" she asked. "Anyhow it's none of his business, what you and I do, what we have together." She smiled warmly, almost seductively. "It's on another plane entirely. Come on, don't look so sad." She moved nearer and gave him a quick, wet kiss. "Everything's going to be all right. Only if I were you I wouldn't go home just yet."

At two a.m. that night, Alan lay awake and in pain in a confusion of blankets and sheets and a sense of having behaved both stupidly and badly. Whether he opened his eyes or shut them, he kept seeing Jane's face white against the darkness, with its expression of shock, hurt, and anger.

Following Delia's advice, he had delayed his return and gone to the faculty club for supper. In his confused state of mind, he had forgotten that sitting in a straight chair for more than a few minutes at a time always aroused the lizard in his back—whom he now sometimes thought of as Old Clootie, the familiar name of the Devil among his Scottish ancestors. At home and in the office he usually stood up or lay down on the sofa to eat.

Last night, even before his food came, he had to stand up and walk about, causing the waiter and the other diners to look at him oddly. Fortunately, no one he knew was in the faculty club, but even so, agony and embarrassment had made it impossible for him to finish the meal, though he managed to drink a Scotch on the rocks and half a bottle of wine. Afterward he stumbled dizzily and painfully out into the lobby and called a taxi. As he did so, inside his spine, Old Clootie flexed his claws and smiled.

For the first few minutes of the ride Alan tried to sit up like a normal person, but was unable to manage it. When Jane drove him to campus he always lay down in the back seat, to minimize the pain.

"Hey, you all right back there?" the taxi driver had inquired.

"Fine, just a little tired," Alan had replied in blurred tones that, he realized, sounded like those of a drunk.

He had arrived home in agony, but still resolved to deny everything. When Jane asked, in a voice that combined fear and rage, where the hell he had been, he had said, as planned, that he had wanted to give her time to cool off.

"Listen, my back is in spasm," he had told her. "I have to take a pill."

"I'm sorry," Jane said almost automatically, in a flat, neutral voice. She followed him into the kitchen and stood waiting while he gulped water and painkillers. "I'm very sorry it hurts, but I need an explanation."

"Maybe it's you who owe me an explanation," Alan said, his words blurred by pain and alcohol. Then, though it felt unreal, he took the offensive and rebuked her for her rude unprofessional behavior and leap to false conclusions. He insisted that his presence in

Delia's office had been an act of concern and friendship—telling himself meanwhile that if he was stretching the truth, it was also out of concern and friendship. He was sparing Jane information that would hurt her unnecessarily.

As he spoke in imitation of a firm, reasonable manner, he felt a rush of pity and affection for his wife: this small brown-haired woman with her neat shirtwaist dress, her fading prettiness and wide blue eyes, reddened as if with weeping. She was a good person who loved him and had been unfailingly kind to him over the long months of his pain. It wasn't her fault that her kindness had begun to feel more and more like a burden.

"I don't believe you," Jane said when he finished, her voice trembling. She sagged against the electric stove as if for warmth and support. "I think you're just saying what Delia told you to say."

"That's ridiculous," Alan replied weakly, alarmed by her guess. "You're really prejudiced against her," he added, regaining control. "You have been from the start."

"No, that's not so—" Jane's voice wobbled.

"You've always been determined to think the worst of her."

"I haven't, I've tried—"

"That first week, you told me she was a complete egotist."

"Well, she is. She never thinks of anyone except herself."

"That's just not true," Alan said. "Delia's actually a very wonderful and generous person."

Jane turned to stare at him. "You're in love with her too," she stated in the tone of someone who has just turned over a rock and found a dead toad under it. "Just like everyone else."

"I—" Alan opened his mouth to deny this, but was unable to do so. "Don't be stupid," he said. "She's been a very good friend to me. To us," he amended. "She's found me a gallery that's already sold over fifteen thousand dollars' worth of my work. She's why we have that pasta-making machine you've wanted for so long."

"I don't care. I hate her, if you want to know the truth," Jane had cried, "and I hate that pasta machine. It's more trouble than it's worth. I can't tell the least difference between what it makes and normal pasta, and I don't believe anyone else can either."

In spite of himself, Alan (who believed he could tell the difference) must have allowed an ambiguous smile to appear on his face at this. Jane may have taken it as a smile of epicurean superiority, for a sudden spasm of rage convulsed her small neat features, and she snatched up the pasta machine and threw it, not exactly at Alan but at the floor next to his right foot, where it landed with a noisy, unpleasant jangle and thud.

"Jesus Christ," he exclaimed, jerking aside in a way that wrenched his back. "For shit's sake, Jane, get ahold of yourself." But already she had turned away from him and was hanging on to the back of a kitchen chair, weeping violently.

"I'm sorry—I shouldn't have—" She stooped to retrieve the broken pasta machine. "But it's because you're lying to me, lying and lying," she sobbed. "If you would just tell the truth, it wouldn't be so awful."

For a moment, Alan had had the impulse to do this, but he stopped himself as he realized that the kitchen was full of other appliances and cookware that might be thrown, that might not miss. If he had been well, he wouldn't have cared, but in his present condition any further injury could make his pain unbearable. Jane is a violent woman, he thought. I've been married to her for sixteen years and I never knew this.

"I am telling the truth," he insisted, beginning to feel like a complete louse.

Jane did not reply, only stood and stared at him, her arms full of wrecked metal parts.

"It's late now," he said, "and I'm in a lot of pain. I think we should just go to bed and sleep on it."

"All right," she said in a voice of great weariness. "But I'm not going to sleep in the same bed as you." With a gesture of angry distaste, she shoved the pasta machine down into the kitchen trash can.

"I didn't say you had to," Alan had retorted. "Go on. We'll feel better in the morning."

"Maybe," Jane said. "You can use the bathroom first," she added. It was the same sentence she had spoken almost every night for a year and a half. Since he hurt his back, it had taken Alan longer to undress and put on his pajamas and brush his teeth and swallow his prescriptions and get into bed and arrange his many pillows and fall asleep. When Jane came to join him, he would usually still be awake. Then they would put their arms around each other, and he would report on his pain, discuss the events of the day, and plan for tomorrow. But now the tone of the familiar phrase was no longer casual and considerate—it was harsh and flat.

And when Alan, with groans and curses, had climbed into the antique four-poster, Jane had not come to lie beside him. As he lay there in the dim glow of the bathroom night-light, he could hear her small slippered feet descending the stairs to the downstairs guest room.

Two-thirty a.m. He turned over, trying not to aggravate Old Clootie, staring into the dark. Why was it, he thought, that Delia, who had never said she loved him or promised him anything, made him feel better whenever he saw her, and Jane—who loved him, and had done so much for him—made him feel worse? Why was it that when he was with Delia, though his back still hurt, it was as if the pain were beside him and not within him—an unwelcome companion, but not a devil possessing and torturing him? Maybe it was because Delia never asked how he was feeling or expressed a condescending pity for him—and in the long run, in Alan's opinion, all pity was condescending.

He turned over again, groaning. Then, finally, the pills he had taken began to work, and he drifted into an uneasy, guilty sleep.

It was late when Alan woke, almost nine. His back still hurt, but his head was clearer. You made a bad mistake last night, he told himself.

You've got to remember that Delia is a visiting scholar at the Unger Center who will only be in town until next May. Whereas Jane is your wife who has promised to be true to you forever, in sickness and in health. You have to make it up with her. You don't have to admit anything, but you have to apologize for upsetting her and tell her that you love her and are very grateful to her. Because it's true—it must be true, even if you don't feel it now.

Alan groaned. The house around him was quiet: probably Jane was still asleep in the downstairs guest room. Well, let her sleep. He hauled himself up, feeling the familiar angry clutch of the lizard in his spine as he did so. He put on a navy-blue plush robe and slippers, used the bathroom, brushed his teeth, and went downstairs to make coffee.

The kitchen was empty, but stuck to the center of the table was a yellow Post-It note:

I've gone to stay at my mother's, will phone later. J.

Oh, Christ, Alan thought. It's too late. I've already burnt my bridges. An image appeared in his mind of an eighteenth-century "Chinese" ornamental bridge he had photographed in an English park for his book on architectural follies. Originally it had been decorated in wood and plaster, with carved dragons painted red and gold and blue. But the arch at the far end (not visible in his photo) had been damaged in a recent fire, and a gilt rope was strung across the near end, warning visitors not to cross. He could not remember now whether the bridge had been scheduled to be repaired or de-molished.

Suppose his bridges were truly burnt, and Jane had left him for good and was out of his life? Suppose he was free to see Delia, to be with her whenever they wanted? It was what she wanted too, he was almost sure of it. The way she sighed when he touched her, the way she widened her silver-gray eyes and gazed into his when they arranged to meet—and when they did meet— Unlike Jane, she was always erotically inventive, sometimes amazingly so. She couldn't really care for that useless person Henry Hull, her whole manner when she spoke of him suggested this. If she were free too—

It would mean trouble and pain, it would mean blame and guilt. But so what? He remembered something Delia had said more than once, that it was not important for an artist to be happy, or to be good. "We're above all that," she had told him. "What's important for us is to do our work." Right now, he was neither happy nor good, but he was working, and if he had Delia—

Alan glanced again at the note on the table, its dark-blue ink, its familiar neat girlish penmanship—and now he noticed another line of writing at the bottom, an afterthought in pencil:

Ham sandwich in fridge.

He knew what that meant: it meant that Jane still felt responsible for his welfare. To be sure of this, he opened the fridge and saw the sandwich, on a white plate with a slice of dill pickle beside it, the whole tightly covered with plastic wrap. He knew that there would be mustard and mayonnaise on the rye bread, and he could see the red-leaf lettuce that he preferred. There was no mistaking the message: whether he wanted her there or not, Jane was still in his life.

THIRTEEN

"Something awful has happened," Jane told Henry as she climbed into his SUV late Saturday morning at the nearly deserted Farmers' Market. Most of the stalls were empty; only a few sellers shivered in down jackets and knitted wool hats behind displays of pumpkins, potatoes, and homemade jams. A thin, mean wind gusted from the lake, where a rim of ice clung to the withered grass of the shore.

"You're shivering," Henry said. "I'll turn up the heat. Now give me your hands. Oh, so cold." He pulled off Jane's driving gloves and took her chilled fingers in his own, warmer ones. "All right. Tell me."

Though she had resolved not to break down, Jane could not keep back a strangulated sob or two as she related the events of yesterday afternoon and evening. Henry did not interrupt, only nodded occasionally, holding or rubbing her hands all the while. Gradually it dawned upon her that he was not registering shock or astonishment. "Yeah," he merely said several times as she told the story, and again when she had finished. "Yeah."

"How do you mean, 'Yeah?'" Jane asked, looking at him. Henry did not answer, only shrugged inside his duffle coat. "You're not surprised," she said suddenly. "You already knew."

"Well. More or less."

"But you didn't say anything to me." Jane pulled her hands away.

"I—I could have been wrong," Henry stammered. "I mean, I didn't know for sure it was Alan this time."

"This time?" She stared. "You mean something like that has happened before?"

In the silence that followed, she heard only the rough hum of the car heater.

"Yeah," Henry said finally. "But see, from Delia's point of view, it's not serious, it's just something she needs sometimes. It doesn't have anything to do with her feelings for me."

"But how could it not?" Jane cried.

"Because it's only play, she says. There's no past or future to it. No depth."

"No depth?"

"Just a little kissing and hugging. So it doesn't count." Henry smiled uncomfortably.

Jane sat back, staring at him. The unwelcome thought had come to her that perhaps Alan and Delia were no more guilty than she and Henry, and that possibly everything that had happened between them was also shallow and temporary. "I see," she said. "I mean, I don't see."

"Neither do I, if you want to know," he said. "Not anymore."

"But at least she agrees that something happened," Jane said. "Alan doesn't?"

Jane shook her head. "That's the worst thing, the lies," she said with a sob. "If he admitted what was going on, if he'd said he was sorry, I could stand it. If he said they were only doing what we've done, I'd have to, I guess—" She swallowed awkwardly. If Alan had told me the truth, I would have had to tell him the truth, she thought suddenly, and then maybe I wouldn't be here.

"But he didn't say that," Henry prompted.

"No, he said that Delia was having a migraine, and he went to see if there was anything he could do for her. Then I broke into the room and screamed and threw things and made her headache much worse. He sort of turned it all upside down so everything was my fault. He said he never knew I could be so irrational and suspicious, and so violent."

"Uh-huh," Henry said. "It sounds like he's been taking lessons from Delia."

"How do you mean?"

"That's what she does. If she doesn't like the truth, she turns it around until she does, and eventually she's convinced that things happened the way she says they did."

"But you believe me, don't you?"

"Yeah, sure. I believe you."

"It's not just the lies," Jane said with a long sigh. "It's as if Alan's changed into a different person. Maybe partly because of the pain, but it's more than that. It's as if he's under some awful spell. When he looks at me, it's so cool and judging, as if I was just somebody he'd hired to work for him, who was making a nuisance of herself. Last night when we were talking in the kitchen I felt all cold and shivery, like the wind was blowing indoors. I can't—I don't—" With a wail, Jane collapsed against Henry.

"There, there," he said, putting his arms around her, stroking her hair.

A few moments passed, then Jane sat up again. "The thing is, I don't think I can stand to live in the same house with him anymore," she said through tears.

"Really?"

"Uh-huh. Not now, at least."

"That's the best news I've heard in years," Henry said. He pulled Jane toward him again and kissed her wet face. "Where will you live, then?" he said presently.

"I can stay on with my parents, in my old room."

"That's so wonderful." He began to kiss her again.

"Janey, darling. Shouldn't we—I mean, would you like to go somewhere where we can be together?" he said presently. "It's so cold here, and anyone can see us." He gestured across the parking lot at the stalls of the Farmers' Market, where a vendor of honey and jam was glancing in their direction.

"I can't," Jane said with a sob. "I'm still sort of under the weather." She registered the incomprehension on his face. "I'm bleeding," she said awkwardly, and wished at once that she had chosen another phrase. But what she had said was true in every sense. She was underneath a storm of bad weather, blown about and half drowned, and bleeding emotionally as well as physically.

"I don't care. I want to be with you." Henry pushed Jane's windbreaker aside and put one heavy warm hand on her cotton shirt, over her left breast. "Maybe we could go to the Center, to the cupola."

"We can't—" Jane felt weak and confused and excited, all at the same time. Even when he was well, Alan had never touched her during what he called "your monthlies," though she had once or twice suggested it long ago. "Anyhow, we can't go to the Center. There's a conference there this weekend; the place is full of French literary theorists."

"Yeah. Very bad vibes." Henry laughed. "Then we'll drive out into the country. I think I know a place." He started the car and turned toward the exit.

I shouldn't do this, Jane thought. I should tell him to stop and let me get out. But another part of her thought, Why not?

"There's an old barn off the Myers Road, I saw it when I was jogging the other day," Henry said presently. "No houses nearby, and nobody's using it except to store hay." Jane said nothing—she felt out of breath, unable to speak, as if she were standing in a strong wind.

"Here you are," Henry said as he shoved open the sliding door of the barn. It was full of hay, but in tight rectangular bales. While Jane stood in the entrance shivering with cold or something more serious, he unfolded a knife and cut the wires on three bales of hay, then

shook them out into a heap. "There you are." Henry slid the barn
door back into place; now the only light came from long vertical
chinks in the sides and a triangular opening at the peak of the roof.
Then he took off his duffle coat and spread it over the hay. "Here.
Sit down, and I'll warm you up."

"Lovely, lovely," Jane murmured nearly an hour later, not for the
first time. She felt strange and light-headed and happy, as if she were
floating on a sea of hay.

"Yeah. There's nothing like the real thing." Henry laughed. "I'd
almost forgotten."

"Me too." It was true what he had hinted before, she thought:
Delia only liked, only allowed, what her mother called "hanky-
panky." "Is it very late?"

"Well, it's"—he held up a bare arm and checked his watch—
"twelve-fifteen."

"Oh, lord." Jane gave a heavy sigh as a weight of obligation and
guilt fell upon her, heavy and scratchy as the hay that towered
around them. "I have to get back to the house." She sat up.

"Really?" Henry yawned and pulled her toward him.

"Yes, I have to pack, and cook something for Alan that he can
warm up over the weekend, and find a graduate student to drive
him to campus and back next week." She gave another, deeper sigh.
What have I done? she thought. *You've done what you've been wanting
to do for months,* a voice said in her head. *Something wonderful and
right, something selfish and wrong.*

"You still think you have to take care of Alan?" Henry raised his
eyebrows.

"Well, yes. For a while anyhow." A sensation of fatigue came
over Jane. "Until I can arrange for someone else to do it. Somebody
has to." She rose to her knees, pulling her clothes together and
brushing herself off. The nest where they had lain was flattened and
trampled, and slightly stained with bodily fluids.

"You'll never be able to get this stuff back into bales," she said.

"No, probably not." Henry grinned. "And I'm not going to try."

"But what will they think, the people who own the barn?"

"They'll think it was tramps."

"I suppose so." It was tramps, Jane thought. I'm a tramp. But it was worth it.

Holding hands, stopping every few feet to kiss, they walked to his car.

"Can you call me this afternoon?" Henry asked as they reached the Farmers' Market.

"Ye-es. I can call from the P&C. But won't Delia be there?"

"Yeah, probably. And we're supposed to go out to dinner tonight. Hell. Tomorrow—can you meet me here about ten?"

"I can't do that." Jane sighed. "My mom will expect me to go to church with her tomorrow morning, because it's Sunday. And then there's Sunday dinner. But maybe later."

"About four?"

"I'll try," she said.

"I'll come then and wait."

"That's good." She gathered her coat around her and slid toward the door.

As she opened it, Henry put out his hand and caught hold of hers. "Oh, Janey. I love you so much," he said.

"Really?" Jane knew that she was not looking her best: her hair was tangled and partly full of hay, her face streaked with the snail tracks of tears.

"Yeah. Really."

"I love you too," she whispered. Then she shut the door behind her and made her way through the fine icy wind toward her car.

"Did you have a good talk with Reverend Bob?" Jane's mother, Carrie, asked as Jane came from the cold dull November day into the warm, well-lit kitchen on Sunday afternoon.

"Yes, very good," Jane lied, glancing at the pink-flowered kitchen clock. In ten minutes Henry Hull would be in the lot behind the empty Farmers' Market, waiting for her. Somehow, she must find an excuse to be there too.

"He's a very nice young man, isn't he?" Carrie said, sifting flour into a mixing bowl. "Of course, nobody can ever replace Reverend Jack." She sighed. "Would you like some coffee?" It was clear that she hoped for details of the consultation.

"No thanks," Jane said. "I have to go back to the house now. I forgot my hair dryer and all my makeup yesterday, and I'll need them for work tomorrow." This was actually true.

"Oh, that's all right." Her mother smiled. "I can lend you—"

"And my prescriptions," Jane hastened to add, though this was a lie: she had already finished her only prescription, for an ear infection picked up at the University swimming pool. "But I'd better go now, before it starts to snow again. I just have to stop in the bathroom."

"Mm." Carrie gave an understanding smile.

Upstairs, Jane's face in the mirror looked tired and pale. If she had thought she could get away with it, she would have used some of her mother's lipstick and blusher, but Carrie was sure to notice and think that Jane wanted to look attractive for Alan.

With every word she said, every gesture she made, Jane thought, she was digging herself deeper into a pit of lies. The phrase was that of the Reverend Bob Smithers, and he had applied it to Alan, but it belonged equally to her. Reverend Bob was in fact a nice young man, but he had been easy to lie to, unlike the Reverend Jack, who would surely have looked directly into Jane's eyes and seen the shadow of Henry Hull there. Reverend Bob sincerely wanted to bring Jane and Alan back together as soon as possible; he had spoken of patience and love and forgiveness. Reverend Bob also wanted Alan to come in for counseling, something that would never happen, since Alan would never agree to be counseled by someone like Bob

But Jane had not told him this. She had pretended to listen and agree, and that too had been a lie. Her patience with Alan and her love for him were nearly exhausted, and she did not want to forgive him. She wanted him to vanish off the face of the earth, so she could be with Henry.

Jane's mother Carrie also hoped that Jane and Alan would get back together eventually, but she felt there was no reason for haste. Alan needed to be taught a lesson, she had said. A bad back was no excuse for bad behavior, and if Jane stayed away for a while he would realize how much he loved her and needed her. The reaction of Jane's father had been different. He was a taciturn man, recently retired from the local post office, who usually offered few opinions on domestic matters. But last night, after his wife had explained the situation to him, he had broken his usual silence.

"You and Alan have joint accounts at the Hopkins County Trust, right, Janey?" he had asked. "Checking and savings?"

Jane had agreed that this was so.

"Okay. Monday morning, you go down there first thing. You open up a new account in your own name, transfer half of both the old accounts into it."

"Oh, I don't think Janey needs to do that," his wife had protested. "Alan isn't going to cheat her out of anything."

"Maybe not. But it's best to be safe. Fellow gets involved with a floozy, he might do anything."

"She's not really a floozy," Jane had said, speaking rather for the honor of the Unger Center than for that of Delia.

But her father had shaken his head. "Saw her photo in the paper. A floozy."

Now Jane dragged a comb through her curly hair and ran downstairs. "I'll be back soon," she said, which was probably another lie, and hurried out.

It was already past four when she reached the Farmers' Market parking lot, but Henry was not there. Immediately a cold wave of fear and depression washed over her. She had to see him, not just because she loved him, but because he was the only person in the world she could talk to now without lying. Over the past couple of months she had gradually become distant from her three closest friends, all of whom often said how much they admired her devotion to Alan in his illness. After she had begun to fall in love with Henry, she didn't want to confide in them, because they would have been surprised and shocked by her disloyalty.

Now, of course, her friends would probably blame Alan for getting involved with Delia, but since Delia was a local and national celebrity, the news would be too good to keep quiet. Anyhow, if she told them about Delia and not about Henry she would be lying again, sinking deeper and deeper into the Reverend Bob's pit of lies, which would probably resemble the construction site she had passed on the way to the Farmers' Market: a big deep muddy hole with orange barriers around it and a pile of dirt at one side. The pit of lies was one of the gateways to hell, according to a sermon she had once heard.

Dusk was falling now, the light thickening in the bony trees by the lake, and Henry still hadn't come. Maybe something had prevented him? Or maybe he had just decided not to come, because seeing her was too risky or too much trouble. He was still safe in his life, Jane thought for the first time, because Delia didn't know anything about her.

Slowly, inexorably, the air darkened, and the slatted stalls of the Farmers' Market began to look more and more like empty chicken coops. *Don't you want to be free?* Henry had said last week. Well, now she was free, but he wasn't, because he was still living with Delia. He hadn't told Delia anything; maybe he wasn't planning to tell her anything. Maybe he wanted to stay with her, even if they weren't really married and she only allowed hanky-panky, because she was so much more rich and glamorous and famous and interesting than Jane. Maybe for him Jane was like what he'd said about Delia's affairs, something he needed sometimes.

Now night had fallen: only a sullen gray light shimmered on the lake beyond the trees. Jane would have to carry out her excuse now. She would have to drive to her house and collect her makeup and her hairbrush, which would mean seeing Alan again and trying not to get into another conversation full of lies, his lies of fact and her lies of omission. Then she would have to drive back to her parents' house and lie some more to them.

FOURTEEN

Three days later, Alan was walking slowly and painfully across campus toward the building where the annual Unger Humanities Lecture would soon be given by a famous New York critic, L. D. Zimmern. It had snowed the night before, and the frozen lawn was glazed gray-white; the sky was covered with a foggy scrim of cloud, also gray-white, in which a small flaw indicated the presence of the distant sun. Alan's mind was also covered with foggy cloud; the only small bright spot in it was the knowledge that he would soon see Delia again. His back hurt worse than it had for weeks.

When Jane had returned to the house without notice late Sunday afternoon, Alan had just burnt both his dinner and his hand by punching in BAKED POTATO instead of WARM on the microwave. Jane had instantly expressed concern and filled a saucepan with cold water and ice cubes, her old standard remedy. As Alan sat at the kitchen table with his hand in the pan of ice water, he had felt a rush of gratitude, even of affection.

"Thank you, that feels a lot better," he told her. And then, after a pause, "Look, I really regret what happened Friday."

"Yes?" Jane's stiff, neutral expression slowly began to soften.

"I—" He opened his mouth to tell her that he was very sorry, but in fact he was involved with, maybe even in love with, Delia Delaney. *The best thing you can do, always, is tell the truth and take the consequences,* his father used to say. But Alan did not do this now, partly because Jane already looked so beaten-down and miserable. He also did not do it because it would cause Delia to regard him with scorn. "It was natural for you to get upset," he said instead. "I know it looked suspicious, but honestly nothing was going on. Delia was having a migraine, and I was just trying to give her some comfort, some sympathy— You know I'm in no shape to—" He swallowed the half lie.

Jane stared at him, her mouth trembling. "I don't believe you," she said finally. "Nobody could believe you. You don't have to take off your clothes to sympathize with somebody. And nobody hides behind a curtain unless they're involved in some hanky-panky," she added, in her mother's phrase and almost her mother's intonation. "It's all dirty lies, and I bet you didn't even think of them yourself. That horrible woman put you up to it."

"Really, Jane," Alan said, trying to speak in a cool and reasonable manner.

"She's using you, just like she uses everybody. She doesn't care for you or anyone but herself, and you'll find that out soon, unless you're too stupid. Oh, the hell with it all." Jane burst into tears; then she turned away and rushed upstairs. When she returned, dragging a carry-on suitcase, she would not even speak, only left, slamming the back door.

"Jane's staying with her parents downtown, and she won't speak to me," he had told Delia on Monday morning.

"Acting out all the old clichés," Delia had said with a slight, scornful laugh.

"How do you mean?"

"Giving you the silent treatment. Gone home to Mother."

"So where should she have gone?"

"Jesus, I don't know." Delia sighed, almost yawned. "New York, Paris? But some people have no imagination."

That's true, he thought. But it's not their fault; and if Jane had really gone to New York or Paris there would be confusion and scandal.

"And now you're supposed to admit your guilt and beg forgiveness, isn't that right?"

"You think that's what I should do?" asked Alan, who had again been considering this move.

"Not if you want any respect at home from now on," Delia told him. "If you wait a while, she'll come around."

It was Wednesday now, and Jane had not come around in either sense of the phrase. She had been at the Center every afternoon, but had made no attempt to speak to him there, though every day a plate containing that evening's supper, wrapped in transparent plastic, had appeared in his fridge. Meanwhile, incredibly rapidly, everything at home had begun to fall apart. The cleaning lady wouldn't come until Friday, and the house was already a mess, littered with discarded papers and dirty dishes. The flowers had died in the vases, and Alan couldn't find the can opener. Yesterday he had spilled a plate of creamed chicken and waffles into his recliner, and though he had done his best to mop it up, the leather was now sticky and smelly. When he went to the supermarket with his student driver he had forgotten to buy bread or milk for his morning cereal, and he was out of clean underwear and socks.

As he reached the entrance to the lecture hall, Alan was surprised to see in the crowd his back-pain pal Bernie Kotelchuk, the retired professor of veterinary medicine, accompanied by his wife Danielle, a retired professor of French.

"You going to the lecture?" he asked.

"Uh-huh." Bernie grinned.

"You're interested in 'William James and Religious Experience?'" Traditionally, the annual Unger Lecture was coordinated with that year's Unger Center theme.

"Nah, not really. But Zimmern is Danielle's ex-husband."

"Really." Alan had been more or less unaware that Danielle had an ex-husband; she seemed so well suited to her current one.

"I wouldn't miss it for anything," said Danielle. Like Bernie, she was ruddy, cheerful, and sturdy. She wore her thick gray hair in a ponytail tied with red and brown yarn, and was wrapped in several layers of hand-knit red and brown sweaters and scarves rather than a coat.

"You know, most women would do anything to avoid having to listen to their ex," Alan said.

"Not me." Danielle smiled. "I'm not angry at Lennie anymore, it's been too long. Anyhow the kids will expect me to give them a report." She moved ahead, toward the double doors.

"So how are you doing?" Bernie asked as they followed.

"Oh, okay," Alan replied, and saw Bernie register the true meaning of this answer according to their unspoken code, perhaps that of all invalids: *Not so good, actually*. "How about you?"

"Not too bad," Bernie said, meaning, *Better, actually*. "I'm driving again, you know."

"Yeah? That's great."

"It's all because of this doohickey." Bernie held up a large brown canvas carrying case. "Changed my life."

"A briefcase changed your life?"

"Yep," Bernie asserted. "Well, nah. It's what's inside. Feel it, see if you can guess." Alan touched the briefcase and encountered a thick, flat, curved piece of hard material, probably wood. It was familiar somehow, but he could not identify it, and shook his head.

"It's a toilet seat," Bernie confided. "This exercise guy at the Y—you know, the one with the red hair and the Star Trek T-shirt— he put me on to it last week. You go to Sears, he said, buy yourself one of these. Take it apart, throw away the lid. Get a bag for the bottom piece. This here, it looks like a briefcase, right? Hell, it is a briefcase. Nobody can tell what's inside. I take it everywhere. All of a sudden, no extra pain when I sit. Danielle doesn't have to drive me anywhere. I can go to the drugstore, work at my desk, drive to school to check on the dog project. Fly on planes, go to conferences, anything I want." He laughed.

In the past, before the lizard moved into his back, nothing on earth would have persuaded Alan to carry around a toilet seat in a canvas bag. But Jane had left him; he was eating scorched or soggy microwaved meals and depending on unreliable student drivers. "You think it would work for me?"

"Could be. Wanna try it?"

Together, Alan and the Kotelchuks moved toward the rear of the room. Bernie placed the briefcase on a seat, and Alan lowered himself onto it cautiously. Usually he could hardly bear to sit on a hard surface for more than a few minutes. But now the pain did not increase; it even seemed to moderate slightly.

"Yeah, that's better," he conceded, standing up out of the way so that Bernie could sit down. Over the past year or so, several people, including Jane, had suggested that he should obtain and carry about with him an inflatable rubber ring of the type used by sufferers from hemorrhoids, or women after a painful childbirth. Alan, whose horror of seeming ridiculous had not diminished, had always refused. But a briefcase—yes, that might be possible, as long as nobody knew what was inside it.

Even before the lecture started, Alan had to get up and walk about at the back of the room. It was the same one in which, not long ago, Delia Delaney had read; but the scene today was very different. Delia, with her red-gold curls loose down her back, her violet eye shadow and trailing lacy scarves, had been a figure of beauty and glamour. Zimmern was an elderly professor of nondescript appearance with a lot of dark-gray hair and a dark-gray suit. Delia's audience had been larger and younger and more than two-thirds female, and included many women whose appearance and getup was as unusual, though far from as alluring, as her own. Today it was the standard mix of humanities students and faculty, with a scattering of

older townspeople and retirees who had perhaps known Zimmern
when he taught here a quarter century ago.

While Delia spoke, Alan had leaned forward to absorb every
word. He had been amazed by the brilliantly theatrical, emotional
quality of her performance, and gloried in the secret knowledge that
earlier in the day he been closer to her than anyone in the room. But
though L. D. Zimmern spoke with wit and erudition, Alan lost
much of his discourse. Instead, his attention oscillated between the
increasingly intolerable pain in his back, his own oppressive domestic situation, and his desire to see Delia again as soon as possible. She
should have been there now, but her husband had called the Center
that morning to say that she had a migraine and wouldn't be able to
make the lecture, though she hoped to be at the official dinner.

In order to see Delia, Alan had planned to go to the reception
and skip the dinner, since he was unable to eat unless he was standing up or lying down. Now, as soon as the lecture was over, he met
the graduate student who had been hired to drive him home, and
arranged for a detour to the local mall, where he purchased a white
plastic toilet seat and a black nylon briefcase. At home he separated
the sections of the toilet seat with some difficulty, threw the top half
in the trash can, concealed the bottom half in the briefcase, and went
into the garage. He had not driven his Volvo for over a year, but until recently Jane had exercised it once a week, and it started readily.

There was still some pain, but it was manageable, Alan decided.
With a sense of freedom and power that he had not had in a long
time, he canceled the taxi he had ordered and drove to the Unger
Center.

His luck held: Delia was there. Unfortunately, though, the reception was over, and she was already sitting at the other end of the
long dining table, not far from Jane, who clearly saw him but did not
speak or wave. Meanwhile, he, as the senior Unger Fellow, had been
placed at the left of Lily Unger, with L. D. Zimmern, the guest of
honor, on her right. It was soon clear that Zimmern and Mrs.

Unger were already acquainted, though they had apparently not met for some time.

"So you never married again," Lily Unger said to Zimmern, in a teasing tone that Alan had never heard her use before.

"No. Tried it once, didn't like it. Same thing with oatmeal."

"Oatmeal?" Lily giggled.

"It's supposed to be good for you, maybe it is, but it's also tasteless and lumpy."

Yeah, you could be right, Alan thought, and then was interrupted by Davi Gakar's wife, on his own left, who wished to talk about the differences between Eastern and Western religion. It was not until she turned to her other neighbor that he was able to speak again to Lily Unger and ask the question that had been on his mind all through the shrimp bisque.

"Who's the old bald guy talking to Delia?"

"Wally Hersh," said Lily, well informed as usual. "He's a big trustee. Also powerful on the Alumni Council."

"Yeah?" Zimmern said. "He looks like a big hamster."

"He does, sort of." Lily giggled.

Alan stared down the table. Wally Hersh was large and beefy, with the muscle-bound physique of a former athlete now running to fat. At the moment, Delia was leaning toward him, laughing. Her red-gold hair was piled on top of her head, and she was wearing a low-cut blouse with a big white lily tucked into the cleavage— apparently one of those that this same Wally Hersh had sent and Jane had thrown at her.

"He was here all last week for the yearly meetings," Lily said. "I don't know why he's still hanging around."

Wally Hersh, who was not only well over sixty, but red-faced and slightly popeyed, was now leaning toward Delia, smiling and patting her soft white hand with his coarse red paw. How can she allow that? Alan thought.

"He'd better watch his step with Delia," Zimmern said. "She can be dangerous."

"Really?" Lily Unger remarked with surprise and some disapproval. "She's been tremendously popular at the Center. A little overemotional, maybe, but very nice and charming to everyone."

"She wasn't nice and charming to me," Zimmern said. "She cut me dead at the reception just now." He gave a short laugh.

"Really?"

"I figure she's still mad about something I wrote once. It was years ago, but apparently she hasn't forgiven me."

"Oh? What did you say?" Alan leaned forward.

"It was when she came out with those Southern mountain tales of ghosts and lost children and unfaithful lovers and black crows that sit on the roof and foretell death. *Heart's Ease,* yeah, that was the title. I called her the intellectual's Dolly Parton."

"You know, there is a resemblance," said Lily Unger, laughing. "She's just as pretty, anyhow."

"You should have seen her twenty years ago," Zimmern told them. "You can't believe how beautiful she was then. And some of those early stories really weren't bad. The trouble was, after a while she began to repeat herself."

"Her reading was a great success," Lily Unger said, a little huffily.

"No doubt. Most people can't tell the difference between the original and a good copy. My theory is, Delia hasn't really taken in anything that happened after she left the mountains of West Virginia. Her life there was so intense, so violent, so primitive. It was full of everything that's in the early stories: passionate crazy people and crazy ideas. If she'd stayed, it probably would have destroyed her. So she escaped, she went to college, and then eventually to New York. Never went back. But she paid a price. The world outside the mountains isn't quite real to her, you can tell that from her later writing. Same thing with Edna O'Brien, same thing with Colette, but worse because Delia's never found another subject the way they did. No, I'm afraid she's had it."

With difficulty, Alan said nothing, fearing that if he spoke he would speak too vehemently, betraying the strength of his feelings.

Lily Unger, however, came at once to Delia's defense. "Well, I must say, I don't agree. I admired her last book very much."

"I'm sure you did," Zimmern agreed politely, but in a manner that somehow cast doubt both on Delia's writing and on Lily Unger's artistic taste and discernment. Then he turned away to a pretty woman on his right, the wife of a dean, whose main interest was the preservation of the natural environment.

"So how are you feeling these days?" Lily Unger asked him kindly. But Alan was almost unable to reply. At the moment, he was hardly aware of the pain in his back, he was so preoccupied with a sour, angry sensation that he had not felt in many, many years—a sensation that he identified, after a moment, as not heartburn but corrosive sexual jealousy. "Oh, not too bad," he lied, smiling with effort and trying without success to wrench his gaze away from the far end of the table, from Delia.

FIFTEEN

"Well, hello there," Henry said as Jane, nearly twenty minutes late, came up to him at a display of home-baked apple and pumpkin pies on Saturday morning. It was a cold, windy day, the last weekend this year for the Farmers' Market. But the sun was bright, and several dozen people were buying root vegetables and eggs and homemade pottery and bread from those stalls that remained open. He touched her cheek lightly, causing a sensation that resembled her sister's description of a hot flash.

It had been a hard week for Jane. Living at her parents' house was awkward and constraining. Though her mother loved her, she could not help treating Jane like the child and adolescent she had once been: asking her to set the table, sending her to the P&C when she ran out of milk, reminding her to dress warmly. Carrie had always had definite ideas about what Jane should do, and what she should do now was go back to Alan. He was her husband and he needed her. She should forgive him and let bygones be bygones.

"How can I forgive him if he won't admit he did anything wrong?" Jane had asked rather desperately.

"He knows he's done wrong," Carrie had said, not ceasing to knit the blue sweater with a pattern of red and white ducks that she was making for Jane's sister's youngest child. "And he knows you know it. I'm sure he feels sorry and ashamed of himself now."

"Maybe," Jane said.

"But a man has his pride," her mother continued, as if Jane had not spoken. "And it's not as if he'd actually been unfaithful. From what you told me, it was probably just a little hanky-panky. All you need to do is say that you want to put this behind you, and go on with your life together."

"Maybe," Jane repeated. But I don't want to go on with that life, she thought. I want to be with Henry, only Mom doesn't know it, because I haven't told her. I'm just as bad as Alan, a liar and an adulteress.

"I'm sure he'll be relieved and grateful. And of course you'll let him know that it mustn't happen again."

"But it will happen again, probably. Because of that awful woman."

"You don't know that, dear." Her mother looped a strand of red wool over the white. "You've had such a good marriage. And everyone admires you so much for the way you've taken care of Alan since he got ill."

"Mh," Jane had said. She wished she could talk to someone besides her mother. But since she began to love Henry, she had stopped confiding in her friends. The only person she could talk to now was Henry, who was half the problem.

"I'm sorry I was late," she said to him now as they moved apart from the crowd around the stalls and stood under the bare yellow branches of a big willow.

"That's okay."

"I brought you some black walnuts, from the tree we saw on Warren Road. Here." She handed over a heavy brown-paper bag. "They're much better than the walnuts you get in the stores. But you need to let them dry out for a few weeks, and then crack them on stone with a hammer."

"Thank you. . . . So how's it going?"

"All right. Well, not all right."

"Really." A dark shadow seemed to cross Henry's face. "Why is that? No, wait. Come and sit down. Let's talk." He led the way to one of the picnic tables by the windswept lake and set his basket of apples and sourdough bread and honey on it. "Okay. Tell me."

"It's all wrong," Jane said, catching her breath. "It's all lies. Everyone thinks I'm a good person, but I'm not. Not anymore. I promised in church to take care of Alan forever, and now our house is falling apart and the fridge is full of mold." A sob escaped her.

"Maybe that serves him right," Henry said.

"Well, in a way it does, that's what my mother says, but not forever. She says it was right that I left, because then he would know I was serious, and he would feel guilty and appreciate me properly. But now she thinks it's time for me to go back, so we can all be together for Thanksgiving. Anyhow, my sister's coming from New Hampshire, and she'll need the spare room."

"It's important for your family, Thanksgiving," he suggested.

"Yes, it is. My sister and her husband and kids always come, and my uncle and two aunts from up the lake, and usually there's cousins too. Isn't Thanksgiving important for your family?"

"Yeah, but I don't always make it to Toronto. I didn't last year, but I'm going up this weekend."

"And will Delia be there?"

"Nah. She's going to New York. She doesn't get on with Canadians." He took an apple out of his basket, looked at it, and returned it. "So your mother thinks you should go back to Alan," he said. "And do you want to go back?"

"No," Jane admitted.

"That's good." Henry smiled for the first time. He put his warm hand on her arm, between the wristband of her blue parka and her driving gloves, and Jane did not have the strength to remove it.

"But it doesn't matter what I want," she said weakly, pushing back her wind-tangled brown curls. "What I want is wicked and selfish."

"You really believe that?"

"Yes—no. I don't know," Jane wailed, and buried her damp face in her hands. Another sob escaped her. "I'm an awful person, really."

"Oh, yeah?"

"I'm so angry all the time, and violent."

"Violent?" Henry laughed.

"Yes. I told you how I nearly threw that big glass vase at Delia."

"But you didn't, because you didn't really want to hurt her." Henry smiled.

"I did too. When she started laughing, as if it was all some big joke, I wanted to hurt her. I only didn't throw the vase because it was a valuable heirloom. It belonged to Matthew Unger's mother, and now it belongs to the Center."

"Oh, Janey. I love you." Henry pulled her toward him and kissed her, but Jane only partly responded, looking over his shoulder for spectators and spies.

"I don't see why," she said miserably when he let go.

"I don't know. I guess it's because you have such sea-blue eyes, and you're so hopelessly honest."

"Only with you. I'm lying to everyone else all the time, because I'm not telling them the truth. I used to be a good person, but now I'm not, I'm angry and mean all the time, really, inside. Alan's in so much pain, and I used to feel so horribly sorry for him, but now I don't care, almost. I don't love him anymore. I don't even like him much."

"That's wonderful," Henry said.

"But it's all wrong. My place is with my husband, my duty is there, that's what my mother says. And her new minister, Reverend Bobby, says the same."

" 'Reverend Bobby?' " Henry laughed.

"I know." In spite of herself, Jane smiled. "He's only about twenty-six years old."

"Well, I don't agree. I think your place is with me," Henry said. "I'm so glad you're here," he added. "I was afraid you weren't coming."

"I almost didn't," Jane admitted. "But I wanted to see you too much."

"Yeah," he agreed. "Me too."

"Even though you never came last Sunday when you said you would. I waited here until it was dark."

"I couldn't. I explained that. Delia was insisting we go to this drinks party, and if I hadn't agreed she would have been suspicious."

"Yes, you told me." Jane raised her streaked face and looked out across the shimmering, wind-troubled water of the lake. "It's not the same for us now, is it?" she said, uttering the thought that had sat on her head like a tight dark hat for the whole week. "I've left Alan, and you haven't left Delia. You haven't even told her you know what happened."

"No," Henry admitted.

"Are you going to?"

"I've got to wait a bit, Janey," he said. "Right now she's tired of me. I figure she's on her way out. But if she knew I was in love with somebody else, she could get jealous and possessive."

Jane frowned. It seemed unlikely to her that anyone could be tired of Henry. He's a coward, she thought miserably. Or he's stalling. He might love me a little, and want to sleep with me, but he wants to avoid trouble even more. "You want to avoid trouble," she said, shivering in the cold wind, which seemed now to come directly from the North Pole.

"Yeah. But it's only for a little while."

"Oh? How long?" Jane was feeling colder and colder, even though Henry's arm was around her shoulders.

"I don't know."

Jane said nothing, but she took a step back.

"We'll be together very soon, I hope. When things are easier."

Jane looked at Henry, his square shoulders, his thick curly hair, and the strong blunt lines of his face. He's here, but he's not really here, she thought. I can't count on him.

SIXTEEN

It had been another strange week for Alan Mackenzie. By Friday he felt as if he had been on a long alternately exhilarating and exhausting nature hike of the sort he remembered from camp, slogging up steep slopes and down into thick swamps. The highs had been his meetings with Delia, his restored ability to drive, and another sale at the gallery in New York. There had also been the soggy lows of persistent backache, obsessive jealousy, a growing despair about his work, and the sudden awkward reappearance of Jane in his life.

On Friday night he lay awake between three and five a.m., suffering from pain and artistic depression. He could not find a comfortable position—the lizard kept shifting its grip, alternately clawing his lower back and left hip. Also something he had eaten, or the drugs he had taken, was causing severe gaseous indigestion. Since Jane had moved to her parents' house the suppers she left had been getting less and less attractive, culminating last evening in a nasty congealed-looking macaroni and cheese casserole with lima beans. Either she was punishing him with worse and worse meals, or she was (no doubt unconsciously) trying to poison him.

If Alan's friends and colleagues knew that his wife had left him and gone home to her mother, dinner invitations would have been forthcoming. But as yet he had not told anyone, because he assumed that, as Delia put it, Jane would soon come around and make this admission unnecessary. Also, he didn't want to answer the inevitable question, *Why has she left you?* either with a lie or with the truth.

Worst of all, as he stared into the cold blackness of the cloudy November night, he had finally admitted to himself that he was sick of miniature ruins of famous public buildings. The first dozen or two had been exciting and satisfying; but lately, as he turned the pages of travel books looking for possible subjects, he had begun to feel weariness, even disgust. Maybe, even probably, his career as an artist was over almost before it had begun. Delia Delaney loved him—anyhow, she had often allowed him to love her. But when she knew he was finished as an artist, she would be disappointed and maybe even scornful, as she had been about her husband's giving up poetry. ("He had a couple of bad reviews, and couldn't take it.")

At five a.m. Alan unwound himself from his snarled sheets and blankets and staggered into the bathroom. In the smudged, foggy glow of the night-light, he saw the face of a hysterical aging loser: in chronic pain, deserted by his wife, probably about to be dropped by his mistress, and without inspiration. Someone who might as well be dead.

But on his way back to bed, dizzy with drugs and nausea and despair, he had a revelation. By accident he switched on the wrong light in the hall and saw, blindingly white against the black of an unused bedroom, part of a wall, an open door, and a wooden goose in graceful flight toward the dark. He stopped in his tracks, flash-frozen. The scene was fragmentary, but also eternal That section of wall, that doorway, that chair, that motionless yet moving white bird, could have been—*could be*, made of plaster or stone or painted metal. It could stand free, as another kind of artificial ruin—perhaps comic, perhaps ironic, perhaps tragic.

And if this vision could be made three-dimensional, so could other fragments of domestic architecture, each with its own complex, interlocking meanings. The monumental, even mythic corner of a kitchen, with dishes in the rack and a window open over the sink, a knife and a half-sliced tomato on the sill. A bathroom with crumpled hanging towels, a dining room with part of a table, dishes, glasses, a napkin thrown down—

Or a section of wall from his childhood bedroom, with a half-open casement window, his narrow maple bed with its ball-topped posts and thrown-back patchwork quilt; his toy Scottish terrier and suspended model airplane, frozen in time like the ruins of Pompeii. All white—or, maybe more interesting, in a spectrum of sepia browns or grayed pastels.

And he needn't limit himself to domestic architecture, or to this country, Alan saw suddenly. The images could come from anywhere and anywhen. All of history and geography was available to him. Colonial, Victorian, Art Nouveau, Art Deco, Modern—Medieval, Renaissance, eighteenth-century—anything, everything. Fragments of schools, stores, libraries, offices, churches—the haunting architectural equivalents of a George Segal sculpture—

Yes. He could do it. And as an architectural historian he could make all these ghostly tableaux authentic, with the right door and window frames, shutters, cornices, chairs, hanging garments, decorative objects.

Though it was still densely dark outside, Alan did not return to bed. Instead he pulled his navy blue wool bathrobe over his pajamas, went into the study, and located a pad and drawing pencils. In too much of a hurry to retrieve his briefcase/toilet seat from downstairs, he stood in front of a file cabinet and made notes and sketches for well over an hour without stopping. Sometimes he paused for a few moments, overcome with awe and gratitude for the revelation that had come to him. Delia was right, he thought: this gift he had received was a by-product of pain and illness.

At dawn, stiff and chilled, he set the sheets of paper he had covered aside, took more codeine, and collapsed into bed, where he slept until noon. Waking, he feared at first that he had dreamed the whole thing. But the drawings were there, and in the light of day they still looked good: better than good. He dressed, made himself tea and toast, and, ignoring the pain in his back as much as possible, got out some paper and old paints, and began to convert his first sketch into a colored drawing. Delia will like this, he thought. She always has a special feeling for birds.

He was halfway through a second—the attic of his parents' house this time, with its little round window, the upper left-hand pane cracked in a partial star, the old brass-hinged and brass-hasped trunk underneath, and the discarded dressmaker's dummy (terrifying at five, still sinister and melancholy when he left for college) leaning toward the light at an angle—when he heard the kitchen door open.

"Hello, it's me," Jane's voice called.

She's brought some even more inedible, poisonous supper, Alan thought. He put down his brush, vexed at the interruption. Then, to prevent his wife from coming upstairs and seeing his new drawings, which she would probably like as little as the earlier ones, he descended to the kitchen. Jane was standing by the sink in front of a brown paper bag of groceries, wearing baggy jeans and a Gore-Tex windbreaker For years he had thought of his wife as amazingly pretty: now she seemed ill-dressed, commonplace, and undersized, and her curly brown hair was much too short. Had she deliberately made herself unattractive, or was it that since he'd known Delia his idea of beauty had shifted?

"Oh, hello there," he said. "Look, you don't have to bring me supper anymore. I can drive now, I can manage on my own."

"That's all right," Jane told him. "I mean, you don't have to. I've decided it's time for me to come home, anyhow." She indicated her suitcase by the back door.

"Oh yes?" Alan smiled only briefly. "That's good," he heard himself say rather flatly. He was surprised at his lack of relief—because this was what he had wanted, wasn't it?

"But we have to talk seriously."

"Mh," he agreed, though what he had to do now was get back to his drawing. The light beige he had chosen for the dressmaker's dummy was wrong: it needed to be darker, or no, better, freckled with pinholes and stains.

"I just have to put these groceries away," Jane said.

"Yeah, okay," Alan said. Delia had been right again, he thought. Jane had come around. But why did she have to come around now, breaking into his work?

His wife closed the door of the fridge and sat on a kitchen stool. "We haven't either of us behaved perfectly," she said in the tone of someone trying to be more than fair.

"Uh, no," Alan agreed. Delia wouldn't think much of this admission, but the last thing he wanted now was a serious talk, and this might save time. He would add a section of the attic ceiling to the piece, he decided: the beams, the raw insulation and the nails coming through from the shingles. Yes, yes!

"But that isn't what's important. I mean, I don't want to let something that only happened once, and I'm sure you regret now, destroy our marriage." Jane unzipped her windbreaker and pulled it off. Underneath she had on a heavy, faded green cotton sweater from L. L. Bean that Delia would probably have died rather than wear.

"No," Alan said weakly, realizing that he was admitting guilt, and also not telling the truth. It happened a lot more than once, it's still happening, and I don't regret it, he thought.

"So I decided we should just never mention it again."

"Mh." He frowned. You won't mention it, he thought, and I won't mention it, but we'll both think of it, and I will be forever in the wrong.

"All I want is, I want you to promise not to see Delia again, ever."

"But Jane, that's not possible," Alan exclaimed, stunned out of his preoccupation. "We're both Fellows at the Center, after all."

"I realize that. I know you'll have to be in the same room sometimes, at the lectures and lunches. You'll have to say hello and be polite if people are watching. But you don't have to be alone with her."

"Uh, no," Alan said. I do have to be alone with her, he thought. She's important to me. You don't understand, and I don't want you to understand. He looked at the conventionally pretty, badly dressed youngish woman who was sitting at the kitchen table. At the moment she seemed like a complete stranger.

For years he had felt love for this woman, and sometimes passionate desire, Alan remembered with surprise. He had been deeply grateful for her love and care in the worst moments of his illness: before, during, and after his operation. But slowly the duty of continuing to feel this gratitude had become oppressive. If Jane moved back, as she seemed determined to do, he would always have this duty. He might be more comfortable physically—meals would be better and the house cleaner—but he would always be one down. Also, it would be more difficult to see or speak to Delia.

"We have to make our marriage work. It's our job, after all, the one we signed up for."

"I guess so." Alan was struck by the conventionality of her rhetoric, as if Jane were quoting the minister of her parents' church, as was possibly the case. It occurred to him that something was lacking from this conversation. Jane had not said that she loved him or had missed him, and he had not said it either.

"We have to try, that's all." She did not look at him, but at the oiled butcher-block surface of the kitchen table, and her tone wavered, almost as if she were about to start crying. Moved by a combination of affection, pity, and good manners, Alan crossed the kitchen floor and awkwardly put his arm around her.

"Mm, hm," he said. Over Jane's shoulder he saw her suitcase slumped against the fridge by the back door. That could be a construction too, he thought. The fridge, the broom and dustpan hanging on the wall, the open door, the wheeled carry-on suitcase with its rectangular handle echoing the shape of the door. Someone is going, someone is coming. Everything in pale blue shades, only the suitcase dark, ink-black, like a hole in the scene. Or maybe everything else dark, and the suitcase ghostly white?

"Mom will be happy. She really wants you to be there for Thanksgiving." For the first time Jane spoke in a somewhat normal voice.

"But I can't do that," Alan said, letting go of his wife and standing back.

Thanksgiving had never been one of his favorite holidays, and he had given no thought to its approach this year. Though he had once found domestic gratitude easy and natural, he had always resented being expected and forced to be grateful in a public manner. He had also never looked forward to holidays with Jane's parents, who always, right from the beginning, had seemed to be judging him and finding him wanting. He wasn't interested in local events, and didn't feel or wish to show enthusiasm for televised sports. He did not like the food Jane's mother made: the creamed overcooked vegetables, the heavy, oversugared pies and cakes. He detested the wine they served on special occasions, cheap sweetened brands called Blue Nun and Grenache Rosé. He did not want to go to church on Thanksgiving with Jane and her overextended family—new aunts, uncles, nieces, nephews, cousins, and in-laws were always turning up. Whenever he went he was bored, with a boredom that sometimes approached actual pain. But if he declined to go, waves of disapproval would wash over him, as they had last year, even though the ache in his back had prevented him from sitting in a pew or at the dinner table for more than ten minutes at a time.

And now it would be worse, because Jane always told her mother everything. Her parents and probably a lot of other relatives would have heard about what she had seen in Delia's office. They would look at him and see a sinner, a lost sheep. Some would condemn him as an adulterer, while others, like the red-faced uncle who ran a construction company, would condemn him for being stupid enough to get caught. He would never be forgiven. So why should he give up anything?

"I have to go to New York," he told Jane. It was hardly a lie, because he would make it true as soon as possible.

Jane gave him a disappointed look, which rapidly moderated into a suspicious one. "Delia Delaney is going to New York for Thanksgiving," she said.

"So?"

"You're going to see her there."

"I hadn't planned to." Since Alan hadn't planned to go to New York, this was strictly true, but might, he realized, soon become false. "I'm going to see my dealer," he said, realizing that this too could become true. "He's sold another picture, and there's some new work I need to show him." A surge of excitement at this idea caused him to smile at Jane, but she did not smile back. Instead, her expression was one of distrust and despondency.

"That's nice," she said without enthusiasm. "Well, I guess I'll go unpack." While Alan watched, unable to stop her, she pulled her carry-on suitcase across the kitchen floor and into the hall. Presently he could hear it bumping up the stairs, one step at a time, each bump the sound of boredom, duty, and depression to come.

SEVENTEEN

On the Tuesday after Thanksgiving, Jane Mackenzie stood in the upstairs hall of the Unger Center in a state of frustrated suspicion. The doors to Alan's and Delia's offices were both shut, and from behind the latter she seemed to hear shuffling and mumbling. Alan was in there, she was almost sure of it—anyhow, he wasn't answering his phone, and neither was Delia. But she couldn't know for sure, even if she had the nerve to use her master key again. Yesterday, while Jane was at lunch, Delia had gotten Susie to send for a locksmith to install a bolt on the inside of her door.

"It's so there won't be people barging in when she's working," Susie had explained. "She has to protect her privacy."

Alan, when Jane had complained of this breach of authority and proper process, had not been sympathetic. In his opinion, Delia was right to have summoned someone out of the yellow pages. "You know how long she would have had to wait if you'd put in a requisition to B and G," he had told her. "It took them over a month to fix the kitchen ceiling. And this isn't an emergency." When Jane suggested that what Delia wanted to lock out was not fans and students, but people who might catch her doing something shameful, Alan told her that she was being ridiculous. It was the same phrase he had used before, when denying that there was anything wrong about his friendship with Delia.

Of course, if she waited long enough, Jane thought, she would or would not see Alan come out of Delia's office. But that would prove nothing, at least in his opinion. Also she had work to attend to, and no respectable reason to be hanging around the upstairs hall of the Center. If anyone saw her now, they would wonder what on earth she was doing there.

She was acting irrationally, Jane knew that. Because it wasn't so much that she cared about Alan, it was that her mind was so full of confusion and doubt. Probably, though she couldn't be sure, he and Delia had been laughing at her and lying to her for weeks, or months maybe. And what was much worse, Henry had probably been lying to her too, saying he loved her but not doing anything about it, not leaving Delia even after he knew he wasn't really married to her and she was cheating on him. Yes, maybe he did sort of love me, Jane thought. But he wasn't going to change his life for that. So it was right that she had stopped seeing him or speaking to him, that she was trying to forget him and put her marriage back together.

The trouble was that she kept thinking about Henry anyhow, remembering places and words and gestures: the barn full of stacked hay, the way he said "Janey," a slow touch on the back of her knee—She couldn't stop thinking about Henry; she couldn't even stop loving him. Meanwhile, her marriage was not back together, it was lying around in disordered ugly metallic bits, like the pasta machine she had once thrown not exactly at Alan.

Gritting her teeth, Jane went back downstairs. She knew what her mother and Reverend Bob would say: they would say that she must not dwell on doubts and suspicions or immoral desires, but must go about her daily life cheerfully and prayerfully, trusting that her love for Alan and his for her would bring them back together in the end. Only she doubted more and more often now that she would ever love Alan again and that he would ever love her.

With a sigh that made Susie look up anxiously, she opened the file of this month's expenses on her computer.

"Jane? Are you all right?" Susie asked.

"Fine," Jane lied. "It's just the bill from the caterers again. I've told them before not to bring milk or sugar, because we have our own, but they keep charging for them—" She allowed herself another sigh, almost a groan.

"Should I make us some tea?"

"No—yes, that would be nice," Jane admitted. "Thank you."

"Red Singer or Early Grey?"

"Red Singer, please." Jane had given up correcting Susie's cute names for her two favorite brands of tea after realizing that they had been invented by Charlie Amir. Susie had forgiven him for the lunge he had made at her earlier in the term, and lately they often had lunch together on campus. "He's really awfully nice," she had said last week, "and really smart and funny. His wife has left him, but he's such a good sport about it."

A few moments later a gust of fresh, cold air entered the hall, followed immediately by Henry Hull, whom Jane had not seen since their meeting by the lake over a week ago, and hardly expected to see alone again, though in spite of herself she kept imagining how this might happen. A hot pulse began to beat in her forehead, and she felt faint. He's here, she thought. He's not as tall as Alan, but there's so much of him somehow, even more than I remembered.

"Oh, hello," she said nervously. "I think Delia's upstairs—" *But don't go there,* she started to say, then thought: No, go. Maybe you'll find out what's happening in that room, if anything's happening.

"I'm not looking for her," Henry said. "Is Susie around?"

"Yes, she's in the kitchen making tea."

"Let's go into the other room, then. There's something I need to tell you."

Jane gave a gasp and trembled slightly, but did not move.

"About Delia and the Center," he added.

"All right." She followed him out of the office and then into the big reception room at the right of the front door. "What is it? I can't stay long."

"Delia's leaving."

"Leaving? Leaving what?"

"Well, everything. You name it. The Center, Corinth University, Hopkins County. Me, probably." Henry leaned against the carved mahogany molding of the doorway and began to unfasten his duffle coat. An awful impulse came over Jane to rest her head against it, as she had so often done before.

"But why?"

"She's decided that Corinth is making her ill. You know she's had two very bad migraines in the last week. She thinks it's the cold and the humidity: she's used to a Southern climate, mild sunny winters. Here it's so dark and damp and cloudy all the time now: like living in an industrial freezer, she says."

"But Delia's signed a contract with the Center till the end of next term. How can she leave now?"

"Easy." He smiled slightly. "She packs her bags, gets on a plane, and flies away. Then afterwards I make excuses for her and close up the house."

"But that's not fair. You shouldn't have to—"

Henry shrugged. "I've done it before. Last time was worse. Delia was teaching a writing seminar at Converse College; it nearly drove her crazy. And when she left in the middle of the fall term, it nearly drove the department crazy." He laughed.

I'll bet, Jane thought, not laughing.

"I thought for a while this gig was going to work out, because she didn't have to teach. And she did stick it out a lot longer. It's better in a way: she's not walking out on a class or anything. The Humanities Council won't be so enraged."

"They'll be enraged," Jane said. "Some of them will, anyhow." She paused, thinking. "You know, Bill Laird predicted something like this months ago. He said Delia wouldn't be able to take the weather."

"It's not only that, though. She can't really work here, she's interrupted all the time. Ever since her lecture people are after her to read manuscripts and recommend agents and publishers and write blurbs."

"When is she leaving?"

"I don't know. End of this week, probably." Henry stared out the window at the icy overcast landscape. "She's been saying for a while how much she longs to be in her house in North Carolina, where she can see the snow fall through the sunlight onto green grass, the way it does there sometimes in December."

Jane disregarded this, struck by the administrative repercussions of Delia's departure. "You know, if Delia leaves, we'll stop paying her."

"Yeah. That bothers her. Maybe it's even kept her here a while longer."

"But that can't matter so much. I mean, she must make a lot from her books."

"Sure, she does. But not as much as she needs to feel safe. See, Delia's been poor much of her life, in ways people like you and me know nothing about. She worries about money a lot. And then, writing is chancy. The creek could dry up, like it did with me. Most writers, if they can't live on their royalties, they get a teaching job, but Delia can't stand teaching."

"So how will she manage?"

"She'll manage. One way or another. You've got to remember, she's famous now. Seven years ago, when we met, she was only starting to be well-known, it was different. Anyhow, back then I was still writing and publishing. We were going to become famous together, that was her idea. Her delusion." He laughed harshly. "Now I think she'd like a really successful husband. Somebody like that Wally Hersh, the trustee she was so sweet to at the dinner for L. D. Zimmern."

"But Delia wouldn't marry someone like that," Jane exclaimed.

"I mean, Wally Hersh is old, he must be well over sixty. And he's so funny-looking. Lily Unger says he looks like a giant hamster."

"But he loves literature; I heard him say so twice." Henry smiled. "And he's rich. If Delia married him she would never have to worry about money again. She could hire help to drive and shop and cook and run errands. Right now she has to find people like me or Selma who will do it for nothing."

"It's not just Selma. Everyone at the Center does things for her."

"Yeah, I know." Henry smiled sourly. He's thinking of what Alan has done for her, Jane thought—we both are.

"You'll be going to North Carolina too," she said, realizing this for the first time and feeling as if she had received a blow just above the heart.

"I don't think so." He shook his head.

"No?" In spite of herself, Jane felt joy—foolish, of course, because what difference could it make to her?

"No. I mean, maybe I should. I understand what Delia's been through, I know how frightened she gets sometimes when she's alone. I have a lot of sympathy for her, but I don't want to live with her anymore."

Jane caught her breath. "You don't?" she echoed, forgetting for a moment that even if Henry were free now, she wasn't.

"No. And I think she doesn't want it either. She's not comfortable being with someone who doesn't worship her, doesn't believe in her absolutely. I try not to let it show, but she knows, and it brings her down."

"It's the same with Alan," Jane said. "I keep trying, but I don't believe in his art. And I don't believe in him. I asked him not to see Delia alone again, but it's still happening. I'm almost sure of it. When I was outside her office just now I heard all this shuffling and breathing inside. I think he's in there with her right now."

"Really." Henry did not look surprised or disturbed.

"Don't you care?" Jane stared at him.

"No. I guess I don't, not anymore. Do you?"

"Yes. It's so insulting, for one thing. I mean, here we are, and right over our heads something's going on, whatever it is. Maybe they're only talking. I don't know. But still—" Jane gasped.

"I see what you mean."

"It's like he doesn't care what I know or what I feel, not really."

"Yeah. That's what it's like." He smiled, but Jane did not smile back.

"You're leaving too," she said, looking at Henry and realizing how awful that would be, how important it had been that she could still see him at the Tuesday lectures and the Thursday lunches, even if they could never speak privately.

"I don't know—it depends—" He stumbled over the words.

"On what?"

"You, mostly."

"Me?" Feeling dizzy, Jane subsided onto the window seat. "How?"

"I'd stay here if I could be with you. Otherwise, it'll be the worst place in the world." He stared at her.

Jane met his glance briefly, then looked away. "I don't—I can't—" she cried.

"I suppose that's understandable," Henry said. "Alan's going to have great success as an artist, Delia tells me. It's already started. He'll make a lot of money too. You don't want to be involved with a failure."

"It's not that, not that at all," Jane said, her voice shaking. "I don't care about that."

"No. I believe you don't," Henry said slowly. "It's something else, then. I guess probably you don't love me enough."

"No, no," Jane cried, choking up. "I love you too much, that's what's so awful. I can't help it. But I'm married to Alan, I can't leave him when he's so ill. I'll blame myself and everybody will blame me—"

"I see. You still want to look good. But is it worth it?"

"It's not—I don't—" Jane was unable to speak.

"Here's your tea," Susie announced, coming into the room. "Oh, hello, Henry. Would you like a cup of tea? There's some nice raisin cookies too, left over from lunch."

"No thank you, I'm just going," Henry said. "So, Jane, you let me know what you decide," he added in a strained, neutral tone. "Give me a call by Friday morning, okay?"

"Okay," Jane echoed weakly.

"That's funny," Susie said as the front door closed heavily behind him. "Henry always loves tea and cookies. What's the matter with him today?"

Jane swallowed, which somehow made her chest hurt terribly. "I have no idea," she lied.

EIGHTEEN

Four days later, on a cold dark morning, Alan Mackenzie was on his way to the drugstore to renew a prescription for his current favorite painkiller. In spite of the errand and the weather, his mood was good. He was in only moderate pain, and his impetuous two-day trip to New York had been a success. Not only had he avoided Thanksgiving dinner with Jane's family, he had visited the Metropolitan Museum for the first time in over two years. He had also seen Jacky Herbert, who had professed to be "very keen" on the drawings for the new Doors and Windows constructions, and had spoken of a show the coming autumn. Jacky was also still negotiating with the "important collector" who might want Alan to design and supervise the building of a ruined tower on his Connecticut estate.

Flush with the checks Jacky had sent earlier, Alan had stayed in an East Side hotel rather than in his friends' cramped guest room on Morningside Drive. With the help of his new toilet-seat-concealing briefcase, he had managed planes, taxis, and restaurants with only intermittent serious pain. He had also seen Delia. She had come to his hotel for tea, and presently lain half-naked on his king-size bed, eating room-service tea sandwiches and drinking champagne, exclaiming over his drawings.

"This one, with the half-open window and the thin blowing

curtains, no wonder Jacky loved it, it's so strange and melancholy and beautiful," she had cried. "I want to use it for the cover of my next book of poems. If you'll let me." She smiled.

"I'd be honored," Alan had said, bending to kiss her in an especially sensitive place.

"Oh yes," she had murmured. "Oh, love."

Back home after Thanksgiving, life was less agreeable. Jane remained sullen and suspicious: she resented his absence from her parents' Thanksgiving dinner, and appeared to silently doubt his assurance that he had not gone to New York to see Delia, even though it was more or less true: the meeting with Delia had been a lucky accident, since Jacky had known where she was staying.

Alan knew he should be grateful to Jane, and he was grateful. But he didn't, he somehow couldn't, go beyond that, not anymore. They were supposed to be working on their marriage, but it was uphill work, and he was getting more and more worn out. Anyhow, love shouldn't be work. As Delia had written in a poem, it should be play and passion and joy.

Once he had loved Jane, Alan remembered; once he had thought her beautiful. But now she seemed small and thin and slight, conventional both in appearance and attitude. "People can change so much," Delia had said, speaking about her own marriage to a professor at the Southern college she had gone to, "and then sometimes they aren't right for each other anymore. It's nobody's fault."

One important change was that Jane now had no understanding or appreciation of his work. She had been very supportive and proud of his books on architecture, which always included a warm acknowledgment of her encouragement and help (research, typing, editing). His longest and most serious book, on eighteenth-century American vernacular architecture, was dedicated to her. At first Alan had thought that maybe she felt left out of his new projects, for which her assistance was not necessary. But it was more than that.

"You don't really like them, do you?" he had asked last week, indicating the new drawings spread out on his drafting table at the Center.

"It's not that, exactly," his wife said, flatly honest as always, but obviously straining to be positive or at least polite. "Probably I just don't understand. I mean, you draw so beautifully—but I don't know . . . All these doors and windows, they're so kind of strange and empty. Scary, even. Maybe if there were people in the rooms . . ."

"But that's part of the point, that there's no one," Alan had tried to explain. "They're the ghosts of rooms. Memories of rooms." But Jane's expression had not altered, and for a moment a cold heavy surge of self-doubt had drenched him, like a storm-weather wave full of seaweed and broken shells.

He needed to see Delia, Alan realized, to hear her tell him again that his work was good. But on Monday she hadn't come in to the Center; according to Susie, she was at home with a bad migraine. On Tuesday she was still absent, and that afternoon, against his better judgment, Alan had called her house.

"Yeah?" It was the voice of Delia's husband, Henry Hull. . . . "No, she can't come to the phone, she's not well." . . . "No, she doesn't want to talk to you or anyone. Look, it would be better if you people at the Center would stop calling, all right? She'll come in when she can." Henry's voice was harsh with irritation, even with active hostility. Did he guess what Alan and Delia meant to each other? Or could Jane have told him about the incident in Delia's office?

Another cold flood of despondency had washed over Alan. But yesterday Delia, restored to health and more beautiful than ever in a new creamy lace shawl, had mopped up the flood. She had repeated her praise of his work and her desire for one of the drawings as a cover for her new book. Warmed by this, and by a half hour of pure pleasure, Alan had exclaimed impulsively that he wished that they could be together more often—always.

"Oh, my dear." Delia smiled and made a small shooing gesture, as if waving invisible moths away. "I'd love that too. But you know it's not possible. I need someone with no serious work of his own, someone who has time to take care of me. We both need that."

"You mean you need Henry." Alan felt a heartburn spurt of jealousy.

"Not necessarily." She sighed softly, and fell silent. "There's a time and place for everyone," she said finally, "and I've begun to wonder if Henry's right for me now. There's so much sorrow and failure around him." She shook her head slowly, causing her tangled curls to rise and subside. "It's sad. He had a gift once, but he wouldn't put it first, so he couldn't hold on to it."

Henry's on his way out, thought Alan. And about time. He was never right for her: a dim, semi-employed Canadian, with an irritatingly ironic manner—a parasite on his beautiful, brilliant wife. "Yeah," he agreed.

Delia gave a long sigh. "You have to put your gift first, always," she said. "Because it's the only thing that will last. You have to sacrifice everything for it, including yourself. You'll be consumed soon enough anyhow, vanished into dust and smoke."

"That's true," Alan said, remembering times in the last year and a half in which he had felt this disappearance imminent, even desirable. "There's not that much time."

"You know, if you're a creative person, when you're with someone who doesn't really understand what you're doing, gradually a kind of horrible vacuum develops. It sucks everything up eventually. Even your soul."

Yes, it's the same for me, he had thought. Jane believed in my books, but she doesn't believe in what I'm doing now. She fears and dislikes it, really. "Jane doesn't like my new drawings much," he said. "Really she doesn't like anything I've done lately."

"That's serious." Delia had stopped smiling. She knew, she told him, how destructive it was to live with someone who didn't believe in your work. "That's how it was with my first husband," she told Alan. "Whenever he talked about my writing it was like frogs croaking in a swamp. He tried to be neutral; he didn't say much, but once you hear that croaking sound, the echoes of it are with you night and day, dragging you down and down into the mud. You have to snatch up everything and get away before it drives you mad."

"You're right," Alan replied. Another vision had come to him, and when he was back in his own office he began a drawing. Its central feature was the big Victorian sofa in the room across the hall, its cushions holding the imprint of Delia's body. Her lace shawl was thrown over the back next to the tall open window, and a book lay facedown on the carpet. The sculpture would be mostly in different shades of white and cream, but tinted here and there with a flush of rose-sepia. Sentimental? Yes, perhaps. But he would make it all the same, Alan thought now as he pulled into the snowy parking lot of the drugstore, for love, for Delia.

Twenty minutes later, as he left the store, his mood had darkened to match the weather. He drove to the Center—exceeding the speed limit—and, without stopping to hang his coat under the stairs or wait for the elevator, ascended directly and painfully to Delia's office. For the first time in months the door was wide open. Delia, in a long pale-gray suede vest and embroidered gray silk skirt, stood gazing out the tall window into the pale-gray sky.

In an uneven, angry voice, he spoke her name.

"Oh, hello," she murmured, turning.

Alan did not bother with a greeting. "I just saw Lily Unger in the drugstore. She says you're leaving town forever this weekend."

"Mm. Yes," Delia admitted.

"You never told me." His tone was harsh, accusing.

"I couldn't." She looked at him, smiling softly and regretfully. 'I promised."

"Promised whom?" Alan raised his voice.

She did not answer, only continued to smile.

"Promised what?" Now he was almost shouting.

"Not to make waves." Delia made the gesture of waves with one hand. "Just to slip away, without causing anyone any trouble. I wanted so much to call you, but I was afraid." She took a swaying step toward him.

"Afraid of what?"

"Everything. Everyone." She came closer. How frail she looks today, almost ill, he thought suddenly. How wide and silver-pale her eyes are, how thick and dark her lashes. "Lily said, if I told anyone, they'd argue and threaten and try to stop me."

"I wouldn't—" Alan began, and fell silent, aware that this was what he had been about to do, in any way possible—that he would try even now.

"You don't really have to leave," he said, trying to speak calmly, convincingly.

"But I do." She had reached his side, and gazed up at him, her rosy mouth half open as if for a passionate kiss. "You know how awful it's been here for me, ever since my reading. I knew what was coming. I asked Henry to explain that there would probably be two or three hundred people. But they wouldn't listen. Sometimes I think it was deliberate."

"Yeah," Alan agreed, realizing that "they" in this context meant Jane.

"Lots of people were turned away, and that made them angry and frantic. They felt they had a right to call me on the phone, and come here to get their books signed and ask the questions they didn't get to ask."

"Yes, you told me," he said impatiently.

"I haven't been able to work since then, not really, you know. Even when I lock the door and don't answer the phone, I know they're out there, on their way. Soon they'll be here and then they'll call, and pound on the door and leave messages and notes. They push them under the door sometimes; I can see them sliding into the room like slimy flat white fish. They all want me to read their manuscripts and recommend agents and editors and publishers and be their best friend. You know how it's been, you've seen them."

"Yeah," Alan admitted, remembering some of the strange-looking fans who, unable to reach Delia, had thrust their way into his office and asked for his help in "getting hold" of her, which he naturally did not give.

"And then, next Tuesday, Selma Schmidt is giving a lecture on me, with the most awful, embarrassing title—have you seen the poster?"

"I saw it. 'The Erotic Goddess: Destruction and Reconstruction in Delaney.'"

"And I'm supposed to just sit there and listen, and tell her afterwards how much I enjoyed it." Delia half laughed, half shuddered. "You know I came to Corinth mostly for the privacy. I thought no one could find me here, so far away in the north. And I wouldn't have to teach. The last time I tried that, it was so frightful. The students wouldn't let me alone, they stayed after class and crowded around, and followed me out to the car. Sometimes they even got into the car and sat there, talking and talking and patting my arm and trying to hold my hand. It was like being in a swarm of mosquitoes, all these little itchy bites."

"But you don't have students here," Alan protested.

"No. It was all right for a while. And there was you." She smiled enchantingly. "But since my lecture it's been horrible, really. I feel as if everyone is snatching at me, wanting to tear me apart. I can't work here. Everything I write is false, fouled. I'm having more and more migraines all the time. I feel so besieged, so invaded." Delia shuddered and pushed a tangle of hair away from her pale, damp forehead.

"I'm very sorry." Alan took her in his arms, and she subsided softly against him, yielding to his kiss.

"The thing is," she whispered, catching her breath in a near-sob, "if I can't write, I'm nobody, I'm nothing. No, worse than that. I'm like those demons in Scandinavian legend that look like beautiful women, but they're all hollow behind."

"Oh, Delia. Of course you're not."

"No, I am, sometimes. When I haven't been working and I go onstage to read, that's how I feel, that I mustn't stop or turn around, or they'll all know." She shuddered. "Sometimes I think I'll never write anything real again."

"Hell, no. Of course you will."

"But not here—I can't do it here. I have to go back to North Carolina, where it's not so cold and dark and ugly. I have to cut myself off from everything, and be absolutely alone in the woods and listen for my voices."

She's really leaving, Alan thought, confused, as if Delia were simultaneously there in his arms and gone.

"Maybe you could work in the house," he told her desperately.

"I couldn't—I hate that place," Delia said, pulling away. "It's full of dead birds. You've seen them."

"Yeah." Alan recalled the cases in the hall and dining room.

"Darling, you've got to understand. You've got to help me." She gazed at him, her huge gray eyes brimming with tears. "You'll help, won't you?"

Alan did not reply. He felt confused, angry, bereft. Then a stunning idea came to him. "Maybe I should leave too," he said. "Maybe we could go together." His head whirled as he tried to think how this could be arranged, how he could fly to North Carolina without terrible pain, how he could rent a studio and get supplies and work there; what he could say to the Council and his department and Jane.

"Not now, dearest. I need to be alone now, to lure my voices back."

"But I—I need—" Alan stuttered and fell silent, unwilling to imitate all the other people who were crowding and pulling at Delia.

"And we'll still be together, really. We're too close now ever to be apart." As if to demonstrate this closeness, Delia moved back toward Alan and placed one soft white hand on his shirt, over his heart. "Part of me will always be with you, wherever I go, and part of you will be with me. You know that."

"Yes, I know—" Alan, moved, put his hand over Delia's, then started back as her office door banged open. What looked at first like a stack of cardboard packing boxes entered the room, followed closely by Selma Schmidt. She was wearing farmer's striped overalls and a melancholy expression, and her frizzy dark hair seemed to take up even more room than usual.

"I got them," she declared. "Exactly the kind you wanted." She set the stack of boxes on the carpet and gave Alan an unfriendly look. Clearly she wished he were not there.

"Oh, that's wonderful," Delia said, gazing at the boxes as if they were birthday presents. "Thank you so much."

"It's so awful that you're leaving, even before my lecture." Selma's voice trembled with what appeared to Alan as an exaggerated parody of his own feelings. "I can't stand it here without you. You don't really have to go, not yet."

"I do, though." Delia treated Selma to one of her wonderful half smiles. "If I'm going to work again, I have to be alone for a while."

"You could be alone here."

"No, not anymore. You know that." She smiled fully now, but sadly; it was the same full, sad smile she had just given Alan. Selma already knew Delia was leaving, he realized with a stab of pain. Delia must have told her, though she didn't tell me.

"If you'll show me the books you want packed, I'll start now," Selma said, casting another hostile, impatient look at Alan. *Why don't you get lost?* this look said clearly. "Then I can take them to the post office today before it closes."

"That's not necessary, dear," Delia said. "Tomorrow will be plenty of time."

If he had been in good shape physically, Alan might have tried to ease Selma aside and packed the books himself; but this was impossible now. Suddenly he had no reason to be in this room. If he stayed there, he could only appear as an observer, a physically incompetent cripple.

"I'll see you later," he uttered, with what he hoped was significant meaning.

"Oh yes." Delia did not smile, but she opened her huge gray eyes and gave him a brief look of profound warmth and meaning. *You understand, my darling,* this look seemed to promise, or to lie. *One day soon we will be together again.*

NINETEEN

At noon that same day, Jane was having lunch on campus with Susie Burdett's mother, Linda, whom she had known since childhood, when Linda had been one of Jane's sister's best friends. She was now a secretary in a doctor's office, still a pretty pale blonde like her daughter and, like her, usually cheerful. Today, however, she was depressed and anxious, because Susie had just told her parents that she and Charlie Amir were in love and planning to get married.

"She wants to ruin her life," Linda wailed, shoving her half-eaten sandwich aside. "She won't listen to us, maybe she'll listen to you. I know she admires you a lot."

"I don't understand," Jane said. "I mean, why shouldn't Susie marry Charlie? He's a nice man, very successful in his career, and I think he loves her."

"Oh yeah. You can tell he's stuck on Susie. And he looks like a friendly, ordinary guy, I admit that. I liked him fine at first. But that's not the point. The point is, what we just found out yesterday, he's a Muslim."

"Yes. And?" Jane sighed under her breath.

"Those are the people that blew up the World Trade Center. And they're awful to women. They each have four wives at once, and they shut them up in the house and make them wear these kind of black tent things when they go out."

"I'm sure Charlie isn't that kind of Muslim," Jane said, hoping this was true. "He's an educated man, a professor of economics. I'm sure he won't have four wives and want Susie to wear a tent."

"Well. Maybe not. But you never can tell. And if she marries him she'll be far away and cut off from her family."

"She'll only be in Columbus, Ohio."

"Yeah, but still . . ." Linda frowned. "You know, I didn't much like that boy she was going with before, with his loud voice and his low-life friends, but if Susie had married him she would at least have stayed in town and we could have seen her all the time. You've got to talk to her. Please. You can convince her to break it off."

"I can't do that, Linda," Jane said. "And I wouldn't, anyhow. Susie and Charlie are in love, and people who are in love deserve to be happy together." As she uttered these words, a desperate sinking feeling came over Jane. "I'm really sorry," she told Linda, her voice weighted down by all the things she was sorry for.

Crossing the campus ten minutes later, Jane reached the Center and found it in disorder. Since Susie had phoned that morning with the news that Delia Delaney was resigning her fellowship and leaving town the next day, she did not have to pretend to be surprised, but she still had to pretend to be dismayed.

From a practical point of view Jane was slightly dismayed, because of the official hassle that would immediately follow. From the impractical point of view she was worse than dismayed. Delia was going away, a good thing; but Henry Hull was presumably going too. She had not called him, so she would probably never see him again in her whole life. It was a bright early winter day outside, but at this thought the rooms of the Center, especially the office, seemed to be full of dark smoke.

"It's so sad," Susie said, raising a gloomy face from her computer. "It just won't be the same around here without Delia."

"No, it won't," Jane agreed. "But we can't brood about that; we have a lot to do today. I'll call Bill and Lily now, and write the e-mails to the other council members and the dean. When you get back from lunch you can send them out, along with hard copies by campus mail. And then you'll need to get in touch with the payroll and insurance people in Knight Hall."

"Oh, but I can't!" Susie wailed. "Delia's just given me her latest revisions, and I promised I'd type them up and print everything out today so she can take it with her to North Carolina."

"Really," Jane sighed. Lately, much of Susie's time had been spent on Delia's letters and manuscripts, to the neglect of her actual job. The filing, for instance, hadn't been done for a week.

"I'm sorry, but that will just have to wait," she said. "We've got to send the official announcements of Delia's resignation to the Humanities Council today, before it's all over the campus as a rumor."

"Oh—but—" Susie wailed. "You know, I don't have to go out for lunch. If I stay here, maybe I can finish up Delia's work. She really needs it now, and she's done so much for me."

What Delia had done for Susie, Jane thought, was to tell her that Charlie Amir was in love with her, not giving a thought to the possible consequences. "Well. If you want to miss lunch, naturally that's up to you," she said.

Bill, when she reached him, was quite untroubled. "I told you so weeks ago," he said, laughing. "I said Delia wouldn't be able to take the winter, didn't I?"

"Yes, you did," Jane admitted.

"You should be pleased, after all the trouble she's caused."

"Well, I am, in a way," Jane agreed wearily, thinking, If only you knew. "But it always looks bad when a famous visitor cancels a lecture or walks out on the University. And now I have to write to everyone on the council, and Dean Lewis, and the people at Knight Hall, and they'll all blame us."

"Of course they won't. Visiting professors do this kind of thing all the time—especially artists. There was a case just the other year in the Music Department, involving a frozen cello, as I remember." He laughed.

"Yes, I heard about it," she said.

"And now you can get a new state-of-the-art copier."

"Well, that's true," Jane said, expressing but not feeling enthusiasm.

What is the matter with me? she thought as she hung up. I used to get a lot of satisfaction out of going into a crisis and putting everything to rights. But now it just makes me tired. I feel as if I were pushing a stone uphill—no, not a stone, something bigger and uglier, like a dead cow.

Next Jane called Lily Unger, who turned out to know the news already. Delia had confided in her yesterday, she admitted, because she knew Lily would understand and would keep her confidence. (*Unlike you and most other people*, was implied.) And Lily did understand, completely. Delia was so sensitive, and Southerners just weren't prepared, biologically or psychologically or even spiritually, for our northern winters, were they?

"I suppose not," Jane said, thinking that Lily was probably parroting Delia's excuses. Well, maybe that was the way to go—the letters could, should, say that Delia was resigning for health reasons.

"So you have to be gentle with her. You have to remember that she's not a tough winter-hardy plant like you, with generations of rural ancestors."

What the hell did that mean? Jane thought. Well, it meant that Lily was a snob, no surprise really. Okay, my grandfather and great-grandfather were farmers, and I'm not a Southerner, but so what?

"Of course, we'll all miss her terribly. But what really counts, after all, is her writing, isn't that true?"

"I suppose so."

"I expect everyone's a bit upset at the Center, though."

"Well, yes. Some of them are," Jane agreed.

"I have friends here to lunch, but I'll be over as soon as I can."

"You don't have to—" Jane began, but Lily had hung up; it was not like her to miss any crisis.

In fact, many people at the Center were upset. At the buffet lunch Davi Gakar, Charlie Amir, Selma Schmidt, two visiting graduate students, and the entire catering staff from the Hotel School had hovered over Delia, regretting her departure, fetching her plates of food, and presenting books for her to autograph. Delia, looking pale and a little weary in a flimsy gray-blue tunic and long skirt, with her golden-spaniel curls pulled into a ponytail and hanging loose down her back, thanked them all effusively, with Southern spaniel charm. She assured Charlie that no one had ever before understood how to make a cup of coffee exactly the way she liked it; she promised Davi to send his children a signed copy of her Southern folktales.

In the office, Susie was eating crackers and drinking soda from a can and sniveling as she typed, and Selma Schmidt, red-eyed and weepy, was banging about pasting address labels onto cartons of Delia's books and papers.

"You don't have to do this today," Jane told her. "I mean, surely some of these books can be stored at Delia's house for a while—" Oh, hell, she thought. It's not Delia's house, it's the Vogelers' house. It's rented until next May fifteenth—but if Delia and Henry leave, who will pay the rent? She realized with a sinking feeling that there was no lease, only a file of letters, several of them signed by her, Jane, as director of the Center. It had never happened before that a Visiting Fellow had left in the middle of the year, and nobody had asked for an official rental agreement. But maybe Delia and Henry were still liable. Or maybe I am, Jane thought, already beginning to feel exhausted. I must talk to Bill Laird. I must remember to make sure that this never happens again.

Only Alan was not caught up in the general low-level hysteria, she realized. At the start of the lunch hour he had made himself a ham and Swiss cheese sandwich from the buffet table, picked up a bottle of sparkling water, and retreated to his office. Maybe he was trying to avoid Delia, as Jane had asked him to do. Maybe she had been wrong and even wicked to suspect and spy on him for the last couple of weeks. Maybe, even, nothing much had been happening that day in Delia's office.

I must give him time, I must try to be more patient and more affectionate with him, Jane told herself, as her mother and Reverend Bobby had been telling her and she had been telling herself ever since she moved back into the house. And why should that be so hard? Alan wasn't difficult and demanding now, not often anyhow. Instead, he was distant and preoccupied. Sometimes he would ask her to fetch something or do an errand for him, but he usually asked politely, even apologetically, and afterward he thanked her politely. "Thank you. You're a very kind person," he had said just the other day, as if she weren't his wife anymore, but a houseguest or a distant relative.

Most of the time, when Alan was home, she couldn't talk to him at all, because he was wearing headphones that looked like black chrome and rubber snails and listening to his CDs, or to the books on tape he kept ordering by mail or taking out of the local and University libraries. "It helps me to concentrate, and forget the pain," he had told her last night when she finally asked if he had to have the headphones on all the time.

When they ate dinner together he took off the headphones, and responded to her questions and comments, but almost never initiated any. And as soon as she put her fork down, he would begin to clear the table and put things away, groaning sometimes with pain as he stooped to place a heavy pan on a low shelf, but refusing her assistance. "No," he would say. "This is my job." Then he would retreat to his study to work on his peculiar new drawings: plans for sculptures of open windows and doors and fragments of empty rooms. All empty, like their marriage, Jane thought as she looked at them, nobody there, nothing left.

More than once, as she sat alone in the evening, or lay awake in bed alone (Alan was still sleeping in the study, and when she had suggested he move back he had said he often got up at night and didn't want to disturb her) the depressing thought came to her that he had never asked her to return to their house, she had just gone and done it.

The worst thing was that she kept thinking about Henry, something she mustn't do. It didn't matter that Henry was so kind and strong and honest and healthy and had curly dark hair and loved her. He was also weak and unreliable. She had to put him out of her mind and keep trying to repair her marriage, as she had promised she would. Alan was ill, he needed her. That was what she had to remember. Things had to get better between them: after all, they had loved each other once, they had been happy together all those years when everything was all right and they were friends.

Trying to shove these repetitive thoughts aside, Jane turned to her computer and began to compose the letter to the dean. But as soon as the words "for health reasons" appeared on the screen, she sighed and stopped. "Susie?" she asked. "Did Delia say why she was leaving?"

"Uh-huh," replied Susie. "Well, not exactly. She just said she had to go because it was so cold and she couldn't work here."

"I see." For the first time it struck Jane that as the director of the Unger Center for the Humanities she, not her assistant, should have been the person to whom Delia announced her resignation. That she had neglected to do this was rude, even insulting. Probably Delia had wanted to avoid speaking to her: in fact, they had both been avoiding each other ever since the awful scene upstairs. All the same, it would have been right.

But of course Delia cared nothing about what was right. If she had, there would already be a proper letter of resignation. Jane groaned as she realized that before she could write to the dean and the council she would have to obtain such a letter.

Lunch was now over, and except for Susie, and Selma with her piles of books and cartons, the ground floor was empty. Pushing the invisible dead cow ahead of her, Jane slowly climbed the stairs and stood in front of Delia's door. From behind it she could hear a murmur of voices, and a sensation of awful events about to repeat themselves caused her to recoil and glance across the hall. But no: Alan was in his office, standing at his drafting table with his back to her.

Taking a deep breath, she knocked. There was no response.

"Delia? Are you there? I'm sorry to disturb you now, but I have to speak to you," Jane said, realizing that this was a lie: she did want to disturb Delia, now and always.

Silence. Then the door opened a few inches, but the face in the gap was that of Lily Unger.

"It's Jane," Lily announced.

There was an indistinct response from within, then the door was opened fully.

"Thank you," Delia said, rising from the sofa. "Darling Lily, thank you so much for everything." She put a hand on Lily's arm and, without seeming to, conveyed her into the hall. "Really, I'll be all right," she added with a long soft sigh. "I'll call you tonight. I promise.

"Oh, Jane. I'm so exhausted," she said, shutting the door. At lunch Delia had looked pale and tense; now she seemed almost ill. An unkind smear of winter light from a gap in the curtains lit her face, exposing bruised violet hollows around the huge gray watery eyes and crepey skin beneath them, roughened rouged cheeks, and a sag of flesh under the chin. Why, she's old, Jane thought. Bill was right; she's much older than she told us: over fifty maybe.

"And I'm cold all the time," Delia moaned. "So cold." She shivered and clutched a slate-gray fringed pashmina shawl more closely around her shoulders. "I think I must be coming down with something."

"I'm sorry to disturb you," Jane repeated, this time sincerely,

"No, I'm happy you're here. It's my appointment book: it was right there on my desk, and now it's vanished. It's black, with a scarlet pimpernel on the cover—for assignations, you know—and my whole future is in there." Her voice rose to a soft wail. "I can't go on without it. Please. My head hurts so—and my eyes. Maybe you can see it somewhere."

She's old and ill, Jane thought, old and ill and frightened; Henry doesn't love her; he loves me. She felt a tremor of compassion. "Well, okay. I'll try," she said. She went to the desk and began to turn over drifts of paper. Many of them, she noticed, were sheets of the expensive heavy lime-green poster stock that Delia kept taking from the supply cupboard, with only a line or two scrawled on each one.

"Maybe it fell off the desk," she suggested, but Delia only looked at her hopelessly. Sighing, Jane dropped to her hands and knees and crawled under the big oak desk, where the wastebasket had been overturned and the oriental carpet was littered with scrap paper. She crawled closer and began shuffling through the debris.

"Wait—is this it?" She held up a small notebook.

"Oh yes! Oh, thank you, thank you." Delia snatched the book, giving Jane a wonderful smile.

"You're welcome," Jane said, backing out awkwardly, smiling too. She remembered something Henry had said, that we always feel kinder toward people after we have helped them. But maybe that could work both ways.

"Well, now you've got to help me," she said, standing up. "I have to write to the dean and the Humanities Council today, and I need an official letter of resignation from you."

"A letter?" Delia put one hand on her forehead, as if a migraine were churning there under the tangled golden tendrils. "I don't understand. I'm not resigning, it's just the cold here, the darkness, it's making me so horribly ill—"

"Susie says you told her you were leaving town tomorrow."

"Oh, I am, I must. But as soon as I'm better—at least, I hope so— Lily says January can be very beautiful here, with radiant sunny days, and the snow gleaming like sugar frosting."

"Yes, it can," Jane admitted. Lily Unger put you up to this just now, she thought. She suggested that if you go on leave, instead of

resigning, your paychecks and health insurance will continue. That's
what you were thanking her for.

"And the spring, too. She says that in April the hill below the
University is covered with golden flowering sythia trees."

"Forsythia," Jane corrected. "It's a bush." Delia's not going forever, she thought. She'll be back, and Henry will come with her, and
I'll see him again. A surge of joy washed over her.

"Oh yes? I should like to see that, so much."

"Well. In that case, we'll need a request for a medical leave of absence. I'll get Susie to type up a letter for you to sign."

"Oh, but I can't do that. I'm not ill, really—it's just that I can't
work here. It's the chill, the darkness. The town is so ugly now, and
so full of ugly boring people. . . ." Delia gazed at Jane, her eyes wide
with appeal.

And I'm one of them, Jane thought. She hardened her heart.
"That's up to you, of course," she said. "But if you're not in residence, and there's no medical leave form on file, the accounting office in Knight Hall will stop processing your paychecks." This
statement was probably a lie: the payroll office would not stop
Delia's checks unless they were told to do so. But when you deal
with immoral people, you become immoral. You touch pitch and
are defiled, as the Reverend Bobby had said just last Sunday.

"They are so petty?" Delia asked, pouting.

"Yes, I'm afraid so."

"Very well." A long, sad sigh. "Wait, don't go. I want to speak to
you. About Alan."

"Yes?" Jane stopped with one hand on the new bolt of the
door. She's going to admit what really happened, she's going to say
she's sorry, she thought, feeling ashamed of her recent spiteful
thoughts.

"You must know—you must realize that Alan has great talent—
even genius," Delia insisted, coming closer and putting one soft
hand on Jane's arm. "He's going to have a great success with his art.
But the more original something is, the longer it takes for it to be

fully recognized. Some stupid people will never understand. They'll say cruel things."

"Yes, so I've heard," Jane said flatly, wondering if Alan had repeated to Delia some of the things she had said about his art. But they weren't cruel, she told herself, just uncomprehending, and anyhow Alan had promised her not to talk to Delia again.

"So it is important that when I'm gone he has someone he can depend on to support him and encourage him. That's what you need to do, even if you don't understand his work." Delia moved nearer, so close that Jane could see the bruised violet skin around her eyes, and her thick mascaraed lashes.

She thinks I'm one of the stupid people, Jane realized. "Naturally I support Alan," she said, becoming indignant. "He's my husband."

"No, I don't think you do. That's why I've had to help and comfort him. But I'm leaving tomorrow, and then it will all be over."

What it, what all? Jane thought, angry and confused. "You mean it's not over now?" she said. "But Alan promised, weeks ago—"

Delia sighed. "Yes, I know," she said. "But men are so weak, don't you agree? It's hard for them to follow through on their promises. And how could I refuse, when he needed my encouragement and affection so desperately?" She had taken hold of the doorknob; now she pulled it open and began to push Jane out. "So you must forgive him, and stay with him and be kind to him," she murmured.

"Don't you tell me what to do!" Jane cried in a furious whisper. But she said it to the closed door; the only response was the sound of the bolt being shoved home. Her heart was pounding, and she was trembling with rage at Delia, and at Alan, who had continued to mess around with Delia—unless she was lying, out of spite. But no: there were the voices behind her door so many afternoons, and his coolness at home. It was Alan who was lying, and had been lying all along, for weeks and months. How could Delia dare to ask her to forgive him? How could she think she could work her phony charm on Jane? How could she not know that Jane would naturally want to do the opposite of what Delia told her to do?

She tried to gather her thoughts, to concentrate on practical matters, but her head was full of confusion. Delia wasn't resigning, so there was no need to write to the dean, and the letters to the council could wait until next week. The only person she needed to speak to today was Bill.

Back in the office, Susie was still typing and eating crackers, and Selma was addressing cartons, as if only a few minutes had passed since she went upstairs. And in fact, that was so, Jane realized. She took two deep breaths, lifted the phone off its cradle, and called Bill's number.

As always, he was calm, even amused. "Well, yes, it was interfering of Lily to talk to Delia about a medical leave," he said. "But you know how Delia is, she gets people to do things for her by looking helpless."

"Yes, I know," Jane said, catching her breath. I felt sorry for her, she thought, and so somehow she got me to crawl under her desk and dig through her dirty trash. "What I don't understand is how she does it."

"I guess she sort of casts a glamour over them, like the gypsies in the old ballad," Bill said, laughing. "But you know, it will be a lot simpler for us if Delia doesn't resign," he added. "Less talk."

"Maybe."

"I know—you're thinking about the new copier. But I expect we can find the money somewhere. . . . For instance we might rent out Delia's office to some other department that needs space for the spring term. There's often extra faculty at the Law School, for instance."

"We can't rent Delia's office; she's going to be here next term," Jane protested.

"Oh, I don't think so." Bill laughed.

"You think she and Henry won't come back at all?" Jane said, her heart sinking.

"I doubt it. Why should she, when she'll be getting her checks anyhow? And then there's her migraines, that the climate here is so bad for."

"Oh, hell," she exclaimed, so sharply that Bill said:

"Jane? What's the matter?"

"It's just—" She tried to lower her voice. "I sort of can't face it." She took another deep breath. "I mean the rescheduling, and the conference we've set up for the spring, so many people coming because they think Delia will be here—"

"Oh, you'll manage, I'm sure of it," Bill told her. "You always do. You're a very good administrator. Well, call me if anything else comes up."

Still holding on to the cordless phone, Jane walked out into the hall. Her heart was still pounding. Everyone is lying to me, and telling me who I am and what I should do, she thought. Everyone except Henry. She moved down the hall to the entrance, gazing through the double doors into a brilliant landscape of graceful bare maple trees and gas-flame-blue sky and distant gold and lavender hills.

No matter what Delia says, it's not ugly here in Corinth, she thought, it's beautiful; and nobody here is boring. I don't have to do what people tell me or be who they tell me I am. And I deserve to be happy, just as much as Susie does. She lifted the phone and punched in Henry's number.

TWENTY

It was a fine early June evening, with a soft salty breeze in the plumed pampas grass by the water, and the organic-food tycoon and art collector Franklin Bannerman was hosting a large drinks party on his Greenwich estate. The occasion, officially, was the completion of a brand-new ruined medieval tower on the shore, designed by the newly fashionable installation artist Alan Mackenzie. The tower itself was not actually ruined, though a few crenellations were missing from its battlements. But only a fragment of the adjoining walls remained—or, rather, had just been built—suggesting the ghostly presence of a much larger structure.

The stonemason and the two architecture graduate students who had helped Alan in the construction were on the terrace mingling with the guests, drinking and scarfing up salmon pâté and creamed chicken in puff pastry. But Alan, tired of walking back and forth, waited beside the warm gray stones of the tower, leaning on his cane, while people in groups of two or more crossed the long velvety lawn to see the structure more closely and ask questions about it, some intelligent and some ridiculous. Those of the men tended to be practical or ribald ("Took you how long to put up this thing?" "Well, Frank finally got himself a really big prick."). Those of the women were more often sentimental or domestic ("Oh, it's lovely, it makes me feel as if I was in a fairy tale" "You ought to put some lights in here, so Frank could use it for parties").

Alan was beginning to think of returning to the terrace for another drink, but decided to give it a few more minutes. His back hurt, as usual, though the pain was somewhat blurred now by alcohol and codeine, and by a sense of professional triumph. Otherwise he felt and looked well: he had lost weight and picked up a tan from working on the tower, and he had a new expensive haircut and an even more expensive beige summer suit.

The last six months had been strange and confused, marked by both gains and losses. His career was going well: several more big drawings had been sold at what he still thought of as inflated prices; and there were two more commissions in prospect, one definite. He had a show scheduled in October at Jacky Herbert's gallery, and there had been short but gratifying pieces about his installations in the *New York Times* and the *Corinth Courier.* On the other hand, he had lost both his wife and his true love, Delia Delaney.

When Delia left Corinth in December she had vanished almost completely, leaving no address or telephone number, only a PO box in Ashland, North Carolina. Alan had written to this box frequently, and received in reply only three warmly affectionate but very brief notes, the last one in March.

> *Wild snowdrops in the sunlit woods today, a message of new life and hope. Winds whispering secrets, songbirds calling and mating in the pines. My pen is in my hand—you are in my thoughts always.*
>
> *Dilly*

Since then, silence. Of course, Delia had warned him; she had explained that in order to work again—to make contact with her spirits, as she put it—she would have to cut herself off from everyone

for a while, even from the people who meant most to her—perhaps
especially from them, she had murmured, with a meaningful glance
at Alan. But she had refused even to guess how long she might be
gone, or when he might see her again. "Darling, I can't know that
now—I can't know anything."

Trying to reconcile himself to her temporary absence, Alan had
frequently reminded himself of all Delia had given him already. It
was because of her that he had a New York gallery and sales at New
York prices. It was because of her that he had crawled out from under the heap of dirt and stones that his life had become, and dared to
commit himself to art and to love. Delia had even persuaded him to
see the clawing lizard in his back as not wholly evil. If he had remained free of it, he would also have remained merely a professor of
architectural history, with an occasional hobby of building and
drawing follies and ruins. She had changed his life—and he had
hoped to change hers.

All through December and January he thought of Delia, his
Dilly, almost constantly, remembering her voice, her touch, her
words so vividly that at first he sometimes forgot that she was gone.
As he walked down the hall at the Unger Center he would often
automatically glance into her room, and only then remember that
she had left. Meanwhile, her freeloader husband, Henry Hull, was
already back in Corinth, living in their rented house. From time to
time Alan saw him hanging around the Center office. It was clear
that Delia had no further use for him—yet Henry, apparently not
realizing this, or hiding his true feelings, maintained a cheerful
manner. A couple of times, when Jane wasn't around, Alan had
stopped to ask him how Delia was doing, and the answer was always the same: "Fine, far as I know." His tone was offhand, but no
doubt he was feeling uneasy and rejected, and with good reason.
You're on your way out, pal, Alan thought. Whether you know it
or not.

At home, Alan never mentioned Delia's name; he tried to behave
politely and pleasantly during this interim period. There was no

point, after all, in making trouble for Jane before it had to be made. Then, one evening just before Christmas, his wife had declared that she wanted to move back into her parents' house, after they left for their annual winter stay in an RV park in Tampa.

The thing was, she told him, she did not think their marriage was working. Though he disliked the idea of his or any marriage as a malfunctioning appliance, Alan could not disagree; he knew that in effect Jane was right. They had been happy together once, but the person who had been happy with Jane and with whom she had been happy was someone else, someone healthier and more conventional—not an invalid and not an artist. Besides, when Delia returned it would be easier if he was living alone.

This time Jane did not bring him a dinner wrapped in foil every day, but she arranged for their cleaning lady to come in three afternoons a week instead of one, to do the laundry, shopping, and errands, and leave a meal for Alan to warm up. Jane also provided him with the take-away menus of several local restaurants. Thanks to the checks that kept coming from the gallery, he could easily afford the extra expense.

He missed her, in a way, but it was also a relief that she was not there every evening serving his dinner and doing the dishes and then sitting alone in the living room switching channels on the TV and hoping that their marriage, that ill-functioning stove or fridge, would recover by itself, when he already knew it would not recover—that what was wrong with it was fatal.

It was a hard, lonely winter. January and February were cold and gray, and Alan was often in pain or blurry from the effects of drugs with threatening names that sounded like diseases. Sometimes he was well enough to draw and paint, or make notes for his study of church architecture, which he had not quite abandoned. At other times he spent whole afternoons lying on the sofa in his office, trying to read a heavy book held awkwardly and painfully on his chest, or listening to tapes of classical music. Over and over again he kept telling himself that one day, after the snow melted, Delia would be there.

Often he imagined this time: their meeting, their walks in the greening woods or in the Corinth Orchard; Dilly in his bed, or bedded among the falling apple blossoms. He even imagined the trouble-free end of his marriage, and of Delia's, and a summer wedding at her cabin in the North Carolina mountains—or perhaps here in Corinth, in the ruined chapel he and his students had built—its stained-glass window of holy chickens now in place. He imagined Delia crowned with flowers whose names and meanings she would know, and their procession through the miniature triumphal arch that had been the first step toward his new career. He was pleased and encouraged when he received a formal request from Delia's publisher asking for the right to use a reproduction of his drawing for *Attic Window* on the cover of her forthcoming book. It proved that, though she might be silent, Delia was indeed thinking of him.

Meanwhile, the news of Alan and Jane's separation had made a considerable stir locally. Acquaintances, including a couple of single women whom he hardly knew, invited him to dinner and attempted to pump him for details and motivation; friends sympathized and attempted to give advice. Bernie and Danielle Kotelchuck gave him roast beef and beer and suggested that he try to make it up with Jane, who, they said, was essentially a very good person. Gilly and her husband Pedro gave him stir-fry and marijuana and suggested that he and Jane go together to a very good crisis mediator they knew. Public opinion, largely, was on Alan's side. Jane, after all, had deserted an invalid husband—a cruel, selfish act. She had also walked out on someone who was beginning to have considerable artistic success—a foolish, impulsive act, possibly motivated by envy. If she had supporters, they did not speak to Alan.

Early in February Jane asked Alan to have lunch with her on campus and suggested that they file for divorce. She didn't think they would be getting back together, she said—and he had to agree. She also declared that she wanted to be fair about everything. They had already split the checking and savings accounts, and she didn't want any part of Alan's TIIA/CREF, which his salary had paid for.

Jane didn't want the house either. She knew Alan loved it, but she never had, really. Yes, it was old and historic, maybe even beautiful, she said. But it was awfully hard to take care of, all those little rooms and steep narrow stairs and low ceilings. It was drafty and badly insulated too, with the plumbing and heating always breaking down, and the soil in the garden was mostly clay. All she wanted was half its assessed value, not counting the follies, so that she could buy a newer, more modern house nearer to town, with good soil and a chimney that didn't smoke. And, if it was all right with him, she'd like to take the furniture and china that had been her grandmother's, and her Cuisinart and all the cookbooks and garden books.

And then, Jane said, when the frost was out of the ground, and she'd found a new place, she'd like to come and dig up some of the plants from her garden: the peonies and daylilies and some of the myrtle, and the asparagus and the raspberry and blackberry canes and the rhubarb.

"Sure, you can have them all, take anything you like," Alan had said, amazed and relieved by the modesty of her demands, and especially by the news that he would not lose his beloved house— wondering if this leniency was in part dictated by the consciousness of public opinion.

After this, when they met at the Unger Center, relations between Alan and Jane remained cordial though cool. Considering what had happened to a couple of his colleagues whose marriages had ended, he felt very fortunate. But he was stunned when, in mid-March, Jane announced that she was planning to marry Henry Hull. In the surprise and heat of the moment, Alan spoke unsympathetically of Henry, calling him a loser and a layabout and asking how she could even consider marrying someone like that. "Yes," Jane remarked in a low, strained voice, "that's what Henry thought you would say. It's what he thinks everybody will say, but it's not true. He has a perfectly good well-paying job, with more editing work than he can possibly take on."

Yes, she admitted, her mother had been kind of upset by the idea of the marriage at first, because she disapproved of divorce, but she'd come around. She liked Henry, and so did Jane's dad, and they could watch sports together. Anyhow, it was what she wanted to do, what was right for her.

Alan could not bring himself to congratulate her. He felt insulted, injured, and worst of all, made to look ridiculous. Naturally he wanted Jane to be happy, or at least content—it was what any reasonable man would want for his ex-wife. He had already hoped that she would meet someone suitable, someone dependable, someone more like her, eventually—but not right away. If she found someone first, it would look as if he, Alan, had been rejected. Of course, really he had found Delia first, but nobody knew that. And now, when Delia returned to Corinth, probably in a few weeks, and their relationship became public, they would be a joke. People would speak of wife-swapping. At the thought, Alan shuddered. Though he knew it to be a weakness, he still had a horror of being laughed at. It was a weakness Delia didn't share: she didn't care if people laughed, she had said once—it just showed how limited and stupid and conventional they were. Sometimes Alan wished he were more like her. Maybe one day he would learn to be.

If Jane and Henry were to marry after he and Delia, it might be seen as the slightly pathetic union of the two rejected, less successful partners—yes, maybe then he could endure it. He had therefore tried to persuade Jane not to announce her plans for six months, suggesting that it would look better. But she had refused. "I don't care anymore if things look good," she had said. "If you pour chocolate sauce over an old cake of soap it will look good, but you wouldn't want to eat it."

The only silver lining to the whole disaster had been the news that Delia had never been married to Henry Hull. This would not only make things simpler for her and Alan, it proved that she had had the self-respect and the good sense not to tie herself legally to someone like that. And indeed, when Jane's plan to marry Henry Hull finally became known, she was further condemned, and so was Henry, especially by the many on-campus fans of Delia Delaney, who of course did not know that Delia loved Alan and that they would soon be together.

Yes, but when? Time was passing: the coarse, gritty, porous heaps of snow by the driveway and in the parking lots at the University were beginning to shrink. Early in April Jane asked Alan if he wouldn't like to move back into his original office at the Center, with its north light and view of the lake and big green sofa. "No, I don't think there's any point in that," he had told her. "After all, it's almost spring now, and Delia should be back soon."

"I'm not sure she will," Jane said.

"Why not?" Though he tried to control it, Alan's voice rose a bit. "Have you heard something?"

"No, nobody has. But Bill Laird thinks she's never coming back, and she hasn't answered any of the official letters I've sent her."

"But that doesn't mean anything. Delia hasn't answered any-body's letters, Susie says." (Except mine, he thought.)

"No," Jane said sourly. "And what that means, if you want to know what Bill thinks, and I agree with him, is that Delia doesn't want to admit she's not coming, because she's on medical leave, and she wants the University to keep sending her paychecks."

"Oh, she wouldn't do that," Alan said. "She wants to be in Corinth as soon as the weather's warm enough for her to stay well." He tried to speak firmly, reminding himself that Jane didn't know the main reason Delia wanted to be there—but something in his voice wobbled slightly, unbalanced for a moment by doubt.

"Maybe," Jane said. "Maybe not."

She knows something—Henry's told her something, Alan thought. And for a moment he felt panic. But once he was back in his office, he lifted the brown paper that covered his drawing board and slid out Delia's three note cards. "Your downcast Dilly," he read, and "You are in my thoughts always," and the doubt and panic passed.

All this had been hard enough. What was worse, what was intolerable, had happened early last month. On a sunny Monday morning, Davi Gakar came into the Unger Center carrying the Style section of Sunday's *New York Times*. Horribly, unbelievably, it contained a wedding announcement headlined "Delia Delaney, Wallace Hersh." Below this was a photograph of Delia looking beautiful and Wally Hersh, the Corinth trustee, looking like a large, fat, old, bald hamster. This was followed by the disgusting, improbable news of a marriage in Palm Beach, where Mr. Hersh lived. He also, it appeared, lived in Manhattan and in Rye, New York, and was the chairman of something called Hersh International Manufacturing, sixty-four years old, and a widower.

Alan's first reaction was that the whole thing must be a hoax of some sort, a hideous joke by a former fraternity brother or business associate, for instance, who wanted to embarrass Wally Hersh. Or someone who had it in for Delia, some crazed fan. The announcement gave her age as fifty-one instead of forty-five, clearly a malicious lie. But then Lily Unger sidled into the Center, looking smug, and said she'd known it all along, or anyhow for a couple of weeks. She had even been invited to the wedding, and would have gone if it wasn't so far and the planes so unreliable at this time of year.

"I predicted it. And of course I was the one who introduced them," Lily said, preening. It was at this point that Alan had had to go upstairs and shut himself in his office, and try not to break anything that would show or make the kind of noise anyone could hear. He slammed his fist into the wall a couple of times, but Matthew Unger's father had built well, and he managed only to dent the plaster and bruise his knuckles badly—there was still a dried smear of blood there by the window.

She was supposed to be working so hard she couldn't see anyone or answer anyone's letters, Alan thought. But all along she must have been writing to Wally Hersh and seeing him. Maybe, even probably, he came to the cabin in the woods, which Alan had only once seen a photograph of, but fantasized about often. He should have suspected it, or something like it. After all, Delia had betrayed Henry Hull with Alan, so what was more likely than that she would betray Alan in his turn? Of course she didn't love Wally Hersh—she had married him for his three houses and his wealth, which (according to Lily Unger) was considerable. Maybe she really was fifty-one years old: the *Times* ought to know, they had files going back years to when she wouldn't have wanted to lie about her age. Bitch, whore, liar.

And she never even wrote to tell me, Alan thought. She's a coward too. Or maybe worse, she had just forgotten him and couldn't be bothered. He recalled something his dealer, Jacky Herbert, had said. "Delia's not capable of multi-tasking. When she's working, she doesn't notice anything that happens around her. Or if you manage to interrupt her, then she turns her attention on you—her complete attention, like a high-powered spotlight, though usually not for long. People are drawn to it like moths, they flutter frantically against the glass, and then the spotlight is turned off and they fall to the ground, scorched."

The next few weeks were agony, both physical and psychological. For a while Alan allowed himself to indulge in fantasies of confrontation, accusation, injury, and even murder. But finally he realized that the only thing he could do now was to curse Delia as a liar and a bitch and a gold digger and then forget her completely— never think of her again. Easier said than done. His back pain flared up, he drank alone in the evenings, and slept badly, the first few hours in a drunken stupor, the rest of the night in nervous fits and starts. At three and four a.m. he stumbled into the kitchen and broke things, mostly glasses and plates, sometimes by accident and sometimes on purpose, while the lizard hissed and clawed in his back.

He couldn't, of course, tell anyone what was the matter, but his friends noticed that he was looking ill and miserable; they suggested false causes and useless cures. The only thing that helped, finally, was work. Cursing Delia, he also remembered something she had said to him once. "It's not important for an artist to be good, or to be happy. If you're serious, you have to give all that up. If you don't, if you keep wanting those things, every time you pick up a pen you'll make the wrong choices."

His back was starting to ache seriously; he needed another drink, Alan thought now, and he looked toward the house to see if anyone else was coming to inspect the tower up close. No—yes, a figure had just detached itself from the crowd on the terrace and was starting across the lawn: a blond woman in a long, filmy white dress. The declining sun was full in his eyes, and for a moment he thought it was Delia. Over the past six months he had imagined that he saw her so often—in New York especially, but also, stupidly, in Corinth. More than once in the past six months he had followed some innocent female stranger down a street or across campus. He blinked hard, impatient with the persistence of his illusion, his obsession.

Then, with a sensation of having been struck hard in the chest, he realized that this time it was not a mirage. Approaching him was the person in the whole world he most and least wanted to see.

While he watched, she came nearer, becoming realer and even more beautiful than he had remembered, with a kind of faultless elegance he had never seen before. The Delia he'd known had been always just a little untidy—her mane of golden hair loosely and seductively disordered, her trailing thrift-shop skirts and fringed scarves slightly creased or disarranged as if she had just gotten out of bed. Once he had quoted to her Herrick's poem, which she of course knew, that begins, "A sweet disorder in the dress . . ." Now her hair had the braided and curled and puffed perfection of the

Botticelli portrait he had been reminded of the day they met, and her dress was an elaborate designer's confection of silk chiffon with layered floating pleats. As she came nearer Alan could see that she was carrying a wineglass in each hand.

For months he had rehearsed what he would say to Delia when and if they met, though the script had changed over time, from passion to interrogation to accusation to rejection. Now he could remember none of the lines, and stood tongue-tied.

"I brought us some champagne," she said, holding out one hand. The familiar sound of her voice, the low, caressing Southern accent, broke Alan's daze, and he struck out, knocking the glass onto the lawn. Almost any other woman—especially Jane, with her instinctive domesticity—would have exclaimed, would have stooped to pick up the broken pieces. Delia paid no attention—she merely set the remaining glass of champagne on a bit of artificial ruined stone wall and gazed at him with her dark-fringed gray eyes.

"Wh-what are you doing here, what the hell are you doing?" he stuttered.

"I came to see you," she murmured. "I made Jacky invite me. I had to come, I had to see you."

"Yeah, well, hell." Alan swallowed. "You could have tried to see me before. You could have written, at least, to tell me you were going to marry Wally Hersh." His voice had strengthened and he pronounced the name with all the scorn he could manage.

"I couldn't, I didn't dare. I was afraid you'd try to stop me. I knew you could stop me." She gazed at him helplessly.

"Oh, shit," Alan said with feeling.

"I thought—I hoped you'd understand." Delia moved nearer; he could smell her subtly flowery, presumably expensive, perfume. "You have to understand. I couldn't bear it if you didn't." Her voice wavered, and her huge pale eyes seemed to fill with tears. But Alan was unmoved. Yeah, maybe I could have stopped you, but you didn't give me a chance to stop you, he thought. Or, more likely, the whole thing is a lie.

"You're not going to tell me you're in love with him?" he said.

"I've been so frightened, always," Delia said, disregarding his question and thus, Alan realized, answering it. "You don't know. All my life."

"Yeah? Frightened of what?"

"Of everything. Of losing everything, being nothing and nobody." She looked at him innocently, helplessly. But she's not innocent, she's not helpless, Alan reminded himself.

"That's ridiculous. You're famous. And you're beautiful," he said, painfully aware of how true this was as she stood before him, the tendrils of her hair and the thin gauze of her long sleeves fluttering in the wind.

"Yes, now I am," Delia admitted, putting one soft hand on his arm and speaking low and intensely. "But that could end anytime. Suppose suddenly I couldn't write anymore. The world forgets so fast; it always wants something new. Everyone knows how it goes. You don't write anything, but you still get a little grant or a little prize here and there, and then pretty soon you've had most of the grants and prizes. You try to make it on readings, but they come less and less often. Soon you're one of those sad former writers you meet at art colonies, living from one residency to another. Then you wake up one morning and you can't even get into a colony, you're old and ugly and poor and mostly forgotten. All you have is a leaky log cabin in the mountains and a lot of used clothes and dead manuscripts. I couldn't bear that. I had to do something."

"But—Wally Hersh—he's—" Alan swallowed the angry words. He did not believe that Delia could ever be old and ugly and forgotten, but he believed in her irrational fear of this future.

"He's very sweet, really." She smiled, sweetly, as if to demonstrate.

"Sweet." Alan tried but failed to say this word neutrally.

"He loves artists and writers. When I took him to the Academy lunch last month and he met John Updike and Dick Wilbur he was really happy. His favorite course in college was English literature."

"So?" He felt rage rising in him.

"You don't understand," Delia almost wailed. "It's different for you, you can always teach and support yourself. And I can't—I've tried, but it destroys me, it destroys my work. You have tenure and health benefits and retirement—you're safe."

"And now you're safe too," Alan said, half in sympathy, half in scorn.

"Yes. You don't know, it's such a relief. It's as if, all my life, I'd been holding my breath, dreading the mail because I know it will be full of bills, maxing out credit cards, giving readings in awful places when I was coming down with the flu, being charming to awful people to get them to help me, fighting through migraines, lying sick as a cow in motels—" She gave a great sigh, then a wonderful smile. "But now I don't have to do any of that. When you have enough money, you can hire people to do whatever you need done, and you don't have to pay them in kisses and compliments—or if you do, it's a bonus for them."

"You have to pay Wally Hersh, though," Alan said flatly, fighting a crazy impulse to grab her and crush her elaborate white frills. "But I suppose it saves time, like consolidating all your debts with a single credit card company."

"No. It's more like owning the company." Delia did not obviously take offense, but she withdrew her hand and took a step away. "It's very beautiful, your tower," she said. "Even more than I thought it would be when Jacky showed me the drawings."

"Thank you," he said repressively, refusing to express pleasure.

"Can you get up to the top?"

"Yes," he admitted. "There's stairs inside."

"Wonderful." She started toward the arched stone entrance, and Alan, after a moment, picked up his cane and followed, drawn by both antagonism and passion. Painfully he climbed the stone steps behind a flurry of white gauze and bare pale rosy legs in high-heeled silver sandals.

"Oh, it's nice up here. There's a lovely view."

"Yeah, that was the idea." Alan followed her gaze across Long Island Sound, now a sheet of rippled gray silk near the shore, touched with ultramarine farther out. Then he looked back to where Delia stood, where the crenellated wall had been deliberately designed and built to look broken away. Suppose I pushed her now, suppose she fell, would she die? he thought. No, probably not, because of the thick bushes just below, sumac and blackberry and wild rose—but she might be injured, or at least badly scratched—

"Jacky says you're doing awfully well with your art," Delia remarked. "He showed me the piece in the *Times*. And he says you've got more commissions after this one."

"Yeah. There's a collector in New Jersey who has a sculpture park; I'm building something for him next month. And there's supposed to be another commission, somewhere in Westchester. Only it's not certain—Jacky won't even tell me the guy's name."

"Yes. The mystery client." Delia smiled. "It's Wally. He wants the ruined Temple of Venus that was in the group show last year."

"Well, he can't have it," Alan said, feeling a surge of rage and losing his cool. "That stupid rich bastard." He swallowed hard, fighting the urge to strike out. "He's bought you, and now he wants to buy me."

"Oh, darling. Don't say that," Delia wailed. "It's my place too. It's for me, really; I've been dreaming about it for months."

"A ruined Temple of Venus," Alan growled. "Well, that's fucking appropriate." He turned away and began slowly and painfully to descend the stone steps, with Delia following close behind.

"It doesn't have to be very ruined," she cried, clutching on to his arm to stop him. "Just a little. And it could be so beautiful, like in your drawing, with the columns and the stone garlands of flowers and fruit, and the faded frescoes—it would be a big project, it could take months to build. And you'd be there, and I'd be there. . . ." She took another step down and moved toward him, then against him. For the first time since December he felt the warm, soft weight of her; he saw, in the shadows of the circular stair, her pale face turned to his.

"Oh, my dear," she whispered. "I've missed you so much."

What the fuck am I doing? Alan thought. How can I trust this bitch, how can I love her? She betrayed Henry Hull, then she betrayed me, and now she's betraying Wally Hersh. But the pull was too strong, and he moved closer.

"You could build it in September," Delia murmured when they paused for breath. "Wally has to be in Hong Kong then, I'll be all alone—but of course you'll have to come to Rye much sooner, to look at the site. There's a little pond that might be just right—"

"I didn't say I would do it," Alan said, crushing Delia's elaborate tiered skirts against the rough stone of the staircase.

"But you will, won't you?" She kissed him again, lightly and warmly, then swayed back. "And then, you know your *Attic Window,* that's going to be on the cover of my new book? I want you to build it by my cabin in North Carolina, just where the mountain falls away, so that what you see through the window is all sky and distant hills."

"Oh yeah?"

"Yes. Absolutely."

"And I suppose then you'll want another piece for Wally Hersh's place in Palm Beach," he said as coolly as he could manage.

"No. I don't like Palm Beach. And Wally's house is really awful, all pink and green Cuban tiles and stucco arches and chandeliers and ugly fountains. My spirits would never come there, not in a thousand years. I'm going to persuade Wally to sell it and move to Key West. That'll be much more welcoming for them."

"Really." Alan descended the last few steps to the ground floor of the tower, trying to get a grip on himself, and stepped outside. "According to what I read, Key West is overrun with homeless chickens and feral six-toed cats, and drugs, and drunken writers and crazy motorcyclists, and the local government is completely corrupt," he said.

"Yes, doesn't it sound wonderful?" Delia laughed. "I'm going to be so happy there. Even happier than Henry and Jane." She paused in the natural frame of the tower's archway, whose gray stone had begun to turn a faint gold in the light of the declining sun.

"You think they're going to be happy?"

"Oh yes, probably. Boringly happy. Or maybe eventually they'll begin to bore each other, who knows?"

"And will you really be happy?"

"Maybe. Sometimes."

"I thought you didn't believe artists should be happy."

"I don't. Not as a steady thing. The world is a bad place for us, mostly. That's why we mustn't miss anything good that comes along. And there's pleasure sometimes, there's joy—like today. I wasn't sure you'd even speak to me."

"Probably I shouldn't have," Alan said.

"Too late now." Delia laughed and came closer. "Let's drink to that." She lifted the remaining champagne glass from where she had set it on an outcrop of artificial ruined wall, sipped, and handed it to Alan. A few bubbles still rose unhurriedly through the liquid, whose color, he thought, could have been described as pale gold—or as piss. "It's hardly gone flat at all," she said.

Alan drank. "No. Only a little." He looked across the lawn toward the party. "I think we'd better get back," he said.

"Yes." Delia sighed. "But I'll call you soon, so we can arrange for you to come to Rye."

Alan said neither yes nor no, but a heavy dark feeling—or was it light, was it joy?—came over him that he was fated to go to Rye, fated to build Delia's ruined Temple of Venus, to join her in her ruin, or whatever it was, maybe for the rest of his life.

"You know," she murmured as they began to cross the lawn, "you could do what I did, if you wanted to. I've met so many women lately—they're widowed or divorced, in their forties and fifties, but quite attractive, and very well off. They try to keep up their spirits, but their children have grown and gone, and they're real lonely and sad. They don't know what to do with themselves. Most of them would jump over the moon for a man like you, an artist, a genius."

"A cripple," Alan said.

"But that just makes it more romantic. Wally loves my migraines, they appeal to his protective instincts. It would be the same for you—artists always have a tragic wound, to go with their invincible bow, you know. They need to be taken care of. Anyhow, that's what my new girlfriends think. When you're in Rye I'll invite two or three of them to lunch, and you'll see."

"I don't want to see," Alan said, stopping and turning to stare at Delia. In her floating white dress, overlaid with gold by the low sun, like the grass and the gray stones of the tower behind her, she looked almost unearthly. "Who are you, Dilly, what are you?" he asked, catching hold of her arm. "Are you a demon come to tempt me to sin?"

"No, I'm your good angel, like I always was," Delia said. "I'm your true love." She gave him a quick, blazing look. Then she laughed and walked on. They were near enough to the terrace now to be seen, and soon many well-dressed, gold-tinged people began to surge toward them: greeting them, congratulating them, separating them.